"Affecting and Beautifully Written!"

—*Publishers Weekly*

"Whatever story she tells, whatever chances she takes, one always has the sense of being in good hands and good, adventurous company. She's one of the best!"

—*Peter S. Beagle*

"Vonda McIntyre gets better as time goes on, which is as it should be with a writer of her skill and sensitivity. This collection demonstrates the widening range of her vision."

—*Roger Zelazny*

"Fascinating . . . stories that touch our feelings as well as our intelligence and our imagination."

—*Marge Piercy*

"The clarity and range of her imagination are exhilarating!"

—*Kirkus Reviews*

"McIntyre will undoubtedly carry off a lot more Nebulas."

—*Fantasy and Science Fiction*

FIREFLOOD
and Other Stories
Vonda N. McIntyre

A TIMESCAPE BOOK
PUBLISHED BY POCKET BOOKS NEW YORK

The following stories in this collection have been previously published:
"Of Mist, and Grass, and Sand" in *Analog*; "Spectra" was first published in *Damon Knight's Orbit 11, An Anthology of New Science Fiction Stories*, by G.P. Putnam's Sons; "Wings" in *The Alien Condition*, edited by Stephen Goldin, published by Ballantine Books; "The Mountains of Sunset, The Mountains of Dawn" in *Fantasy & Science Fiction;* "The End's Beginning" in *Analog*; "Screwtop" in *The Crystal Ship*, edited by Robert Silverberg, published by Thomas Nelson, Inc.; "Only at Night" in *Clarion*, edited by Robert Scott Wilson, published by New American Library; "Recourse, Inc." in *Alternities*, edited by David Gerrold, published by Dell; "The Genius Freaks" in *Damon Knight's Orbit 12*, published by G.P. Putnam's Sons; "Aztecs" in *2076: The American Tricentennial*, edited by Edward Bryant, published by Pyramid Books; "Fireflood" first published in *Fantasy & Science Fiction*.

A Timescape Book published by
POCKET BOOKS, a Simon & Schuster division of
GULF & WESTERN CORPORATION
1230 Avenue of the Americas, New York, N.Y. 10020

Published by arrangement with Houghton Mifflin Company
Library of Congress Catalog Card Number: 79-17774

ISBN: 0-671-83631-5

First Timescape Books printing March, 1981

10 9 8 7 6 5 4 3 2 1

TIMESCAPE and design are trademarks of Simon & Schuster.
POCKET and colophon are trademarks of Simon & Schuster.

Printed in the U.S.A.

To Frances Collin

Contents

FIREFLOOD
and Other Stories

Fireflood

Dark moved slowly along the bottom of a wide, swift river, pushing against its current. The clean water made long bubbling strokes over her armor, and round stones scraped against her belly scales. She could live here, hidden in rapids or pools, surfacing every few hours to replenish her internal supplies of oxygen, looking little different from a huge boulder. In time she could even change the color of her armor to conform perfectly to the lighter, grayer rock of this region. But she was moving on; she would not stay in the river long enough to alter her rust-red hue.

Vibrations warned her of rapids. She took more care with her hand- and footholds, though her own mass was her main anchor. Stones rumbling gradually downstream did not afford much purchase for her claws. The turbulence was treacherous and exciting. But now she had to work harder to progress, and the riverbed shifted more easily beneath her. As the water grew swifter it also became more shallow, and when she sensed a number of huge boulders around her, she turned her back to the flow and reared up above the surface to breathe.

The force of the current sent water spraying up over her back, forming a curtain that helped conceal her. She breathed deeply, pumping air through her storage lungs, forcing herself not to exceed her body's most efficient absorption rate. However anxious she was to get underwater again, she would do herself no good if she used more oxygen than she stored during the stop.

Dark's armor, though impenetrable and insensitive to pain, detected other sensations. She was constantly aware of the small point of heat—call it that, she had no more accurate word—in the center of her spinal ridge. It was a radio transceiver. Though she could choose not to hear its incoming messages, it sent out a permanent beacon of her presence that she could not stop. It was meant to bring aid to her in emergencies, but she did not want to be found. She wanted to escape.

Before she had properly caught her breath, she sensed the approach of a helicopter, high above and quite far away. She did not see it: the spray of water glittered before her shortsighted eyes. She did not hear it: the rush of the river drowned out all other sounds. But she had more than one sense that had as yet no name.

She let herself sink beneath the water. An observer would have had to watch a single boulder among many to see what had happened. If the searchers had not homed in on the transmitter she could still get away.

She turned upstream again and forged ahead toward the river's source.

If she was very lucky, the helicopter was flying a pattern and had not actually spotted her transmitter at all. That was a possibility, for while it did not quite have the specificity of a laser, it worked on a narrow beam. It was, after all, designed to send messages via satellite.

But the signal did not pass through water and even as the searchers could not detect her, she could not see or feel them through the rough silver surface of the river. Trusting her luck, she continued on.

The country was very different from where she had trained. Though she was much more comfortable underground than underwater, this land was not ideal for digging. She could survive as well beneath liquid, and travel was certainly quicker. If she could not get to the surface to breathe, the time it would take her to stop and extract oxygen directly was about the same. But the character of water was far too constant for her taste. Its action was predictable and its range of temperature was trivial compared to what she could stand. She preferred to go under ground, where excitement spiced the exploration. For, though she was slow, methodical, and nearly indestructible, she *was* an explorer. It was just that now she had nowhere to explore.

She wondered if any of her friends had made it this far. She and six others had decided, in secret, to flee. But they offered each other only moral support; each had gone out alone. Twenty more of her kind still remained scattered in their reserve, waiting for assignments that would never come and pretending thay had not been abandoned.

Though it was not yet evening, the light faded around her and left the river bottom gray and black. Dark slowly and cautiously lifted her eyes above the water. Her eyes peered darkly from beneath her armor. They were deep blue, almost black, the only thing of beauty about her: the only thing of beauty about her after or before her transformation from a creature who could pass for human to one who could not. Even now she was not sorry to have volunteered for the change. It did not further isolate her; she had always been alone. She had also been useless. In her new life, she had some worth.

The riverbed had cut between tall, thick trees that shut out much of the sunlight. Dark did not know for certain if they would interfere with the radio signal as well. She had not been designed to work among lush vegetation and she had never studied how her body might interact with it. But she did not believe it would be safe for her to take a quiet stroll among the giant cedars. She tried to get her bearings, with sun time and body memory. Her ability to detect magnetic fields was worthless here on Earth; that sense was designed for more delicate signals. She closed it off as she might shut her eyes to a blinding light.

Dark submerged again and followed the river upward, keeping to its main branch. As she passed the tributaries that ran and rushed to join the primary channel the river became no more than a stream itself, and Dark was protected only by thin ripples.

She peered out again.

The pass across the ridge lay only a little ahead and above her, just beyond the spring that created the river. To Dark's left lay a wide field of scree, where a cliff and hillside had collapsed. The river flowed around the pile, having been displaced by tons of broken stone. The rubble stretched on quite a way, at least as far as the pass and, if she were lucky, all the way through. It was ideal. Sinking barely underwater, she moved across the current. Beneath her feet she felt the stones change from rounded and water-worn to sharp and freshly broken. She reached the edge of the slope, where the shattered rock projected into the river. On the downstream side she nudged away a few large stones, set herself, and burrowed quickly into the shards.

The fractured crystalline matrix disrupted her echo perception. She kept expecting to meet a wall of solid rock that would push her out and expose her, but the good conditions existed all the way through the pass. Then, on the other side, when she chanced a peek out into the world, she found that the texture of the ground changed abruptly on this side of the ridge. When the broken stone ended, she did not have to seek out another river. She dug straight from the scree into the earth.

In the cool dry darkness, she traveled more slowly but more safely than in the river. Underground there was no chance of the radio signal's escaping to give her away. She knew exactly where the surface was all the time. It, unlike the interface of water and air, did not constantly change. Barring the collapse of a hillside, little could unearth her. A landslide was possible, but her sonar could detect the faults and weaknesses in earth and rock that might create a danger.

She wanted to rest, but she was anxious to reach the flyers' sanctuary as quickly as she could. She did not have much farther to go. Every bit of distance might make a difference, for she would be safe only after she got inside the boundaries . . . She could be safe there from normal people: what the flyers would do when she arrived she could not say.

Dark's vision ranged much farther through the spectrum than it had when she was human. In daytime she saw colors, but at night and underground she used infrared, which translated to distinguishable and distinctive shades of black. They were supposed to look like colors, but she saw them all as black. They told her what sort of land she was passing through and a great deal about what grew above. Nevertheless, when the sun went down she broke through thick turf and peered around at the forest. The moon had not yet risen, and a nearby stream was almost as dark as ice. The fir trees kept the same deep tone as in bright sunlight. Still, all the colors were black.

Dark breathed deeply of the cold air. It was stuffy underground, though she had not had to switch to reducing her own oxygen. That was for deeper down, in altogether more difficult regions.

The air smelled of moss and ferns, evergreen trees, and weathered stone. But under it all was the sulfurous volcano, and the sweet delicate fragrance of flyers.

Sinking down into the earth once more, Dark traveled on.

The closer Dark got to the volcano, the more jumbled and erratic grew the strata. Lava flows and land movement, glaciers and erosion had scarred and unsettled and twisted the surface and all that lay beneath it. Deep underground Dark encountered a tilted slab of granite, too hard for her to dig through quickly. She followed it upward, hoping it would twist and fold back down again. But it did not, and she broke through topsoil into the chill silence of a wilderness night. Dirt and pebbles fell away from her shoulder armor. From the edge of the outcropping she looked out, in infrared, over her destination.

The view excited her. The tree-covered slope dropped to tumbled masses of blackened logs that formed the first barrier against intrusion into the flyers' land. Beyond, at the base of the volcano, solidified lava created another wasteland. The molten rock had flowed from the crater down the flank of the mountain; near the bottom it broke into two branches which ran, one to each side, until both ended like true rivers, in the sea. The northern shore was very close, and the pale nighttime waves lapped gently on the dim cool beach. To the south the lava had crept through a longer sweep of forest, burning the trees in its path and toppling those beyond its head, for a much longer distance to the ocean. The wide solid flood and the impenetrable wooden jumble formed a natural barricade. The flyers were exiled to their peninsula, but they stayed there by choice. The humans had no way of containing them short of killing them. They could take back their wings or chain them to the ground or imprison them, but they wished to isolate the flyers, not murder them. And murder it would be if they denied the creatures flight.

The basalt streams glowed with heat retained from the day, and the volcano itself was a softly radiant cone, sparkling here and there where upwellings of magma approached the surface. The steam rising from the crater shone brightly, and among its clouds shadows soared in spirals along the edges of the column. One of the shadows dived dangerously toward the ground, risking destruction, but at the last moment it pulled up short to soar skyward again. Another followed, another, and Dark realized they were playing a game. Entranced, she hunched on the ridge and watched the flyers play. They did not notice her. No doubt they could see better than she, but their eyes would be too dazzled by the heat's luminous blackness to notice an earthbound creature's armor-shielded warmth.

Sound and light burst upon her like explosions. Clearing the ridge that had concealed it, a helicopter leaned into the air and ploughed toward her. Until this moment she had not seen or heard or sensed it. It must have been grounded, waiting for her. Its searchlights caught and blinded her for a moment, till she shook herself free in an almost automatic reaction and slid across the bare rock to the earth beyond. As she plunged toward the trees the machine roared over her, its backwash blasting up a cloud of dirt and leaves and pebbles. The copter screamed upward, straining to miss treetops. As it turned to chase her down again, Dark scuttled into the woods.

She had been careless. Her fascination with the volcano and the flyers had betrayed her, for her stillness must have convinced the humans that she was asleep or incapacitated.

Wondering if it would do any good, she burrowed into the earth. She felt the helicopter land, and then the lighter vibrations of footsteps. The humans could find her by the same technique, amplifying the sounds of her digging. From now on they did not even need her beacon.

She reached a boundary between bedrock and earth and followed its lessened resistance. Pausing for a moment, she heard both movement and its echoes. She felt trapped between sounds, from above and below. She started digging, pushing herself until her work drowned out all other noises. She did not stop again.

The humans could move faster down the steep terrain than she could. She was afraid they would get far enough ahead of her to dig a trench and head her off. If they had enough equipment or construction explosives, they could surround her, or simply kill her with the shock waves of a shaped charge.

She dug violently, pushing herself forward, feeling the debris of her progress slide over her shoulder armor and across her back, filling in the tunnel as quickly as she made it.

The roots of living trees, springy and thick, reached down to slow her. She had to dig between and sometimes through them. Their malleable consistency made them harder to penetrate than solid rock, and more frustrating. Dark's powerful claws could shatter stone, but they tangled in the roots and she was forced to shred the tough fibers a few strands at a time. She tired fast, and she was using oxygen far more quickly than she could take it in underground.

Dark slashed out angrily at a thick root. It crumbled completely in a powdery dust of charcoal. Dark's momentum, meeting no resistance, twisted her sideways in her narrow tunnel. She was trapped. The footsteps of the humans caught nearly up to her, and then, inexplicably, stopped. Scrabbling frantically with her feet and one clawed hand, her left front limb wedged uselessly beneath her, she managed to loosen and shift the dirt in the small enclosed space. Finally, expecting the humans to start blasting toward her at any moment, she freed herself.

Despite the ache in her left shoulder, deep under her armor, she increased her pace tremendously. She was beneath the dead trees now, and the dry porous earth contained only the roots of trees that had burned from top to deep underground, or roots riddled with insects and decay. Above her, above ground, the tree trunks lay in an impassable tangle, and that must be why the humans had paused. They could not trench her now.

Gauging her distance to the basalt flow by the pattern of returning echoes, Dark tunneled through the last few lengths of earth. She wanted to go under the stone barrier and come up on the other side in safety. But the echoes proved that she could not. The basalt was much thicker than she had hoped. It was not a single flow but many, filling a deep-cleft valley the gods only knew how far down. She could not go under and she did have time or strength right now to go through.

It was not the naked sheet of stone that would keep the humans from her, but the intangible barrier of the flyers' boundary. That was what she had to reach. Digging hard, using the last of her stored oxygen, Dark burst up through the earth at the edge of the lava flow and scrambled out onto the hard surface. Never graceful at the best of times, she was slow and unwieldy on land. She lumbered forward, panting, her claws clacking on the rock and scraping great marks across it.

Behind her the humans shouted, as their detectors went off

so loudly even Dark could hear them, and as the humans saw Dark for themselves, some for the first time.

They were very close. They had almost worked their way through the jammed tree trunks, and once they reached solid ground again they could overtake her. She scrambled on, feeling the weight of her armor as she never did underground. Its edges dragged along the basalt, gouging it deeply.

Two flyers landed as softly as wind, as milkweed floss, as pollen grains. Dark heard only the rustle of their wings, and when she looked up from the fissured gray rock, they stood before her, barring her way.

She was nearly safe: she was just on the boundary, and once she was over it the humans could not follow. The delicate flyers could not stand up against her if she chose to proceed, but they did not move to let her pass. She stopped.

Like her, the flyers had huge eyes, to extend the spectrum of their vision. Armored brow ridges and transparent shields protected Dark's eyes and almost hid them. The flyers' eyes were protected, too, but with thick black lashes that veiled and revealed them.

"What do you want, little one?" one of the flyers said. Its voice was deep and soft, and it wrapped its body in iridescent black wings.

"Your help," Dark said. "Sanctuary." Behind her, the humans stopped too. She did not know if they still had the legal right to take her. Their steel net scraped along the ground, and they moved hesitantly closer. The black flyer glared, and the human noises ceased. Dark inched forward, but the flyers did not retreat at all.

"Why have you come?" The black flyer's voice withheld all emotion, warmth, or welcome.

"To talk to you," Dark said. "My people need your help."

The raven-winged flyer did not move, except to blink its luminous eyes. But its blue-feathered companion peered at Dark closely, moved a step one way, a step the other, and ruffled the plumage of its wings. The blue flyer's movements were as quick and sharp as those of a bird itself.

"We have no help to offer you," the black flyer said.

"Let me in, let me talk to you." Her claws ground against stone as she moved nervously. She could not flee, and she did not want to fight. She could crush the humans or the flyers, but she had not been chosen for her capacity for violence. Her pursuers knew that perfectly well.

Again the nets scraped behind her as the humans moved forward.

"We've only come for her," one of them said. "She's a fugitive—we don't want to involve you in any unpleasantness." The powerful searchlight he carried swept over Dark's back, transfixing the flyers, who turned their faces away. The harsh white illumination washed out the iridescent highlights of the black feathers but brightened the other's wings to the brilliant color of a Stellar's jay.

"Turn out your lights," the jay said, in a voice as brash and demanding as any real bluejay's. "It's dawn—you can see well enough."

The human hesitated, swung the light away, and turned it off. He motioned to the helicopter and its lights faded. As the jay had said, it was dawn, misty and gray and eerie. The flyers faced Dark's adversaries again.

"We have no more resources than you," the raven flyer said. "How do you expect us to help you? We have ourselves. We have our land. You have the same."

"Land!" Dark said bitterly. "Have you ever seen my land? It's nothing but piles of rotting stone and pits full of rusty water—" She stopped; she had not meant to lose her temper. But she was hunched on the border of captivity, straining toward sanctuary and about to be refused.

"Send her out so we can take her without violating your boundaries. Don't let her cause you a lot of trouble."

"A little late for such caution," Jay said. "Redwing, if we bow to their threats now, what will they do next time? We should let her in."

"So the diggers can do to our refuge what they did to their own? Pits, and rusting water—"

"It was like that when we came!" Dark cried, shocked and hurt. "We make tunnels, yes, but we don't destroy! Please hear what I've got to say. Then, if you ask me to go . . . I'll obey." She made the promise reluctantly, for she knew that once she had lived near the volcano, she would need great will to leave. "I give you my word." Her voice quivered with strain. The humans muttered behind her; a few steps inside the boundary, a few moments inside and then out—who, besides Dark, would accuse them of entering the flyers' territory at all?

Jay and Redwing glared at each other, but suddenly Jay laughed sharply and turned away. He stepped back and swept one wingtip along the ground, waving Dark into his land. "Come in, little one," he said.

Hesitantly, afraid he would change his mind, Dark moved forward. Then, in a single moment, after her long journey, she was safe.

"We have no reason to trust it!" Redwing said.

"Nor any reason not to, since we could just as well be mashed flat between stone and armor. We do have reason not to help the humans."

"You'll have to send her back," the leader of the humans said. He was angry; he stood glowering at the very edge of the border, perhaps a bit over. "Laws will take her, if we don't now. It will just cost you a lot more in trouble."

"Take your threats and your noisy machine and get out of here," Jay said.

"You *will* be sorry, flyer," the humans' leader said.

Dark did not really believe they would go until the last one boarded the helicopter and its roar increased, it climbed into the air, and it clattered off into the brightening gray morning.

"Thank you," Dark said.

"I had ulterior motives," Jay said.

Redwing stood back, looking at Jay but not at Dark. "We'll have to call a council."

"I know. You go ahead. I'll talk to her and meet you when we convene."

"I think we will regret this," Redwing said. "I think we are closer to the humans than to the diggers." The black flyer leaped into the air, wings outspread to reveal their brilliant scarlet underside, and soared away.

Jay laid his soft hand on Dark's shoulder plate to lead her from the lava to volcanic soil. His skin felt frail, and very warm: Dark's metabolism was slower than it had been, while the flyer's chemistry had been considerably speeded up. Dark was ugly and clumsy next to him. She thought of digging down and vanishing but that would be ill-mannered. Besides, she had never been near a flyer before. Curiosity overcame her. Glancing surreptitiously sideways, beneath the edge of her armor, she saw that he was peeking at her, too. Their gazes met; they looked away, both embarrassed. Then Dark stopped and faced him. She settled back to regard him directly.

"This is what I look like," she said. "My name is Dark and I know I'm ugly, but I could do the job I was made for, if they'd let me."

"I think your strength compensates for your appearance," the flyer said. "I'm Jay." Dark was unreasonably pleased that she had guessed right about his name.

"You never answered Redwing's question," Jay said. "Why come *here?* The strip mines—"

"What could you know of strip mines?"

"Other people lived near them before they were given over to you."

"So you think we should stay there!"

Jay replied to her abrupt anger in a gentle tone. "I was going to say, this place is nicer than the strip mines, true, but a lot of places nicer than the strip mines are more isolated than we are. You could have found a hidden place to live."

"I'm sorry," Dark said. "I thought—"

"I know. Never mind."

"No one else like me got this far, did they?"

Jay shook his head.

"Six of us escaped," Dark said. "We hoped more than one would reach you. Perhaps I'm just the first, though."

"That could be."

"I came to ask you to join us," Dark said.

Jay looked at her sharply, his thick flaring eyebrows raised in surprise. He veiled his eyes for a moment with the translucent avian membranes, then let them slowly retract.

"Join you? In . . . your preserve?" He was polite enough to call it this time by its official name. Though she had expressed herself badly, Dark felt some hope.

"I misspoke myself," she said. "I came—the others and I decided to come—to ask you to join us politically. Or at least support us."

"To get you a better home. That seems only fair."

"That isn't quite what we're hoping for. Or rather it is, but not the way you mean."

Jay hesitated again. "I see. You want . . . what you were made for."

Dark wanted to nod; she missed the shorthand of the language of the human body, and she found she was unable to read Jay's. She had been two years out of contact with normal humans; or perhaps it was that Jay was a flyer, and his people had made adjustments of their own.

"Yes. We were made to be explorers. It's a useless economy, to keep us on earth. We could even pay our own way after a while."

Dark watched him closely, but could not tell what he

thought. His face remained expressionless; he did not move toward her or away. Then he sighed deeply. That, Dark understood.

"Digger—" She flinched, but inwardly, the only way she could. He had not seemed the type to mock her. "—the projects are over. They changed their minds. There will be no exploring or colonizing, at least not by you and me. And what difference does it make? We have a peaceful life and everything we need. You've been badly used but that could be changed."

"Maybe," Dark said, doubting his words. The flyers were beautiful, her people were ugly, and as far as the humans were concerned that made every difference. "But we had a prupose, and now it's gone. Are you happy, living here with nothing to do?"

"We're content. You people are all ready, but we aren't. We'd have to go through as much change again as we already have."

"What's so bad about that? You've gone this far. You volunteered for it. Why not finish?"

"Because it isn't necessary."

"I don't understand," Dark said. "You could have a whole new living world. You have even more to gain than we do, that's why we thought you'd help us." Dark's planned occupation was the exploration of dead worlds or newly formed ones, the places of extremes where no other life could exist. But Jay's people were colonists; they had been destined for a world that was being made over for them, even as they were being suited for what it would become.

"The terraforming is only beginning," Jay said. "If we wait until it's complete—"

"But that won't be for generations."

Jay shrugged. "We know."

"You'll never see it!" Dark cried. "You'll be dead and dust before it changes enough for people like you are now to live on it."

"We're virus-changed, not constructed," Jay said. "We breed true. Our grandchildren may want another world, and the humans may be willing to help them go. But we intend to stay here." He blinked slowly, dreamily. "Yes, we *are* happy. And we don't have to work for the humans."

"I don't care who I work for, as long as I can be something better than a deformed creature," Dark said angrily. "This world gives my people nothing and because of that we're dying."

"Come now," Jay said tolerantly.

"We're dying!" Dark stopped and rocked back on the edge of her shell so she could more nearly look him in the eye. "You have beauty all around you and in you, and when the humans see you they admire you. But they're afraid of us! Maybe they've forgotten that we started out human or maybe they never considered us human at all. It doesn't matter. I don't care! But we can't be anything, if we don't have any purpose. All we ask is that you help us make ourselves heard, because they'll listen to you. They love you. They almost worship you!" She paused, surprised by her own outburst.

"Worship us!" Jay said. "They shoot us out of the sky, like eagles."

He looked away from her. His gaze sought out clouds, the direction of the sun, for all she knew the eddies of the wind. Dark thought she sensed something, a call or a cry at the very edge of one of her new perceptions. She reached for it, but it eluded her. It was not meant for her.

"Wait for me at sunset," Jay said, his voice remote. He spread his huge furled wings and sprang upward, the muscles bunching in his short, powerful legs. Dark watched him soar into the sky, a graceful dark blue shape against the cloud-patterned gold and scarlet dawn.

Dark knew she had not convinced him. Whe he was nothing but a speck she eased herself down again and lumbered up the flank of the volcano. She could feel it beneath her feet. Its long rumbles pulsed through her, at a far lower frequency than she ever could have heard as a human. It promised heat and danger; it excited her. She had experienced no extremes, of either heat or cold, pressure or vacuum, for far too many months.

The ground felt hollow beneath Dark's claws: passages lay beneath her, and lava beaten to a froth by the violence of its formation and frozen by exposure into spongy rock. She found a crevice that would leave no trace of her passing and slid into it. She began to dig, slowly at first, then faster, dirt and pulverized stone flying over her shoulders. In a moment the earth closed in around her.

Dark paused to rest. Having reached the gas-formed tunnels, she no longer had to dig her way through the substance of the mountain. She relaxed in the twisted passage, enjoying the brilliance of the heat and the occasional shining puff of air that came to her from the magma. She could analyze the gases by taste: that was another talent the humans had given her. Vapors toxic to them were merely interesting scents to her. If necessary she could metabolize some gases; the ability would have been necessary in many of the places she had expected to see, where sunlight was too dim to convert, where life had vanished or never evolved and there were no organic chemicals. On the outer planets, in the asteroids, even on Mars, her energy would have come from a tenuous atmosphere, from ice, even from the dust. Out there the challenging extremes would be cold and emptiness, unless she discovered hot, living veins in dying planets. Perhaps now no one would ever look for such activity on the surface of an alien world. Dark had dreamed of the planets of a different star, but she might never get a chance even to see the moon.

Dark sought a living vein in a living world: she moved toward the volcano's central core. Her people had been designed to resist conditions far more severe than the narrow range tolerated by normals, but she did not know if she could survive this great a temperature. Nor did she care. The rising heat drew her toward a heightened state of consciousness that wiped away caution and even fear. The rock walls glowed in the infrared, and as she dug at them, the chips flew like sparks. At last, with nothing but a thin plate of stone between her and the caldera, she hesitated. She was not afraid for her life. It was almost as if she were afraid she *would* survive: afraid the volcano, like all else, would finally disappoint her.

She lashed out with her armored hand and shattered the fragile wall. Steam and vapor poured through the opening, flowing past her. Before she stopped normal breathing she chanced a quick, shallow mouthful and savored the taste and smell, then moved forward to look directly into the crater.

Whatever she had imagined dissolved in the reality. She was halfway up the crater, dazzled from above by light and from below by heat. She had been underground a long time and it was almost exactly noon. Sunlight beat down through clouds of steam, and the gases and sounds of molten rock reached up to her. The currents swirled, hot and hotter, and in the earth's wound a flood of fire burned.

She could feel as well as see the heat, and it pleased her intensely that she would die if she remained where she was.

Internal oxygen sustained her: a few deep breaths of the mountain's uncooled exhalations and she would die.

She wanted to stay. She did not want to return to the surface and the probability of rejection. She did not want to return to her people's exile.

Yet she had a duty toward them, and she had not yet completed it. She backed into the tunnel, turned around, and crawled away, hoping someday she could return.

Dark made her way back to the surface, coming out through the same fissure so the land would not change. She shook the dirt off her armor and looked around, blinking, waiting for her eyes to reaccustom themselves to the day. As she rested, colors resolved out of the after-image dazzle of infrared: the blue sky first, then the deep green trees, the yellow of a scatter of wildflowers. Finally, squinting, she made out dark specks against the crystal clarity of the sky. The flyers soared in small groups or solo, now and again two coming together in lengthy graceful couplings, their wings brushing tips. She watched them, surprised and a little ashamed to be aroused despite herself. For her kind, intercourse was more difficult and more pedestrian. Dark had known how it would be when she volunteered; there was no secret about it. Like most of the other volunteers, she had always been a solitary person. She seldom missed what she had so seldom had, but watching the flyers she felt a long pang of envy. They were so beautiful, and they took everything so for granted.

The winged dance went on for hours, until the sun, reddening, touched mountains in the west. Dark continued to watch, unable to look away, in awe of the flyers' aerial and sexual stamina. Yet she resented their extended play, as well; they had forgotten that an earthbound creature waited for them.

The several pairs of coupled flyers suddenly broke apart, as if on signal, and the whole group of them scattered. A moment later Dark sensed the approach of the humans' plane.

It was too high to hear, but she knew it was there. It circled slowly. Sitting still, not troubling now to conceal the radio-beacon in her spine, Dark perceived it spiraling in, with her as its focus. The plane descended; it was a point, then a silver shape reflecting scarlet sunset. It did not come too close; it did nothing immediately threatening. But it had driven the flyers out of Dark's sight. She hunkered down on the stone promontory, waiting.

Dark heard only the sudden rush of air against outstretched wings as Jay landed nearby. His approach had been completely silent, and intent as she was on the search plane, she had not seen him. She turned her attention from the sky to Jay, and took a few steps toward him. But then she stopped, shamed once more by her clumsiness compared to the way he moved. The flyers were not tall, and even for their height their legs were quite short. Perhaps they had been modified that way. Still, Jay did not lumber. He strode. As he neared her he furled his wings over his back, folding them one bit at a time, ruffling them to smooth the feathers, folding a bit more. He reminded her not so much of a bird, as of a spectacular butterfly perched in the wind, flicking his wings open and closed. When he stopped before her his wings stilled, each bright blue feather perfectly placed, framing him from behind. Unconcealed this time by the wings, his body was naked. Flyers wore no clothes: Dark was startled that they had nothing to conceal. Apparently they were as intricately engineered as her own people.

Jay did not speak for so long that Dark, growing uncomfortable, reared back and looked into the sky. The search plane still circled loudly.

"Are they allowed to do that?" she said.

"We have no quick way of stopping them. We can protest. No doubt someone already has."

"I could send them a message," she said grumpily. That, after all, was what the beacon was for, though the message would not contain the sort of information anyone had ever planned for her to send.

"We've finished our meeting," Jay said.

"Oh. Is that what you call it?"

Dark expected a smile or a joke, but Jay spoke quite seriously.

"That's how we confer, here."

"Confer—!" She dropped back to the ground, her claws digging in. "You met without letting me speak? You told me to wait for you at sunset!"

"I spoke for you," Jay said softly.

"I came here to speak for myself. And I came here to speak for my kind. I trusted you—"

"It was the only way," he said. "We only gather in the sky."

Dark held down an angry retort. "And what is the answer?"

Jay sat abruptly on the hard earth, as if he could no longer support the weight of his wings on his delicate legs. He drew his knees to his chest and wrapped his arms around them.

"I'm sorry." The words burst out in a sigh, a moan.

"Call them," Dark said. "Fly after them, find them, make them come and speak to *me*. I will not be refused by people who won't even face me."

"It won't help," Jay said miserably. "I spoke for you as well as I could, but when I saw I would fail I tried to bring them here. I begged them. They wouldn't come."

"They wouldn't come . . ." She had risked her life only to have her life dismissed as nothing. "I don't understand," she whispered.

Jay reached out and touched her hand: it still could function as a hand, despite her armor and her claws. Jay's hand, too, was clawed, but it was delicate and fine-boned, and veins showed blue through the translucent skin. Dark pulled back the all too solid mass of her arm.

"Don't you, little one?" Jay said, sadly. "I was so different, before I was a flyer—"

"So was I," Dark said.

"But you're strong, and you're ready. You could go tomorrow with no more changes and no more pain. I have another stage to go through. If I did it, and then they decided not to send us after all—Dark, I would never be able to fly again. Not in this gravity. There are too many changes. They'd thicken my skin, and regress me again so my wings weren't feathered but scaled—they'd shield my eyes and reconstruct my face for the filters."

"It isn't the flying that troubles you," Dark said.

"It is. The risk's too great."

"No. What troubles you is that when you were finished, you wouldn't be beautiful anymore. You'd be ugly, like me."

"That's unfair."

"Is it? Is that why all your people flock around me so willingly to hear what I have to say?"

Jay stood slowly and his wings unfolded above him: Dark thought he was going to sail away off the side of the mountain, leaving her to speak her insults to the clouds and the stones. But, instead, he spread his beautiful black-tipped blue wings, stretched them in the air, and curved them around over Dark so they brushed the ridge of her spine. She shivered.

"I'm sorry," he said. "We have grown used to being beautiful. Even I have. They shouldn't have decided to make us in stages, they should have done it all at once. But they didn't, and now it's hard for us, being reminded of how we were."

Dark stared at Jay, searching for the remnants of how he had been until he became a flyer, understanding, finally, the reasons he had decided to become something other than human. Before, she had only perceived his brilliant plumage, his luminous eyes, and the artificial delicacy of his bones. Now she saw his original proportions, the disguised coarseness of his features, and she saw what he must have looked like.

Perhaps he had not actually been deformed, as Dark had been. But he had never been handsome, or even so much as plain. She gazed at him closely. Neither of them blinked: that must be harder for him, Dark thought. Her eyes were shielded, his were only fringed with long, thick, dark eyelashes.

His eyes were too close together. That was something the virus-forming would not have been able to cure.

"I see," she said. "You can't help us, because we might succeed."

"Don't hate us," he said.

She turned away, her armor scraping on rock. "What do you care, if a creature as repellent as I hates you?"

"I care," Jay said very quietly.

Dark knew she was being unfair, to him if not to his kind, but she had no sympathy left. She wanted to hide herself somewhere and cry.

"When are the humans coming for me?"

"They come when they please," he said. "But I made the others promise one thing. They won't ask you to leave till morning. And if we can't find you, then—there's time for you to get away, if you hurry."

Dark spun around, more quickly than she thought herself able to. Her armor struck sparks, but they glowed only briefly and died.

"Where should I go? Somewhere no one at all will ever see

me? Underground, all alone, forever?" She thought of the mountain and its perils, but it meant nothing now. "No," she said. "I'll wait for them."

"But you don't know what they might do! I told you what they've done to us—"

"I hardly think they'll shoot me out of the sky."

"Don't joke about it! They'll destroy anything, the things they love and the things they fear . . ."

"I don't care anymore," Dark said. "Go away, flyer. Go away to your games, and to your illusions of beauty."

He glared at her, turned, and sprang into the air. She did not watch him go, but pulled herself completely inside the shadows of her armor to wait.

Sometime during the night she drifted off to sleep. She dreamed of the fireflood: she could feel its heat and hear its roar.

When she awoke, the rising sun blazed directly into her eyes, and the steel blades of a helicopter cut the dawn. She tried and failed to blot out the sound of the humans' machine. She began to shiver, with uncertainty or with fear.

Dark crept slowly down the side of the mountain, toward the border where the humans would land. The flyers would not have to tell her to leave. She wondered if she were protecting herself, or them, from humiliation.

Something touched her and she started, drawing herself tightly into her armor.

"Dark, it's only me."

She peered out. Jay stood over her with his wings curved around them both.

"You can't hide me," she said.

"I know. We should have, but it's too late." He looked gaunt and exhausted. "I tried, Dark, I did try."

On the humans' side of the lava flow, the machine landed and sent up a fine spray of dust and rock particles. People climbed out, carrying weapons and nets. Dark did not hesitate.

"I have to go." She raised her armor up off the ground and started away.

"You're stronger than we are," Jay said. "The humans can't come and get you and we can't force you to leave."

"I know." The invisible boundary was almost at her feet; she moved reluctantly but steadily toward it.

"Why are you doing this?" Jay cried.

Dark did not answer.

She felt Jay's wingtip brush the edge of her armor as he walked alongside her. She stopped and glanced up at him.

"I'm coming with you," he said. "Till you get home. Till you're safe."

"It's no more safe for you. You can't leave your preserve."

"Nor could you."

"Jay, go back."

"I'll not lose another friend to the humans."

Dark touched the boundary. As if they were afraid she would still try to escape them, the humans rushed toward her and flung the net over her, pulling in its edges so it caught beneath her armor. They jostled the flyer away from her side.

"This isn't necessary," she said. "I'll come with you."

"Sorry," one finally said, in a grudging tone. "It's necessary."

"Her word's good," Jay said. "Otherwise she never would have come out to you at all."

"What happened to the others?" Dark asked.

One human shrugged.

"Captured," another said.

"And then?"

"Returned to the sanctuary."

Dark had no reason not to believe them, simply because they had no reason to spare her feelings if any of her friends were dead.

"You see, Jay, there's no need for you to come."

"You can't trust them! They'll lie to you for your cooperation and then kill you when I've left you with no witness."

That could be true; still, she lumbered toward the helicopter, more hindered than helped by the humans' tugging on the steel cables. The blades circled rhythmically over her.

Jay followed, but the humans barred his way.

"I'm going with her," he said.

She glanced back. Somehow, strangely, he looked even more delicate and frail among the normal humans than he had when she compared him to her own massive self.

"Don't come any farther, flyer."

He pushed past them. One took his wrist and he pulled away. Two of the humans grabbed him by the shoulders and pushed him over the border as he struggled. His wings opened out above the turmoil, flailing, as Jay fought to keep his balance. A blue feather fluttered free and spiraled to the ground.

Dragging her own captors with her, pulling them by the net-lines as they struggled and failed to keep her on their side, Dark scuttled toward Jay and broke through the group of humans. The flyer lay crumpled on the ground, one wing caught awkwardly beneath him, the other curved over and around him in defense. The humans sprang away from him, and from Dark.

"Jay," she said. "Jay . . ."

When he rose, Dark feared his wing was crushed. He winced when he lifted it, and his plumage was in disarray, but, glaring at the humans, he extended and flexed it and she saw to her great relief that he was all right. He glanced down at her and his gaze softened. Dark reached up toward him, and their clawed hands touched.

One of the humans snickered. Embarrassed, Dark jerked her hand away.

"There's nothing you can do," she said. "Stay here."

The net jerked tighter around her, but she resisted it.

"We can't waste any more time," the leader of her captors said. "Come on, now, it's time to go."

They succeeded in dragging her halfway around, and a few steps toward the helicopter, only because she permitted it.

"If you won't let me come with her, I'll follow," Jay said. "That machine can't outpace me."

"We can't control anyone outside your preserve." Strangely, the human sounded concerned. "You know the kind of thing that can happen. Flyer, stay inside your boundaries."

"You pay no heed to boundaries!" Jay cried, as they pulled and pushed Dark the last few paces back into their own territory. She moved slowly, at her own speed, ignoring them.

"Stay here, Jay," she said. "Stay here, or you'll leave me with guilt as well as failure."

Dark did not hear him, if he answered. She reached the copter, and steeled herself against the discomfort of its noise and unshielded electrical fields. She managed to clamber up into the cargo hold before they could subject her to the humiliation of being hoisted and shoved.

She looked out through the open door. It was as if the rest of the world were silent, for she could hear and sense nothing but the clamor immediately around her. On the lava ridge, Jay stood still, his shoulders slumped. Suddenly his wings flared out, rose, descended, and he soared into the air. Awestruck once more, Dark watched through the mesh of the net. Jay sailed in a huge circle and glided into the warm updraft of the volcano.

The rotors moved faster, blurring and nearly disappearing. The machine rose with a slight forward lurch, laboring under the weight of the hunting party and Dark as well. At the same time, Jay spiraled upward through the glowing steam. Dark tried to turn away, but she could not. He was too beautiful.

The distance between them grew greater, until all Dark could see was a spark of bright blue appearing, then vanishing, among the columns of steam.

As the helicopter swung round, she thought she saw the spiral of Jay's flight widen, as if he were ignoring the threats the humans had made and cared nothing for warnings, as if he were drifting gently toward the boundaries of his refuge, gradually making up his mind to cross them and follow.

Don't leave your sanctuary, Jay, Dark thought. You don't belong out here.

But then, just before the machine cut off her view, he veered away from the mountain and in one great soaring arc passed over the boundary and into the humans' world.

Of Mist, and Grass, and Sand

The little boy was frightened. Gently, Snake touched his hot forehead. Behind her, three adults stood close together, watching, suspicious, afraid to show their concern with more than narrow lines around their eyes. They feared Snake as much as they feared their only child's death. In the dimness of the tent, the flickering lamplights gave no reassurance.

The child watched with eyes so dark the pupils were not visible, so dull that Snake herself feared for his life. She stroked his hair. It was long and very pale, a striking color against his dark skin, dry and irregular for several inches near the scalp. Had Snake been with these people months ago, she would have known the child was growing ill.

"Bring my case, please," Snake said.

The child's parents started at her soft voice. Perhaps they had expected the screech of a bright jay, or the hissing of a shining serpent. This was the first time Snake had spoken in their presence. She had only watched, when the three of them had come to observe her from a distance and whisper about her occupation and her youth; she had only listened, and then nodded, when finally they came to ask her help. Perhaps they had thought she was mute.

The fair-haired younger man lifted her leather case. He held the satchel away from his body, leaning to hand it to her, breathing shallowly with nostrils flared against the faint smell of musk in the dry desert air. Snake had almost accustomed herself to the kind of uneasiness he showed; she had already seen it often.

When Snake reached out, the young man jerked back and dropped the case. Snake lunged and barely caught it, gently set it on the felt floor, and glanced at him with reproach. His partners came forward and touched him to ease his fear. "He was bitten once," the dark and handsome woman said. "He almost died." Her tone was not of apology, but of justification.

"I'm sorry," the younger man said. "It's—" He gestured toward her; he was trembling, and trying visibly to control the reactions of his fear. Snake glanced down, to her shoulder where she had been unconsciously aware of the slight weight and movement. A tiny serpent, thin as the finger of a baby, slid himself around her neck to show his narrow head below her short black curls. He probed the air with his trident tongue in a leisurely manner, out, up and down, in, to savor the taste of the smells. "It's only Grass," Snake said. "He cannot harm you." If he were bigger, he might frighten; his color was pale green, but the scales around his mouth were red, as if he had just feasted as a mammal eats, by tearing. He was, in fact, much neater.

The child whimpered. He cut off the sound of pain; perhaps he had been told that Snake, too, would be offended by crying. She only felt sorry that his people refused themselves such a simple way of easing fear. She turned from the adults, regretting their terror of her but unwilling to spend the time it would take to convince them their reactions were unjustified. "It's all right," she said to the little boy. "Grass is smooth, and dry, and soft, and if I left him to guard you, even death could not reach your bedside." Grass poured himself into her narrow, dirty hand, and she extended him toward the child. "Gently." He reached out and touched the sleek scales with one fingertip. Snake could sense the effort of even such a simple motion, yet the boy almost smiled.

"What are you called?"

He looked quickly toward his parents, and finally they nodded. "Stavin," he whispered. He had no strength or breath for speaking.

"I am Snake, Stavin, and in a little while, in the morning, I must hurt you. You may feel a quick pain, and your body will ache for several days, but you will be better afterward."

He stared at her solemnly. Snake saw that though he understood and feared what she might do, he was less afraid than if she had lied to him. The pain must have increased greatly as his illness became more apparent, but it seemed that others had only reassured him, and hoped the disease would disappear or kill him quickly.

Snake put Grass on the boy's pillow and pulled her case nearer. The lock opened at her touch. The adults still could only fear her; they had had neither time nor reason to discover any trust. The woman of the partnership was old enough that they might never have another child, and Snake could tell by their eyes, their covert touching, their concern, that they loved this one very much. They must, to come to Snake in this country.

It was night, and cooling. Sluggish, Sand slid out of the case, moving his head, moving his tongue, smelling, tasting, detecting the warmths of bodies.

"Is that—?" The eldest partner's voice was low, and wise, but terrified, and Sand sensed the fear. He drew back into striking position and sounded his rattle softly. Snake spoke, moving her hand, and extended her arm. The pit viper relaxed and flowed around and around her slender wrist to form black and tan bracelets. "No," she said. "Your child is too ill for Sand to help. I know it is hard, but please try to be calm. This is a fearful thing for you, but it is all I can do."

She had to annoy Mist to make her come out. Snake rapped on the bag, and finally poked her twice. Snake felt the vibration of sliding scales, and suddenly the albino cobra flung herself into the tent. She moved quickly, yet there seemed to be no end to her. She reared back and up. Her breath rushed out in a hiss. Her head rose well over a meter above the floor. She flared her wide hood. Behind her, the adults gasped, as if physically assaulted by the gaze of the tan spectacle design on the back of Mist's hood. Snake ignored the people and spoke to the great cobra, focusing her attention by her words. "Ah, thou. Furious creature. Lie down; 'tis time for thee to earn thy dinner. Speak to this child, and touch him. He is called Stavin." Slowly, Mist relaxed her hood and allowed Snake to touch her. Snake grasped her firmly behind the head, and held her so she looked at Stavin. The cobra's silver eyes picked up the yellow of the lamplight. "Stavin," Snake said, "Mist will only meet you now. I promise that this time she will touch you gently."

Still, Stavin shivered when Mist touched his thin chest.

Snake did not release the serpent's head, but allowed her body to slide against the boy's. The cobra was four times longer than Stavin was tall. She curved herself in stark white loops across his swollen abdomen, extending herself, forcing her head toward the boy's face, straining against Snake's hands. Mist met Stavin's frightened stare with the gaze of lidless eyes. Snake allowed her a little closer.

Mist flicked out her tongue to taste the child.

The youngest partner made a small, cut-off, frightened sound. Stavin flinched at it, and Mist drew back, opening her mouth, exposing her fangs, audibly thrusting her breath through her throat. Snake sat back on her heels, letting out her own breath. Sometimes, in other places, the kinfolk could stay while she worked. "You must leave," she said gently. "It's dangerous to frighten Mist."

"I won't—"

"I'm sorry. You must wait outside."

Perhaps the younger man, perhaps even the woman, would have made the indefensible objections and asked the answerable questions, but the older man turned them and took their hands and led them away.

"I need a small animal," Snake said as he lifted the tent flap. "It must have fur, and it must be alive."

"One will be found," he said, and the three parents went into the glowing night. Snake could hear their footsteps in the sand outside.

Snake supported Mist in her lap and soothed her. The cobra wrapped herself around Snake's narrow waist, taking in her warmth. Hunger made the cobra even more nervous than usual, and she was hungry, as was Snake. Coming across the black sand desert, they had found sufficient water, but Snake's traps were unsuccessful. The season was summer, the weather was hot, and many of the furry tidbits Sand and Mist preferred were estivating. When the serpents missed their regular meal, Snake began a fast as well.

She saw with regret that Stavin was more frightened now. "I am sorry to send your parents away," she said. "They can come back soon."

His eyes glistened, but he held back the tears. "They said to do what you told me."

"I would have you cry, if you are able," Snake said "It isn't such a terrible thing." But Stavin seemed not to understand, and Snake did not press him; she knew that his people taught themselves to resist a difficult land by refusing to cry, refusing to mourn, refusing to laugh. They denied themselves grief, and allowed themselves little joy, but they survived.

Mist had calmed to sullenness. Snake unwrapped her from her waist and placed her on the pallet next to Stavin. As the cobra moved, Snake guided her head, feeling the tension of the striking muscles. "She will touch you with her tongue," she told Stavin. "It might tickle, but it will not hurt. She smells with it, as you do with your nose."

"With her tongue?"

Snake nodded, smiling, and Mist flicked out her tongue to caress Stavin's cheek. Stavin did not flinch; he watched, his child's delight in knowledge briefly overcoming pain. He lay perfectly still as Mist's long tongue brushed his cheeks, his eyes, his mouth. "She tastes the sickness," Snake said. Mist stopped fighting the restraint of her grasp, and drew back her head. Snake sat on her heels and released the cobra, who spiraled up her arm and laid herself across her shoulders.

"Go to sleep, Stavin," Snake said. "Try to trust me, and try not to fear the morning."

Stavin gazed at her for a few seconds, searching for truth in Snake's pale eyes. "Will Grass watch?"

She was startled by the question, or, rather, by the acceptance behind the question. She brushed his hair from his forehead and smiled a smile that was tears just beneath the surface. "Of course." She picked Grass up. "Thou wilt watch this child, and guard him." The snake lay quiet in her hand, and his eyes glittered black. She laid him gently on Stavin's pillow.

"Now sleep."

Stavin closed his eyes, and the life seemed to flow out of him. The alteration was so great that Snake reached out to touch him, then saw that he was breathing, slowly, shallowly. She tucked a blanket around him and stood up. The abrupt change in position dizzied her; she staggered and caught herself. Across her shoulders, Mist tensed.

Snake's eyes stung and her vision was oversharp, fever-clear. The sound she imagined she heard swooped in closer. She steadied herself against hunger and exhaustion, bent slowly, and picked up the leather case. Mist touched her cheek with the tip of her tongue.

She pushed aside the tent flap and felt relief that it was still night. She could stand the heat, but the brightness of the sun curled through her, burning. The moon must be full; though the clouds obscured everything, they diffused the light so the sky appeared gray from horizon to horizon. Beyond the tents, groups of formless shadows projected from the ground. Here, near the edge of the desert, enough water existed so clumps and patches of bush grew, providing shelter and sustenance for all manner of creatures. The black sand, which sparkled and blinded in the sunlight, at night was like a layer of soft soot. Snake stepped out of the tent, and the illusion of softness disappeared; her boots slid crunching into the sharp hard grains.

Stavin's family waited, sitting close together between the dark tents that clustered in a patch of sand from which the bushes had been ripped and burned. They looked at her silently, hoping with their eyes, showing no expression in their faces. A woman somewhat younger than Stavin's mother sat with them. She was dressed, as they were, in a long loose robe, but she wore the only adornment Snake had seen among these people: a leader's circle, hanging around her neck on a leather thong. She and Stavin's eldest parent were marked close kin by their similarities: sharpcut planes of face, high cheekbones, his hair white and hers graying early from deep black, their eyes the dark brown best suited for survival in the sun. On the ground by their feet a small black animal jerked sporadically against a net, and infrequently gave a shrill weak cry.

"Stavin is asleep," Snake said "Do not disturb him, but go to him if he wakes."

Stavin's mother and the youngest partner rose and went inside, but the older man stopped before her. "Can you help him?"

"I hope so. The tumor is advanced, but it seems solid." Her own voice sounded removed, slightly hollow, as if she were lying. "Mist will be ready in the morning." She still felt the need to give him reassurance, but she could think of none.

"My sister wished to speak with you," he said, and left them alone, without introduction, without elevating himself by saying that the tall woman was the leader of this group. Snake glanced back, but the tent flap fell shut. She was feeling her exhaustion more deeply, and across her shoulders Mist was, for the first time, a weight she thought heavy.

"Are you all right?"

Snake turned. The woman moved toward her with a natural elegance made slightly awkward by advanced pregnancy. Snake had to look up to meet her gaze. She had small fine lines at the corners of her eyes, as if she laughed, sometimes, in secret. She smiled, but with concern. "You seem very tired. Shall I have someone make you a bed?"

"Not now," Snake said, "not yet. I won't sleep until afterward."

The leader searched her face, and Snake felt a kinship with her in their shared responsibility.

"I understand, I think. Is there anything we can give you? Do you need aid with your preparations?"

Snake found herself having to deal with the questions as if they were complex problems. She turned them in her tired mind, examined them, dissected them, and finally grasped their meanings. "My pony needs food and water—"

"It is taken care of."

"And I need someone to help me with Mist. Someone strong. But it's more important that they aren't afraid."

The leader nodded. "I would help you," she said, and smiled again, a little. "But I am a bit clumsy of late. I will find someone."

"Thank you."

Somber again, the older woman inclined her head and moved slowly toward a small group of tents. Snake watched her go, admiring her grace. She felt small and young and grubby in comparison.

Sand began to unwrap himself from her wrist. Feeling the anticipatory slide of scales on her skin, she caught him before he could drop to the ground. Sand lifted the upper half of his body from her hands. He flicked out his tongue, peering toward the little animal, feeling its body heat, smelling its fear. "I know thou art hungry," Snake said, "but that creature is not for thee." She put Sand in the case, lifted Mist from her shoulder, and let her coil herself in her dark compartment.

The small animal shrieked and struggled again when Snake's diffuse shadow passed over it. She bent and picked it up. The rapid series of terrified cries slowed and diminished and finally stopped as she stroked it. Finally it lay still, breathing hard, exhausted, staring up at her with yellow eyes. It hand long hind legs and wide pointed ears, and its nose twitched at the serpent smell. Its soft black fur was marked off in skewed squares by the cords of the net.

"I am sorry to take your life," Snake told it. "But there will be no more fear, and I will not hurt you." She closed her hand gently around it and, stroking it, grasped its spine at the base of its skull. She pulled, once, quickly. It seemed to struggle, briefly, but it was already dead. It convulsed; its legs drew up against its body, and its toes curled and quivered. It seemed to stare up at her, even now. She freed its body from the net.

Snake chose a small vial from her belt pouch, pried open the animal's clenched jaws, and let a single drop of the vial's cloudy preparation fall into its mouth. Quickly she opened the satchel again and called Mist out. The cobra came slowly, slipping over the edge, hood closed, sliding in the sharp-grained sand. Her milky scales caught the thin light. She smelled the animal, flowed to it, touched it with her tongue. For a moment Snake was afraid she would refuse dead meat, but the body was still warm, still twitching reflexively, and she was very hungry. "A tidbit for thee." Snake spoke to the cobra: a habit of solitude. "To whet thy appetite." Mist nosed the beast, reared back, and struck, sinking her short fixed fangs into the tiny body, biting again, pumping out her store of poison. She released it, took a better grip, and began to work her jaws around it; it would hardly distend her throat. When Mist lay quiet, digesting the small meal, Snake sat beside her and held her, waiting.

She heard footsteps in the coarse sand.

"I'm sent to help you."

He was a young man, despite a scatter of white in his black hair. He was taller than Snake, and not unattractive. His eyes were dark, and the sharp planes of his face were further hardened because his hair was pulled straight back and tied. His expression was neutral.

"Are you afraid?"

"I will do as you tell me."

Though his form was obscured by his robe, his long fine hands showed strength.

"Then hold her body, and don't let her surprise you." Mist was beginning to twitch from the effects of the drugs Snake had put in the small animal. The cobra's eyes stared, unseeing.

"If it bites—"

"Hold, quickly!"

The young man reached, but he had hesitated too long. Mist writhed, lashing out, striking him in the face with her tail. He staggered back, at least as surprised as hurt. Snake kept a close grip behind Mist's jaws, and struggled to catch the rest of her as well. Mist was no constrictor, but she was smooth and strong and fast. Thrashing, she forced out her breath in a long hiss. She would have bitten anything she could reach. As Snake fought with her, she managed to squeeze the poison glands and force out the last drops of venom. They hung from Mist's fangs for a moment, catching light as jewels would; the force of the serpent's convulsions flung them away into the darkness. Snake struggled with the cobra, aided for once by the sand, on which Mist could get no purchase. Snake felt the young man behind her, grabbing for Mist's body and tail. The seizure stopped abruptly, and Mist lay limp in their hands.

"I am sorry—"

"Hold her," Snake said. "We have the night to go."

During Mist's second convulsion, the young man held her firmly and was of some real help. Afterward, Snake answered his interrupted question. "If she were making poison and she bit you, you would probably die. Even now her bite would make you ill. But unless you do something foolish, if she manages to bite, she will bite me."

"You would benefit my cousin little, if you were dead or dying."

"You misunderstand. Mist cannot kill me." She held out her hand so he could see the white scars of slashes and punctures. He stared at them, and looked into her eyes for a long moment, then looked away.

The bright spot in the clouds from which the light radiated moved westward in the sky; they held the cobra like a child. Snake found herself half-dozing, but Mist moved her head, dully attempting to evade restraint, and Snake woke herself abruptly. "I must not sleep," she said to the young man. "Talk to me. What are you called?"

As Stavin had, the young man hesitated. He seemed afraid of her, or of something. "My people," he said, "think it unwise to speak our names to strangers."

"If you consider me a witch you should not have asked my aid. I know no magic, and I claim none."

"It's not a superstition," he said. "Not as you might think. We're not afraid of being bewitched."

"I can't learn all the customs of all the people on this earth, so I keep my own. My custom is to address those I work with by name." Watching him, Snake tried to decipher his expression in the dim light.

"Our families know our names, and we exchange names with our partners."

Snake considered that custom, and thought it would fit badly on her. "No one else? Ever?"

"Well . . . a friend might know one's name."

"Ah," Snake said. "I see. I am still a stranger, and perhaps an enemy."

"A *friend* would know my name," the young man said again. "I would not offend you, but now you misunderstand. An acquaintance is not a friend. We value friendship highly."

"In this land one should be able to tell quickly if a person is worth calling 'friend.'"

"We take friends seldom. Friendship is a great commitment."

"It sounds like something to be feared."

He considered that possibility. "Perhaps it's the betrayal of friendship we fear. That is a very painful thing."

"Has anyone ever betrayed you?"

He glanced at her sharply, as if she had exceeded the limits of propriety. "No," he said, and his voice was as hard as his face. "No friend. I have no one I call friend."

His reaction startled Snake. "That's very sad," she said, and grew silent, trying to comprehend the deep stresses that could close people off so far, comparing her loneliness of necessity and theirs of choice. "Call me Snake," she said finally, "if you can bring yourself to pronounce it. Saying my name binds you to nothing."

The young man seemed about to speak; perhaps he thought again that he had offended her, perhaps he felt he should further defend his customs. But Mist began to twist in their hands, and they had to hold her to keep her from injuring herself. The cobra was slender for her length, but powerful, and the convulsions she went through were more severe than any she had ever had before. She thrashed in Snake's grasp, and almost pulled away. She tried to spread her hood, but Snake held her too tightly. She opened her mouth and hissed, but no poison dripped from her fangs.

She wrapped her tail around the young man's waist. He began to pull her and turn, to extricate himself from her coils.

"She's not a constrictor," Snake said. "She won't hurt you. Leave her—"

But it was too late; Mist relaxed suddenly and the young man lost his balance. Mist whipped herself away and lashed figures in the sand. Snake wrestled with her alone while the young man tried to hold her, but she curled herself around Snake and used the grip for leverage. She started to pull herself from Snake's hands. Snake threw them both backward into the sand; Mist rose above her, openmouthed, furious, hissing. The young man lunged and grabbed her just beneath her hood. Mist struck at him, but Snake, somehow, held her back. Together they deprived Mist of her hold and regained control of her. Snake struggled up, but Mist suddenly went quite still and lay almost rigid between them. They were both sweating; the young man was pale under his tan, and even Snake was trembling.

"We have a little while to rest," Snake said. She glanced at him and notice the dark line on his cheek where, earlier, Mist's tail had slashed him. She reached up and touched it. "You'll have a bruise," she said. "But it will not scar."

"If it were true, that serpents sting with their tails, you would be restraining both the fangs and the stinger, and I'd be of little use."

"Tonight I'd need someone to keep me awake, whether or not they helped me with Mist." Fighting the cobra produced adrenalin, but now it ebbed, and her exhaustion and hunger were returning, stronger.

"Snake . . ."

"Yes?"

He smiled, quickly, half embarrassed. "I was trying the pronunciation."

"Good enough."

"How long did it take you to cross the desert?"

"Not very long. Too long. Six days."

How did you live?"

"There is water. We traveled at night, except yesterday, when I could find no shade."

"You carried all your food?"

She shrugged. "A little." And wished he would not speak of food.

"What's on the other side?"

"Mountains. Streams. A few groups of people, traders, the station I grew up and took my training in. And farther on, another desert, and a mountain with a city inside."

"I would like to see a city. Someday."

"The desert can be crossed."

He said nothing, but Snake's memories of leaving home were recent enough that she could imagine his thoughts.

The next set of convulsions came, much sooner than Snake had expected. By their severity she gauged something of the stage of Stavin's illness, and wished it were morning. If she were to lose him, she would have it done, and grieve, and try to forget. The cobra would have battered herself to death against the sand if Snake and young man had not been holding her. She suddenly went completely rigid, with her mouth clamped shut and her forked tongue dangling.

She stopped breathing.

"Hold her," Snake said. "Hold her head. Quickly, take her, and if she gets away, run. Take her! She won't strike at you now, she could only slash you by accident."

He hesitated only a moment, then grasped Mist begind the head. Snake ran, slipping in the deep sand, from the edge of the circle of tents to a place where bushes still grew. She broke off dry thorny branches that tore her scarred hands. Peripherally she noticed a mass of horned vipers, so ugly they seemed deformed, nesting beneath the clump of dessicated vegetation. They hissed at her; she ignored them. She found a narrow hollow stem and carried it back. Her hands bled from deep scratches.

Kneeling by Mist's head, she forced open the cobra's mouth and pushed the tube deep into her throat, through the air passage at the base of Mist's tongue. She bent close, took the tube in her mouth, and breathed gently into Mist's lungs.

She noticed: the young man's hands, holding the cobra as she had asked; his breathing, first a sharp gasp of surprise, then ragged; the sand scraping her elbows where she leaned; the cloying smell of the fluid seeping from Mist's fangs; her own dizziness, she thought from exhaustion, which she forced away by necessity and will.

Snake breathed, and breathed again, paused, and repeated, until Mist caught the rhythm and continued it unaided.

Snake sat back on her heels. "I think she'll be all right," she said. "I hope she will." She brushed the back of her hand across her forehead. The touched sparked pain: she jerked her hand down and agony slid along her bones, up her arm, across her shoulder, through her chest, enveloping her heart. Her balance turned on its edge. She fell, tried to catch herself but moved too slowly, fought nausea and vertigo and almost succeeded, until the pull of the earth seemed to slip away in pain and she was lost in darkness with nothing to take a bearing by.

She felt sand where it had scraped her cheek and her palms, but it was soft. "Snake, can I let go?" She thought the question must be for someone else, while at the same time she knew there was no one else to answer it, no one else to reply to her name. She felt hands on her, and they were gentle; she wanted to respond to them, but she was too tired. She needed sleep more, so she pushed them away. But they held her head and put dry leather to her lips and poured water into her throat. She coughed and choked and spat it out.

She pushed herself up on one elbow. As her sight cleared, she realized she was shaking. She felt as she had the first time she was snake-bit, before her immunities had completely developed. The young man knelt over her, his water flask in his hand. Mist, beyond him, crawled toward the darkness. Snake forgot the throbbing pain. "Mist!" She slapped the ground.

The young man flinched and turned, frightened; the serpent reared up, her head nearly at Snake's standing eyelevel, her hood spread, swaying, watching, angry, ready to strike. She formed a wavering white line against black. Snake forced herself to rise, feeling as though she were fumbling with the control of some unfamiliar body. She almost fell again, but held herself steady. "Thou must not go to hunt now," she said. "There is work for thee to do." She held out her right hand to the side, a decoy, to draw Mist if she struck. Her hand was heavy with pain. Snake feared, not being bitten, but the loss of the contents of Mist's poison sacs. "Come here," she said. "Come here, and stay thy anger." She noticed blood flowing down between her fingers, and the fear she felt for Stavin was intensified. "Didst thou bite me, creature?" But the pain was wrong: poison would numb her, and the new serum only sting . . .

"No," the young man whispered from behind her.

Mist struck. The reflexes of long training took over. Snake's right hand jerked away, her left grabbed Mist as she brought her head back. The cobra writhed a moment, and relaxed. "Devious beast," Snake said. "For shame." She turned and let Mist crawl up her arm and over her shoulder, where she lay like the outline of an invisible cape and dragged her tail like the edge of a train.

"She did not bite me?"

"No," the young man said. His contained voice was touched with awe. "You should be dying. You should be curled around the agony, and your arm swollen purple. When you came back—" He gestured toward her hand. "It must have been a bush viper."

Snake remembered the coil of reptiles beneath the

branches, and touched the blood on her hand. She wiped it away, revealing the double puncture of a snakebite among the scratches of the thorns. The wound was slightly swollen. "It needs cleaning," she said. "I shame myself by falling to it." The pain of it washed in gentle waves up her arm, burning no longer. She stood looking at the young man, looking around her, watching the landscape shift and change as her tired eyes tried to cope with the low light of setting moon and false dawn. "You held Mist well, and bravely," she said to the young man. "I thank you."

He lowered his gaze, almost bowing to her. He rose, and approached her. Snake put her hand gently on Mist's neck so she would not be alarmed.

"I would be honored," the young man said, "if you would call me Arevin."

"I would be pleased to."

Snake knelt down and held the winding white loops as Mist crawled slowly into her compartment. In a little while, when Mist had stabilized, by dawn, they could go to Stavin.

The tip of Mist's white tail slid out of sight. Snake closed the case and would have risen, but she could not stand. She had not quite shaken off the effects of the new venom. The flesh around the wound was red and tender, but the hemorrhaging would not spread. She stayed where she was, slumped, staring at her hand, creeping slowly in her mind toward what she needed to do, this time for herself.

"Let me help you. Please."

He touched her shoulder and helped her stand. "I'm sorry," she said. "I'm so in need of rest . . ."

"Let me wash your hand," Arevin said. "And then you can sleep. Tell me when to awaken you—"

"I can't sleep yet." she collected herself, straightened, tossed the damp curls of her short hair off her forehead. "I'm all right now. Have you any water?"

Arevin loosened his outer robe. Beneath it he wore a loincloth and a leather belt that carried several leather flasks and pouches. His body was lean and well-built, his legs long and muscular. The color of his skin was slightly lighter than the sun-darkened brown of his face. He brought out his water flask and reached for Snake's hand.

"No, Arevin. If the poison gets in any small scratch you might have, it could infect."

She sat down and sluiced lukewarm water over her hand. The water dripped pink to the ground and disappeared, leaving not even a damp spot visible. The wound bled a little more, but now it only ached. The poison was almost inactivated.

"I don't understand," Arevin said, "how it is that you're unhurt. My younger sister was bitten by a bush viper." He could speak as uncaringly as he might have wished. "We could do nothing to save her—nothing we have would even lessen her pain."

Snake gave him his flask and rubbed salve from a vial in her belt pouch across the closing punctures. "It's a part of our preparation," she said. "We work with many kinds of serpents, so we must be immune to as many as possible." She shrugged. "The process is tedious and somewhat painful." She clenched her fist; the film held, and she was steady. She leaned toward Arevin and touched his abraded cheek again. "Yes . . ." She spread a thin layer of the salve across it. "That will help it heal."

"If you cannot sleep," Arevin said, "can you at least rest?"

"Yes," she said. "For a little while."

Snake sat next to Arevin, leaning against him, and they watched the sun turn the clouds to gold and flame and amber. The simple physical contact with another human being gave Snake pleasure, though she found it unsatisfying. Another time, another place, she might do something more, but not here, not now.

When the lower edge of the sun's bright smear rose above the horizon, Snake rose and teased Mist out of the case. She came slowly, weakly, and crawled across Snake's shoulders. Snake picked up the satchel, and she and Arevin walked together back to the small group of tents.

Stavin's parents waited, watching for her, just outside the entrance of their tent. They stood in a tight, defensive, silent group. For a moment Snake thought they had decided to send her away. Then, with regret and fear like hot iron in her mouth, she asked if Stavin had died. They shook their heads, and allowed her to enter.

Stavin lay as she had left him, still asleep. The adults followed her with their stares, and she could smell fear. Mist flicked out her tongue, growing nervous from the implied danger.

"I know you would stay," Snake said. "I know you would help, if you could, but there is nothing to be done by any person but me. Please go back outside."

They glanced at each other, and at Arevin, and she thought for a moment that they would refuse. Snake wanted to fall into the silence and sleep. "Come, cousins," Arevin said. "We are in her hands." He opened the tent flap and motioned them out. Snake thanked him with nothing more than a glance, and he might almost have smiled. She turned toward Stavin, and knelt beside him. "Stavin—" She touched his forehead; it was very hot. She noticed that her hand was less steady than before. The slight touch awakened the child. "It's time," Snake said.

He blinked, coming out of some child's dream, seeing her, slowly recognizing her. He did not look frightened. For that Snake was glad; for some other reason she could not identify she was uneasy.

"Will it hurt?"

"Does it hurt now?"

He hesitated, looked away, looked back. "Yes."

"It might hurt a little more. I hope not. Are you ready?"

"Can Grass stay?"

"Of course," she said.

And realized what was wrong.

"I'll come back in a moment." Her voice changed so much, she had pulled it so tight, that she could not help but frighten him. She left the tent, walking slowly, calmly, restraining herself. Outside, the parents told her by their faces what they feared.

"Where is Grass?" Arevin, his back to her, started at her tone. The fair-haired man made a small grieving sound, and could look at her no longer.

"We were afraid," the eldest partner said. "We thought it would bite the child."

"I thought it would. It was I. It crawled over his face, I could see its fangs—" Stavin's mother put her hands on her younger partner's shoulders, and he said no more.

"Where is he?" She wanted to scream; she did not.

They brought her a small open box. Snake took it and looked inside.

Grass lay cut almost in two, his entrails oozing from his body, half turned over, and as she watched, shaking, he writhed once, flicked his tongue out once, and in. Snake made some sound, too low in her throat to be a cry. She hoped his motions were only reflex, but she picked him up as gently as she could. She leaned down and touched her lips to the smooth green scales behind his head. She bit him quickly, sharply, at the base of the skull. His blood flowed cool and salty in her mouth. If he were not dead, she had killed him instantly.

She looked at the parents, and at Arevin; they were all pale, but she had no sympathy for their fear, and cared nothing for shared grief. "Such a small creature," she said. "Such a small creature, who could only give pleasure and dreams." She watched them for a moment more, then turned toward the tent again.

"Wait—" She heard the eldest partner move up close behind her. He touched her shoulder; she shrugged away his hand. "We will give you anything you want," he said, "but leave the child alone."

She spun on him in a fury. "Should I kill Stavin for your stupidity?" He seemed about to try to hold her back. She jammed her shoulder hard into his stomach, and flung herself past the tent flap. Inside, she kicked over the satchel. Abruptly awakened, and angry, Sand crawled out and coiled himself. When someone tried to enter, Sand hissed and rattled with a violence Snake had never heard him use before. She did not even bother to look behind her. She ducked her head and wiped her tears on her sleeve before Stavin could see them. She knelt beside him.

"What's the matter?" He could not help but hear the voices outside the tent, and the running.

"Nothing, Stavin," Snake said. "Did you know we came across the desert?"

"No," he said with wonder.

"It was very hot, and none of us had anything to eat. Grass is hunting now. He was very hungry. Will you forgive him and let me begin? I will be here all the time."

He seemed so tired; he was disappointed, but he had no strength for arguing. "All right." His voice rustled like sand slipping through the fingers.

Snake lifted Mist from her shoulders, and pulled the blanket from Stavin's small body. The tumor pressed up beneath his rib cage, distorting his form, squeezing his vital organs, sucking nourishment from him for its own growth, poisoning him with its wastes. Holding Mist's head, Snake let her flow across him, touching and tasting him. She had to restrain the cobra to keep her from striking; the excitement had agitated her. When Sand used his rattle, the vibrations made her flinch. Snake stroked her, soothing her; trained and bred-in responses began to return, overcoming the natural instincts. Mist paused when her tongue flicked the skin above the tumor, and Snake released her.

The cobra reared, and struck, and bit as cobras bite, sinking her fangs their short length once, releasing, instantly biting again for a better purchase, holding on, chewing at her prey. Stavin cried out, but he did not move against Snake's restraining hands.

Mist expended the contents of her venom sacs into the child, and released him. She reared up, peered around, folded her hood, and slid across the mats in a perfectly straight line toward her dark close compartment.

"It's done, Stavin."

"Will I die now?"

"No," Snake said. "Not now. Not for many years, I hope." She took a vial of powder from her belt pouch. "Open your mouth." He complied, and she sprinkled the powder across his tongue. "That will help the ache." She spread a pad of cloth across the series of shallow puncture wounds, without wiping off the blood.

She turned from him.

"Snake? Are you going away?"

"I will not leave without saying goodbye. I promise."

The child lay back, closed his eyes, and let the drug take him.

Sand coiled quiescently on the dark matting. Snake patted the floor to call him. He moved toward her, and suffered himself to be replaced in the satchel. Snake closed it and lifted it, and it still felt empty. She heard noises outside the tent. Stavin's parents and the people who had come to help them pulled open the tent flap and peered inside, thrusting sticks in even before they looked.

Snake set down her leather case. "It's done."

They entered. Arevin was with them too; only he was empty-handed. "Snake—" He spoke through grief, pity, confusion, and Snake could not tell what he believed. He looked back. Stavin's mother was just behind him. He took her by the shoulder. "He would have died without her. Whatever happens now, he would have died."

She shook his hand away. "He might have lived. It might have gone away. We—" She could speak no more for hiding tears.

Snake felt the people moving, surrounding her. Arevin took one step toward her and stopped, and she could see he wanted her to defend herself. "Can any of you cry?" she said.

"Can any of you cry for me and my despair, or for them and their guilt, or for small things and their pain?" She felt tears slip down her cheeks.

They did not understand her; they were offended by her crying. They stood back, still afraid of her, but gathering themselves. She no longer needed the pose and calmness she had used to deceive the child. "Ah, you fools." Her voice sounded brittle. "Stavin—"

Light from the entrance struck them. "Let me pass." The people in front of Snake moved aside for their leader. She stopped in front of Snake, ignoring the satchel her foot almost touched. "Will Stavin live?" Her voice was quiet, calm, gentle.

"I cannot be certain," Snake said, "but I feel that he will."

"Leave us." The people understood Snake's words before they did their leader's; they looked around and lowered their weapons, and finally, one by one, they moved out of the tent. Arevin remained. Snake felt the strength that came from danger seeping from her. Her knees collapsed. She bent over the satchel with her face in her hands. The older woman knelt in front of her, before Snake could notice or prevent her. "Thank you," she said. "Thank you. I am so sorry . . ." She put her arms around Snake, and drew her toward her, and Arevin knelt beside them, and he embraced Snake too. Snake began to tremble again, and they held her while she cried.

Later she slept, exhausted, alone in the tent with Stavin, holding his hand. The people had caught small animals for Sand and Mist. They had given her food, and supplies, and sufficient water for her to bathe, though the last must have strained their resources.

When she awakened, Arevin lay sleeping nearby, his robe open in the heat, a sheen of sweat across his chest and stomach. The sternness in his expression vanished when he slept; he looked exhausted and vulnerable. Snake almost woke him, but stopped, shook her head, and turned to Stavin.

She felt the tumor, and found that it had begun to dissolve and shrivel, dying, as Mist's changed poison affected it. Through her grief Snake felt a little joy. She smoothed Stavin's pale hair back from his face. "I would not lie to you again, little one," she whispered, "but I must leave soon. I cannot stay here." She wanted another three days' sleep, to finish fighting off the effects of the bush viper's poison, but she would sleep somewhere else. "Stavin?"

He half woke, slowly. "It doesn't hurt anymore," he said.

"I am glad."

"Thank you . . ."

"Goodbye, Stavin. Will you remember later on that you woke up, and that I did stay to say goodbye?"

"Goodbye," he said, drifting off again. "Goodbye, Snake. Goodbye, Grass." He closed his eyes.

Snake picked up the satchel and stood gazing down at Arevin. He did not stir. Half grateful, half regretful, she left the tent.

Dusk approached with long, indistinct shadows; the camp was hot and quiet. She found her tiger-striped pony, tethered with food and water. New, full water-skins bulged on the ground next to the saddle, and desert robes lay across the pommel, though Snake had refused any payment. The tiger-pony whickered at her. She scratched his striped ears, saddled him, and strapped her gear on his back. Leading him, she started east, the way she had come.

"Snake—"

She took a breath, and turned back to Arevin. He was facing the sun; it turned his skin ruddy and his robe scarlet. His streaked hair flowed loose to his shoulders, gentling his face. "You must leave?"

"Yes."

"I hoped you would not leave before . . . I hoped you would stay, for a time . . ."

"If things were different, I might have stayed."

"They were frightened—"

"I told them Grass couldn't hurt them, but they saw his fangs and they didn't know he could only give dreams and ease dying."

"But can't you forgive them?"

"I can't face their guilt. What they did was my fault, Arevin. I didn't understand them until too late."

"You said it yourself, you can't know all the customs and all the fears."

"I'm crippled," she said. "Without Grass, if I can't heal a person, I cannot help at all. I must go home and face my teachers, and hope they'll forgive my stupidity. They seldom give the name I bear, but they gave it to me—and they'll be disappointed."

"Let me come with you."

She wanted to; she hesitated, and cursed herself for that weakness. "They may take Mist and Sand and cast me out, and you would be cast out too. Stay here, Arevin."

"It wouldn't matter."

"It would. After a while, we would hate each other. I don't know you, and you don't know me. We need calmness, and quiet, and time to understand each other well."

He came toward her, and put his arms around her, and they stood embracing for a moment. When he raised his head, there were tears on his cheeks. "Please come back," he said. "Whatever happens, please come back."

"I will try," Snake said. "Next spring, when the winds stop, look for me. The spring after that, if I do not come, forget me. Where I am, if I live, I will forget you."

"I will look for you," Arevin said, and he would promise no more.

Snake picked up her pony's lead, and started across the desert.

Spectra

I am dreaming. I reach out for something I have lost, something beautiful. I cannot remember what it is, but I know that it is there. Sounds echo in the background. My hands are stopped. I push against the barrier, straining, helpless. I open my eyes to darkness, and remember. I am lying in my sleeping place, with my hands pressed hard against the ceiling just above me, as if I could push it away and be free again. My hands move across the smooth cold surface to corners, as far apart as the width of my shoulders, down the walls to the narrow spaces at my sides. My hands stop, and I lie still.

There is a quick sharp pain in my leg as the cannulae withdraw from the valve implanted in my ankle. The bell that woke me rings again, the bell that calls us to our work. The panel opens at my feet, and light pierces the dark hole in which I am imprisoned. I turn over and crawl out, backward, bending my elbows so I don't scrape my back on the ceiling. I stand on the walkway among the formless gray shapes of the others. Our routine is unchanging, unchangeable. The walkway slides, taking us toward our consoles. Everyone around me whispers and laughs, but I am silent.

They all claim they know what beauty is. They say they see it every work period. They say the patterns that direct us calm and gratify and excite them. They are proud they are better than machines. They say it is ecstasy. If all I could remember was the blackness and the shadows and the broken bars of light, perhaps I could be as content, but I can never feel what they do.

The walkway stops. I turn, walk two steps, and slide into the seat of my console. The fear that touches me every day reaches deeper. I have tried to avoid the helmet before, and learned better. It engulfs my head, cutting off the shadows of my sight. The probes reach out and touch the metal sockets that replace my eyes. I flinch back, but I cannot move away. The probes enter, and the patterns begin.

I work hard. I do my duty. I watch the patterns of darkness and light and do what they tell me. But I want to see the day again.

The sky and the trees are what I remember most. The trees brushed their points against blue, all around our house. The bark was rough and the needles soft and sharp. When I climbed the trees my hands became sticky with golden pitch that left the smell of evergreen on my fingers. The sky was the color of my mother's eyes (I wonder if they took hers away, too?). I only saw the end of the sky once, when I walked too far and the forest stopped. I was very young. I stood at the edge of a cliff accompanied by wind and sun. And I saw that the sky ended in a yellow-brown roiling cloud. I ran home crying, real tears salty on my tongue, drying stiff on my face. My mother comforted me. She said the cloud would never come any nearer. I did not walk that way anymore, even when I was older and should not have been afraid.

A mild electric shock jerks me to awareness. Some error has been made. Three of us work on each set of patterns, as a check against mistakes. I look again, consciously, at the image in my brain. I do what it indicates. My error is confirmed and corrected. I cannot escape my punishment by drawing away or by bracing myself. It jolts through me, and my fingers clench. It is not too strong this time, but if I err again it will be worse. I think that's because they know that sometimes I make mistakes on purpose. The others say they never make mistakes. I don't believe it. I hate their silly patterns. It took them a long time to teach me how to figure out what each set of lines told me to do. They are all different, and I didn't want to learn.

When I was little I could make figures in the dark by pressing my fingers against the corners of my eyes. All the colors came, the ones that are in rainbows (it's so hard to remember rainbows . . . which was on top, violet or red?) and some that aren't. The jagged lines and circles and flowing creatures moved and danced and kept me company at night.

Now, when I'm supposed to be asleep, I remember my childhood companions and I touch my eyes. I always hope that the colors will return and that I'll see the day again. It's hard to remember what colors really look like. I hope, but I touch my closed eyelids and see nothing, and what I feel is hard and dead. Crystals and circuits and lenses that allow me to resolve dark bands into fine lines. It all seems very important to them. It is meaningless to me, and that makes me angry. Sometimes I claw at my eyes in the night. I know I should not . . .

One day as I was coming home I heard voices. Hidden by the corner of our house, I watched. I heard them call my mother selfish. They said we couldn't stay there anymore. She said they were wrong and they knocked her down. I cried stop it! stop it! and beat my fists against their chests. They pulled me away. I looked down and saw how small and frail she was. I tried to hit them again, but they laughed at me and knocked me down too, and when I woke up I was here, and the world was gray shadows. I wonder what they did to my mother . . .

The bands of light and dark fade. I stop. If I tried to keep working without information I would be punished again. It is time for exercise. They want to keep us healthy. The eyepieces withdraw from my dead sockets and the helmet lifts from my head. The world turns to gray, featureless, formless shapes. In this it is worse than when I am working, when the magnified patterns are sharp and clear.

I turn around on my chair and stand up. Two steps forward. The floor moves. The first time it moved beneath my feet I fell down. They had warned me about it. They were watching me my first day, so they punished me. After that I did not fall. The floor takes us all to a large room where the paleness of the walls is a little grayed by distance, and I can hear echoes.

The gray shapes of the others move around me. I know they cannot tell, and I think no one who can see is watching, but I am ashamed to be naked. We put our hands on metal bars and push. Around and around, until we perspire and the air drafts make us cold.

We all have glowing symbols on our backs, each different, so we may be identified. I can feel no difference on my skin, so I don't know how they are made. I push, and walk around and around. There is no symbol near me that I recognize. I hear conversations going on but they are all about the ecstasy of the lights and who had the most unusual pattern. My sweat tickles me, and I want to scratch. Finally the bars slow and lock. The shadows seem to spin around me. I almost fall. The pressure of the others forces me to keep my balance.

We make our way to the moving hall again. I feel disoriented and dizzy. We squeeze our eyelids shut and water gushes over us, cleaning the sweat away. The water is always too hot. Air dries us. Sometimes it is too cold, and we are not really dried at all.

I remember swimming in a deep dark pond near our little house. I wasn't ashamed to be naked there, and I liked the breezes that spread me with goosebumps. I remember grass and pebbles under my feet, and sun cushioning the wind on my back.

The helmet lowers and clasps my head unmoving. The eyepieces extend, enter, attach, and I am once more a receptacle for lines of black and bars of light. I no longer have to think carefully about what I am doing. I think of later, when I can lie down and rest. There will be no patterns and no shadows against the blackness where my sight should be. I think of the insubstantial varicolored companions of my childhood. I am lonely . . . I think of another way to touch my eyelids, a way I've never tried before, so my night friends may perhaps come back. I tell myself that I will be disappointed, but I do not believe it. I believe it will work. I want to close my eyes now and try, but my eyes cannot close here, and if I take my hands from the controls I will be punished again. I work with anticipation now, and eagerness, as if by doing so the time will pass more quickly.

I make an error. I cringe from the shock and my mouth is metallic. My mind has ignored a dark line. I do not understand how I could have missed it. I try again. The punishment surprises and hurts me. I do not know what I have done wrong. The shock recurs. My actions become almost erratic. Perhaps it is their error—

The eyepieces withdraw abruptly. There is something wrong. The senseless punishments frighten me. The helmet releases me. I turn and get up and take two steps, because I know that's what I'm supposed to do. The floor begins to move. I can hear nothing but its glide, see nothing but the uniform paleness of walls passing me. There are no shadow people here, no people like me. Dark lines flash around me, around and around, spinning, enclosing me. I know what is the matter. There's something wrong with the things I use for eyes. I know they will blame me. I'm terrified that they will take away the last remnants of my sight. But now I think, if theirs will not work they will have to give me my real eyes back.

The floor stops. I am reeling. A door opens and a shadow person takes my arm and pulls me inside. I close my eyelids, screw up my face, keep my eyes shut tight. I want my real eyes back. Yours will not work much longer. I will not let you fix them, give me back my eyes.

They tell me to open my eyes. I almost smile. I can't open something I don't have. They tell me again. They slap me. I put up my arms to shield my face, and they slap me again. I can only make dry sobs. My eyelids open and the heavy things behind them drive the ugly shadows and lights into my brain. I am taken to a table and made to lie down. They put straps around me so I can't move, and they start to probe my eyes.

It hurts. It takes a long time, and I can't even see their shadows. It hurts.

They finish, they untie me, they thrust me out. I hear them laughing as I stumble onto the moving floor. It is an ugly sound. My head aches. I go back to my place and sit down. The lights are too bright, the blacks too dark, but I'm not allowed to stop. My hands are trembling. I remember that I've thought of a new way to make myself see, and for a while I can forget the pain.

Finally my time is up. The floor takes us back to our sleeping places. I crawl inside, crouching. I must fit my ankle against the cannulae or the panel at my feet will not slide shut, and I will be punished. I remember soft fragrant pallets of pine boughs and the pleasant soft scratchiness of those needles. Tonight I do not fear the pain. I do what is expected of me and wait for the panel to cut off the light.

I reach up and touch my eyes. Anticipation tickles my throat. It will be so good to see the colors again and remember what they really are. I know this way will work. I reach up—

My hands jerk away. They cannot punish me here. They cannot. This is my place, my time . . . I reach again, and the shock is stronger. My fingers jerk back reflexively and the back of my head hurts from the pressure of the bed. My hands creep up once more. The shock is so strong that the spark flashes back to my brain. I smell seared flesh, and my fingers are numb. I put them to my lips. I can taste blood. I know they will hurt tomorrow, when I must use them at my work.

But even if they did not hurt, I could not touch my eyes. The shadow people will not let me. If only they would, I know that I could see.

I want to cry. I wish that I had tears.

Wings

Long after the last visitors had left the temple, after time had begun to pass almost unnoticed in a deep, unrippled stream, a shape appeared, far distant, unrecognizable through the thin-film watered-silk patterns of the auroras. It ignored the passages between the light-curtains, which led eventually, slowly, to the only structure on the hills, the only thing on which they could focus. As the shape pushed through the membranes, they roiled darkly, discolored, touching and attaching again. The keeper of the temple could follow the angry violet path of their healing, and his own wounds ached in sympathy. He hugged his long arms closer around his bony knees, and watched the approaching shape with great, reflective eyes, slowly blinking.

The keeper had been alone for so long that his isolation had become a habit; for a moment, he hoped the shape might be a wanderer, lost but needing to continue, so he could point it a direction and send it on its way. He could see, by then, that it was a person. Its progress was direct, purposeful. The keeper wondered how it had found its way, without following the labyrinth. The sky was obscured among the curtains.

He saw that it was tired. It neither faltered nor staggered, but came quite slowly. As it approached, the auroras seemed to impede it. It broke through the final veil, stumbled, fell

60

against the low wall, reached to cross it, failed. The keeper could only see its hand, two black fingers and a thumb, tips of silver claws, against gray stone.

He rose and limped across the courtyard, walking faster than when he wished to conceal the limp. A pulse beat in the wrist he touched, too slow, too weak. His hands lingered, touching delicate bones through thin bands of muscle and mole-smooth skin. He rediscovered the sensation of touch, the friction of fur as short as it can be against the same, the warmth of contact. It had been a long time since he had touched another person, even in greeting. His heartbeat quickened.

The thin shape breathed twice, shallowly, quickly, as he touched it. He saw the unnatural angles of its broken bones, and turned it over gently, caressing, so he could pick it up.

He drew back, guiltily. This person was a youth, barely a youth, one who had not yet made a decision.

His hands were more gentle as he picked the youth up—gentle, as one carries a child.

He placed the youth on his own hard bed outside the temple. The collapse must have been from pain. The long third finger of the left hand was broken, and the wing it supported lay crumpled like a smashed ion sail. The keeper opened the dark wing, pulling long frail fingers away from the back of the arm where they had tried to fold. No bone had pierced the skin, nor were the soft membranes torn away or even cut. The wing might heal. The keeper set himself to straightening the bones.

He hoped that care would overcome lack of knowledge, and prevent the youth from being crippled. When he was almost finished, he realized he was being watched. He glanced up.

He managed not to look quickly away. The youth had pastel-green eyes that made his well-formed face ugly. The keeper looked back at the youth's broken wing, as if that were the natural thing to do. "I've done the best I could with thy hand," he said, speaking as one speaks to children and youths.

"I tried to fly over the auroras." The tone was defiant, proud, expecting castigation.

"That is dangerous," the keeper said mildly. Above the temple, the atmosphere was as confused as the light-curtained passages.

"I hoped I would be killed."

"Deep despair for one so young."

"It's dying," the youth said. "Everything's dying."

The keeper saw that the youth was half-irrational from pain and exhaustion. "Sleep," he said.

"Don't you believe me? Didn't you know? You're supposed to be a seer."

"Thou are very cynical."

The youth did not answer, turned away, tried, clumsily, to flex the splinted wing.

"It is less solid than the earth," the keeper said. "Thou shouldst be gentle."

"Why did you help me? Why should you care?" the youth cried in confusion, hatred, grief.

"Go to sleep," the keeper said.

He moved inside the temple to perform his duties. They were few, and empty tradition. The god had departed, long before its last, ridiculed worshippers, as gods always do. The keeper knew that, and allowed himself no illusions about his status. It was his by chance and luck and response to pain, not divine gift. He poured libations to a memory, to a real god, the soul of unconscious things, not outgrown but driven away.

When he had finished his rituals, he returned to the youth, who slept the healing sleep. The keeper felt the throat-pulse and temperature and found neither sufficiently elevated. The precarious, rapid metabolism of their species had to accelerate when called on to heal. The keeper hunched down beside the bed, newly concerned. The youth's fine wide broken wing lay stretched open across the gray stone courtyard, useless as insulation, losing heat. The keeper did not stir for quite a long time. Finally he moved, painfully, and lay down on the narrow pallet. Quite chastely, and with some guilty reluctance, he enfolded the youth in his own one good wing. Then he, too, slept.

Much time had passed since anyone had come to induce prophecies, to wait as he hunched before the altar, sleep-watching, tranced. Now, lying beside the youth, he could feel a vision at the edge of his mind, but it was too distant and too weak to grasp. All the youth's resources were focused within; none were left for resonances. After exhausting himself struggling toward the vision in sleep, the keeper only dreamed. He awoke with memories of close, beckoning stars and high thin air, and a twisting sense of loss. He had dreamed of flying with his mate, so high that below them the earth curved away, yellow and brown and white-wisped with clouds. The sky was purple and gold in the daytime, shading to pale blue on the horizons, black and silver at night. He had loved his mate, but she was dead, and he had loved the night, but it was beyond his reach.

The keeper lay still, unwilling to move and renew his pain. But he must; his own warmth had helped a little, but the youth's body needed food to maintain itself.

The keeper's supplies were not well suited to providing sufficient energy. No one brought meat anymore, and he could not hunt. He was crippled, fit only to serve an abandoned god. He lifted his wing, folded it silently, and rose, to prepare seed paste and broth. He moved slowly, masking pain with caution, and the appearance of grace. Before, when people had come, his manner toward them had been equally graceful, and the children had lost their reticence after only a little while. The adults preferred to pretend apprehension and fear, for they came to the temple to keep their excitement high, to combat impatience, as they would glide over a live volcano or chase a whirlwind. Sometimes the fear could be real. If they stayed long enough, he might tell them their deaths with enigmatic visions they would not recognize until they were imminent. That was the way of seers. But the people were gone; they did not need him anymore. They had not really needed him for a long time, and perhaps they had never needed him at all.

The keeper carried the broth outside and held the shallow bowl to the youth's lips. The youth, half-awake, eyes half-open, seemed not to notice the vegetable taste. The keeper felt the thin tight muscles and smooth skin against his supporting hand, but at the same time saw the ugly eyes again. They were like the soft jellied plants or creatures that grew in the dark, and died in the sunlight. He envied the youth's wings, but pitied the eyes. His patient could never fly much higher than the clouds without going blind.

The youth muttered incomprehensibly and flailed at the keeper's hand so the nearly empty bowl clattered across the stone paving. The keeper sat back on his heels, but the youth was asleep again. After a little while, the keeper lay down on the pallet again and opened his good wing. He slid his hand across the youth's chest, slowly, gently, following sharp lines of ribs, soft skin. The youth shifted. Suddenly guilty, the keeper clenched his touching-fingers into a fist, and lay rigid.

Among the auroras, one day was indistinguishable from the next. The curtains of light screened out the sun and brightened the darkness. Without darkness or light as a rough guide, the keeper had no idea how long the youth slept. He only knew that his time became more difficult. He could not avoid touching the youth, who needed to be fed and kept warm and clean, and whose wing's tendons and muscles would contract without massage. He worked hard over the youth, trying to ignore his feelings, trying to control them.

Yet, who would know if he drew his hands along the thin body, half-extended the short silver talons, drew narrow lines of love against the skin? He could embrace the sleeper, extending both his wings, and no one would pull away at the rough contact of tattered webbing. Children fondled and explored each other's androgynous genitals—why should he restrain himself? Whispered words might influence a decision yet to be made, words and the persuasion of experienced hands, even through sleep. And if the youth awakened, what right could anyone so ugly have to object? Who else but a cripple would take such a mate? Who was left to care?

He opened his eyes against his fantasies, and felt ashamed. The auroras—his pride, his prison—throbbed just beyond the low stone wall.

When he felt most cynical and most alone, he sometimes calmed himself with assurances that he was the most worthy of his people, strong enough (for was he not alive?) to afford kindness and even mercy. Yet of the few crimes his people recognized, the action he contemplated now was the worst.

He had been lonely for a long time. He had understood his solitude, but never accepted it. He was a proud thing, despite his wounds. He might have been bitter and cruel, or vain and futile, but he had even been too proud for that, too proud to allow despair to change him even when there was no one left to see. Now he began to fear that his strength and pride were near exhausted. Attracted, despite the ugliness of the pastel eyes, the keeper could feel himself falling in love. He forced himself to begin thinking of the youth in the masculine. When the youth . . . when *he* awoke, that could be even more influencing than treating him as sexed while he was asleep, but his awakening would force the keeper away from his fantasies.

And perhaps the youth would approach him, in the way that was right and proper, and then the fantasies would no longer be needed.

He knew the bones had knit, well or badly, when the youth's temperature sank toward normal even while he covered him. He folded his wing and rolled away, unwilling to be so near when the youth awoke. He got up, slowly, and limped into the temple.

Later, finishing his duties before the ancient altar, he heard a stirring outside.

The youth, awake, was pulling at the splint. The keeper squatted down beside him and pushed his hand away.

"I'm healed, aren't I? Or I wouldn't have woken up."

The keeper, in his fantasies, had forgotten or discounted the youth's hostility; he was taken aback by it now. "I hope that thou art healed," he said evenly. He removed the splint and gently stretched the wing. The web was soft, and cool. It was almost as hard to take his hands away, even though the youth was awake. The line of the bone was clean, sharp under skin, light. The bone was unscarred, still hollow. "Thou must move it several days before requiring it to bear thy weight."

The youth touched the break with his other hand, stood, and opened his wings to their wide full span, reaching. He smiled, but the keeper could detect a slight sag in his wing, a weakening of unused muscles, a contraction of tendons. "I think thou wilt fly again," he said, and it was the truth.

The youth suddenly dropped his wings, staggering, smile gone, weakened by his mild exertion so soon after awakening. All his bones protruded; his body had half-starved itself, and would need time to recover. The keeper reached up, steadied him, but the youth winced when the flap of wing that did not fold brushed against him. The keeper glanced up; after meeting his gaze, the youth looked away.

"We should, perhaps, be tolerant of each other's weaknesses," the keeper said, cruelly, hurt.

"Why? Nothing forced you to help me. I don't owe you anything."

The keeper levered himself to his feet, walked a few steps, stopped. "No," he said. "I could have let thee heal with thy bones twisted." He heard the sweep of wings opening slowly, wing tips brushing the ground.

"I would have died," the youth said, as if he had committed some crime by living.

"So they thought of me," the keeper said, facing him, "when they left me on the hunting plain for the scavengers."

The youth said nothing for a time. The keeper wondered how he had survived infancy: someone must have cared a great deal, or no one had cared at all. He must have been fiercely protected or virtually ignored until his sentience awoke and he was too old to expose. Letting him die would have been kinder than leaving him to live as an outcast.

"And they left you here. Why do you help, instead of hating?"

"Perhaps I'm weak, and cannot stand the sight of pain."

The youth glanced up, purposely looking straight at the keeper's eyes, holding his own gaze steady. His expression was quizzical. They both knew the keeper would never have lived if he had been weak. It was the youth who looked away first, perhaps from a habit of hiding his eyes so people would tolerate him.

The youth opened his wing, one long finger at a time. The webbing was so smooth, so glossy, that the auroras reflected off it, scarlet and yellow, like flames. "It hurts," he said.

"Still, thou must move it. It may help if I aid thee in stretching it." He opened his own broken wing a little, showing the bones pulled out of shape by shortened tendons. "I knew what should have been done while I slept."

The youth looked at the wing for a long moment, fascinated, horrified. "Please fold it."

The keeper pulled his fingers against the back of his arm, bending his elbow so they would fit. The torn flap hung loose.

"I'm sorry."

"Never mind."

Their conversations were crystalline. The keeper would have preferred to cease touching the youth completely, but he needed to help with the wing, and he refused to allow himself to take out his disappointment on a person. He had hoped his own deformities might cease to matter; that they did not was hardly the youth's fault. The revulsion in him was perhaps less than in others, and perhaps growing weaker, but still present, undeniable, unavoidable.

The keeper began to believe that he himself might as well have died. He had been strong enough to break his fall, strong enough to crawl under a thorn bush away from scavengers, strong enough to sleep eleven days and live. He remembered waking up, peering out through barbed twisting branches at the people hunched watching him and listening to his prophetic mutterings. One held laths and another funeral veils, waiting to brace his wings open and launch him if he died. Even then, with his skin stretched taut over his starved bones, he had been strong enough to crawl toward them, to make a purposeful move to tell them that he would live, that they could rightly help him and take him as their seer. But he was not strong enough for this loneliness and desertion.

A shrill squeal roused him from a doze, leaving him half-awake, confused, exhausted. He heard another sound, a cry abruptly cut off. He folded his wings and moved into the courtyard.

He found the youth sitting against the wall of the temple, sucking the neck vein of a rabbit-deer so freshly dead that one hind foot still trembled in a muscle spasm. "Where didst thou get that? Animals never come past the auroras."

The youth began, delicately, to pull the small animal apart at the major joints. "Maybe it thought you'd tell it its future." He extended his silver claws and began to shred the meat from a narrow bone.

"I do not mock thee."

The youth worried the carcass with his hands for a time. He looked up, and the auroras caught his eyes and brightened them horribly. "Didn't you hate them when you realized they were going to leave you behind? Didn't you want to slash them and tear them and demand what right they had to pretend you didn't matter?"

After a moment, the keeper said, "I grieved."

He had walked into the temple and stood near the back wall, before the stone figure that was crumbling with age and neglect. The keeper was the first in centuries to offer it anything even resembling belief. Slowly, painfully, he had relaxed his wing-fingers, until the scarred membranes lay half-folded around him. "Why did they help me?" he had cried. "If they did not need an oracle, why did they help me, and if they needed one, why did they leave me behind?" But the old god had made no answer, for if the keeper's belief were real, it had not been enough to call the god back.

"I grieved," the keeper said again.

He expected disdain, but the youth looked down and stroked the stained pelt of the rabbit-deer. "Our world is grieving, too," he said softly. "They stole the spirit out of it, and sucked all the life away. All our people ever did was try to escape it, yet it mourns."

The keeper touched his shoulder, gently, "It must seem lonely to thee. But in time—"

The youth made a sound of disgust. "There isn't any time. I hope . . . I hope they have to turn back. I hope they have to come running back to this world they loathed, because they'll find it dead and wasted and unfit to sustain them, and they'll die."

"There will be no turning back in this generation. I dreamed the deaths of some of those who left, and there will be no disaster. The ships will continue, at least through our lifetimes."

The youth stood up, walked a few steps, taut-muscled, angry, spread his wings, allowed the tips to dust the stones. His claws were still bloody. "You'd have everyone substitute your fantasies for their own."

"They are all I have to offer, anymore."

"But they weren't enough for our people, and all you do is grieve." The youth turned and folded his wings against his arms with that graceful smooth snap. "Something will happen, someday, and they'll have to return. They'll spread the sails and catch the rays of some distant sun, and they'll feel grateful that they have some place to come home to. But they never bothered to look at it, they only cared about ways to leave it. So now it's dying, and when they crawl back there won't be anything left."

The keeper realized what the youth was saying. "Thou must have had delusions in thy sorrow and pain," he said. "A world cannot die."

The youth glared at him, and his gaze did not shift, as if in anger he could forget his shame. "This world is dying. If you would sleep and attune yourself to it, the way you did for people, you'd see it. Or come outside your prison and look around."

"I never leave the temple grounds."

The youth closed his eyes, resigned. "Then sit and wait, until the auroras die too." He left the keeper alone, and walked away with the tips of his beautiful wings trailing in the dust.

The keeper wanted to dismiss the youth as unbalanced, but nothing was that easy. It was true that their people had cared more for the sky and the nearby stars than for the world they rested on. It was only natural that this be so for a people who could soar so high that the ground curved away below them, admitting without defense its smallness and insignificance. Only natural for a people whose children make toy gliders with lifting wings by instinct. The stars were so close, they hung in the sky calling, hypnotic. The keeper and his mate, in their ion boat, sailing past the bay between the world and its moon, had navigated by sight and feel alone. And he had seen the ion ships, when the idea was still a fancy, in visions. Before the first was even finished, he had seen the thousand of them, carrying all the people, spread their huge sails and catch the sun's rays and begin to move, very, very slowly, toward a star the passengers already knew had planets they could touch their feet to and leave again.

His people had known much of stars. But he could not say that the world was not dying.

After a little while, he stood up slowly and went to find the youth. "What dost thou mean to do?"

He reached down and picked up a small stone. "What is there to do? I almost wish you had let me die." He hefted the pebble, as if he would throw it into the auroras. The keeper flinched, and saw him hesitate. He thought he would still throw it, but the youth lowered his hand and tossed the pebble back to the ground. "If I knew what to do, I'd do nothing."

"There are still people—"

"You and I may be the last, for all I know. Maybe all the others have killed themselves. I'd have it lonely to deny the rest a sanctuary."

"Must we both be lonely?"

The youth turned his back, hunched his shoulders. The keeper thought he was offended by the implication. "I meant no impropriety—"

"Traditions are as dead as the god in your temple." He shrugged his wings. "You would have me stay."

"I would ask nothing."

"You'd hope."

"One cannot control one's dreams."

"I'll stay for a while."

Later the keeper slept, alone in the close and oppressive darkness of the temple. He expected a vision of the youth, alone in some future that did not include the keeper. He had never seen any part of his own destiny in his prophecies; that made him strangely afraid that no one could ever stay with him. He did not believe he could influence the future. Perhaps the future must influence him.

He saw his world, for the first time since he had come to the temple, and he saw that the youth had been right. Skeletons of rabbit-deer lay scattered on the hunting plain, and the vines that climbed the rock pinnacles of nests shriveled and died. Even the thorn bushes, which could grow where nothing else lived, dried, crumbled, burned. The death of their world would be slow, but the places he saw, deserted, were dying. He could not truly tell, but he thought he would die first. His visions had never frightened him before; now he came out of sleep screaming.

Soft wings rustled beside him. "Did you dream?"

"I did as thou asked," the keeper whispered, lying very still.

"And I was right."

"Yes."

"Is anyone else alive?" In the darkness, the young voice was fervent.

"I saw no one," the keeper said.

"Ah," the youth said, satisfied.

"I am not omniscient."

"You'd see what's important."

"Other people were left."

"They had nothing to keep them alive. Not your strength, nor my hate."

"Thou hast made us too unique."

"I hope not," the youth said. "I think your vision was right, and your hopes are wrong."

The keeper sat up, unwilling to sleep again. "I will never know."

"It would hurt you to know that truth." The tone held compassion that sounded strange after the exultation in death, but the keeper was grateful for it. He watched the shadow of the youth move across the stone floor to the entrance and stand in the wavering light. He rose and followed him, stopping close behind him in his shadow. The youth began to talk, slowly, tentatively. "When the last of them left, I followed them as far as I could, until the sun was so bright I thought I'd go blind . . . I couldn't see them, but I don't think any of them looked back."

"They did not," the keeper said, and the other did not

question his knowledge. "It isn't the character of our people to look back. I think they'll never need to."

"And if they don't—my determination is foolish?"

The keeper spoke very cautiously, afraid to go too far. "Perhaps. Or futile. Thou wouldst deny thyself rather than them."

"I will . . . think about that."

Behind him, the keeper nodded to himself. "Wouldst thou eat?"

"All right."

The youth had not noticed the food while he was sleeping, but awake he had found it less than pleasing. "I'll go out and hunt as soon as I can fly again," he said.

"I'm used to this. The auroras make a long path for thee to walk."

"It's better than staying here."

"I'm used to that, too. But hunt, if that is thy wish."

"Soon?"

"Yes. It is almost ready."

"It's still stiff."

"Thou must stop favoring it." He sipped at his broth. "I will massage it again."

The touching was very much like the motions of love. The keeper could not remember touching any person before this youth since the night his mate had died. They had been flying. She was aged, but still beautiful, and she had decided to die.

It was the way of things. He had chosen her, and made his decision by his bond to her, when she was adult and he, not yet "he," was youth. Half a lifetime before, she, not yet "she," had courted and had bonded with another male, and in time he had aged and died.

Now, she did not wish to grow helpless. She would do what their people had always done, and forever would do, when it was time to die. And he would accept her decision, and carry her veils, as the mates of aging ones always had, and always would. Their children, one youth, one newly adult, bade her farewell. There would have been three, but their second was born with a twisted wing, so they had exposed it.

They flew together for a long time. No clouds obstructed their view of the hunting plain. Had they been hungry they could have feasted on warm meat and fresh blood, but this last night together they did not hunt. They drank thick salty wine and soared higher, giddy. She brushed her wingtip against his cheek, dropped back and down and caressed his chest and belly. She laughed, and made lewd and joyous remarks about whoever would become the next member of their long marriage line. She wished him happiness, and pulled a silver veil from his ankle band. He garlanded her with others. Defying her infirmities, she flew higher. He followed her, feeling the air grow thinner, dangerous, and suddenly cried out in ecstacy.

He had never flown so high. He had heard about this from others, but no one could ever have seen, before, the colors behind his eyes. In reflex, his pupils contracted to pinpoints. He strained upward. His mate cried out to him, "Do you see?" and he called, "I see!" and she said, very softly, it seemed, "Be careful, my love, for I am blind." He looked toward her voice. Very dimly he could see her, tiny, higher than she had ever gone before, higher than he had ever seen anyone fly, wide-eyed against the radiation, the veils seeming only to drift beside her. He saw her wings begin to stiffen, and he knew that she was dead.

As another shower of subatomic particles exploded themselves in his eyes, brighter than any spark through the shielding of their ion boat, he realized he had flown past his wings' ability to carry him, and felt himself begin to fall.

When his struggle against the vertical wind ripped his wing, perhaps he should have allowed himself to die. Fighting, he slowed his fall, but in the end the earth had grasped and shattered him.

"Keeper—"

The word, and a touch on his hand, brought him back. He glanced up, startled. The youth's face showed apprehension, irresolution. He drew in his wing-fingers, folding the smooth membrane. "It's not stiff anymore."

"I was remembering," the keeper said. "Thy words gave me hope, and I . . . I am sorry—"

"It doesn't matter." He let his touching fingers and half-exposed talons linger on the keeper's hand. "Nothing should be forced to die twice," he said. "If we continued our people, the world would kill our children, or the children would kill the world again."

"Thou are not fair," the keeper said. "Some expression of my memory has frightened thee, but I asked for nothing."

"It's true that I'm frightened." He touched the keeper's throat, slid his hand to his shoulder, down his arm, back along the wing-fingers, and this time he didn't wince. "Of your kindness and your strength."

"I do not understand thee."

"I'd change for you, I think."

The keeper sat back, reluctantly, away from the youth's hands. "Then thou wilt leave?"

"I must."

The auroras led the youth on a long, twisting, directionless path to the hills. Outside, the thorn bushes should have been flowering. The youth stood at the edge of the temple's guardians and looked out over the land, at the brown and black thickets of twisted, dying branches. The wind blew hot against his body, and nothing moved as far as he could see. He felt death, and with it an ugly triumph that had ceased to give him pleasure. He glanced back, and almost turned, but reached high instead and snapped open his wings. The wind caught the webbing. He could feel the place where his bones had broken, and hesitated.

Disgusted by his fear, he launched himself from the top of the hill, slipped sideways in a current, angled up, and flew.

After the youth left, time passed strangely; it might have been a long or a short time later that the old breaks in the keeper's bones began to ache constantly. He had begun to age, and once aging started in his people, it progressed rapidly. His sharp sight began to dim. Only cowards and weaklings lived long enough to go blind naturally. He knew he should allow himself to live no longer, but still he did nothing. He did not wish to die on the earth, and he dreamed of dying properly, radiation-blind, flying.

He felt gentle hands that roused him from a doze, or perhaps it was all a dream.

"Keeper, I am back."

He raised his head and looked calmly into a face made ugly by its eyes. "It is thou."

"No more," he said. "Not 'thou' for a long time."

The keeper seemed not to hear. "Hast thou seen everything die, then?"

The other supported him, and he smelled fresh blood. "No. You were right. There are others. Around them, the earth lives." He held the warm body of a small animal to the keeper's lips. "Drink it," he said "Last time I was selfish."

Blood ran hot in the keeper's throat; he had almost forgotten the hunt. "Why art thou here?"

"For the same reason I left."

"How long has it been?"

"A year."

"Ah." Dark eyelids closed over darker eyes, tired. "It seemed longer."

"It seemed very short, to me."

The keeper did not speak or move for a long time. "I am dying. Will you carry my veils?"

He saw that the old one, half-dreaming, thought he could still fly. "I will. The stars will touch you." He gently lowered him. "I'll build you a glider, keeper," he whispered. He lay down beside him to wait, and opened his wing across him. He hoped the keeper could still feel it, and know the presence of one who loved him.

The Mountains of Sunset,
the Mountains of Dawn

The smell from the ship's animal room, at first tantalizing, grew to an overpowering strength. Years before, the odor of so many closely caged animals had sickened the old one, but now it urged on her slow hunger. When she was a youth, her hunger demanded satiation, but now even her interior responses were aging. The hunger merely ached.

Inside the animal room, three dimensions of cages stretched up the floor's curvature, enclosing fat and lethargic animals that slept, unafraid. She lifted a young one by the back of its neck. Blinking, it hung in her hand; it would not respond in fear even when she extended her silver claws into its flesh. Its ancestors had run shrieking across the desert when the old one's shadow passed over them, but fear and speed and the chemical reactions of terror had been bred out of these beasts. Their meat was tasteless.

"Good day."

Startled, the old one turned. The youth's habit of approaching silently from behind was annoying; it made her fancy that her hearing was failing as badly as her sight. Still, she felt a certain fondness for this child, who was not quite so weak as the others. The youth was beautiful: wide wings and delicate ears, large eyes and triangular face, soft body-covering of fur as short as fur can be, patterned in tan against the normal lustrous black. The abnormality occurred among the first ship-generation's children. On the home world, any infant so changed would have been exposed, but on the sailship infanticide was seldom practiced. This the old one disapproved of, fearing a deterioration in her people, but she had grown used to the streaked and swirling fur pattern.

"I greet thee," she said, "but I'm hungry. Go away before I make thee ill."

"I've become accustomed to it," the youth said.

The old one shrugged, leaned down, and slashed the animal's throat with her sharp teeth. Warm blood spurted over her lips. As she swallowed it, she wished she were soaring and eating bits of warm meat from the fingers of a mate or a lover, feeding him in turn. Thus she, when still a youth and not yet "she," had courted her eldermate; thus her youngermate had never been able to court her. Two generations of her kind had missed that experience, but she seemed to regret the loss more than they did. She dismembered and gutted the animal and crunched its bones for marrow and brains.

She glanced up. The youth watched, seeming fascinated yet revolted. She offered a shred of meat.

"No. Thank you."

"Then eat thy meat cold, like the rest of them."

'I'll try it. Sometime."

"Yes, of course," the old one said. "And all our people will live on the lowest level and grow strong, and fly every day."

"I fly. Almost every day."

The old one smiled, half cynically, half with pity. "I would show thee what it is to fly," she said. "Across deserts so hot the heat snatches thee, and over mountains so tall they outreach clouds, and into the air until the radiation explodes in thine eyes and steals thy direction and shatters thee against the earth, if thou art not strong enough to overcome it."

"I'd like that."

"It's too late." The old one wiped the clotting blood from her hands and lips. "It's much too late." She turned to leave; behind her, the youth spoke so softly that she almost did not hear. "It's my choice. Must you refuse me?"

She let the door close between them.

In the corridor, she passed others of her people, youths and adults made spindly by their existence on the inner levels of the ship, where the gravity was low. Many greeted her with apparent deference, but she believed she heard contempt. She ignored them. She had the right; she was the oldest of them all, the only one alive who could remember their home.

Her meal had not yet revived her; the slightly curved floor seemed to rise in fact rather than in appearance. The contempt she imagined in others grew in herself. It was past her time to die.

Ladders connected the levels of the ship, in wells not designed for flying. With difficulty, the old one let herself down to the habitation's rim. She felt happier, despite the pain, when the centrifugal force increased her weight.

The voyage had been exciting, before she grew old. She had not minded trading hunting grounds for sailship cubicles: the universe lay waiting. She entered the ship young and eager, newly eldermated, newly changed from youth to adult; loved, loving, sharing her people's dreams as they abandoned their small, dull world.

The old one's compartment was on the lowest level, where the gravity was greatest. Slowly, painfully, she sat cross-legged beside the window, unfolding her wings against the stiffness of her wing-fingers to wrap the soft membranes around her body. Outside, the stars raced by, to the old one's failing sight a multicolored, swirling blur, like mica flakes in sand.

The habitation spun, and the sails came into view. The huge reflective sheets billowed in the pressure of the stellar winds, decelerating the ship and holding it against gravity as it approached the first new world the old one's people would ever see.

She dreamed of her youth, off lying high enough to see the planet's curvature, of skimming through high-altitude winds, gambling that no capricious current could overcome her and break her hollow bones. Other youths fell in their games; they died, but few mourned: that was the way of things.

She dreamed of her dead eldermate, and reached for him, but his form was insubstantial and slipped through her fingers.

Claws skittered against the door, waking her. Her dreams dissolved.

"Enter."

The door opened; against the dimness of her room light shadowed the one who stood there. The old one's eyes adjusted slowly; she recognized the piebald youth. She felt that she should send the youth away, but the vision of her eldermate lingered in her sight, and the words would not come.

"What dost thou wish?"

"To speak with you. To listen to you."

"If that's all."

"Of course it isn't. But if it's all you will allow, I will accept it."

The old one unwrapped her wings and sat slowly up. "I outlived my youngermate," she said. "Wouldst thou have me disgust our people again?"

"They don't care. It isn't like that anymore. We've changed."

"I know . . . my children have forgotten our customs, and I have no right to criticize. Why should they listen to a crippled parent who refuses to die?"

The youth heel-sat before her, silent for a moment. "I wish . . ."

She stretched out her hand, extending the sharp claws. "Our people should never have left our home. I would long be dead, and thou wouldst not have met me."

The youth took her hand and grasped it tightly. "If you were dead—"

She drew back, opening long fingers so her wing spread across her body. "I will die," she said. "Soon. But I want to fly again. I will see one new world, and then I will have seen enough."

"I wish you wouldn't talk of dying."

"Why? Why have we become so frightened of death?"

The youth rose, shrugging, and let the tips of the striped wings touch the floor. The vestigial claws clicked against the metal. "Maybe we're not used to it anymore."

The old one perceived the remark's unconscious depth. She smiled, and began to laugh. The youth looked at her, as if thinking her mad. But she could not explain what was so funny, that they had reached for the perils of the stellar winds, and found only safety and trepidation.

"What's the matter? Are you all right? What is it?"

"Nothing," she said. "Thou wouldst not understand." She no longer felt like laughing, but exhausted and ill. "I will sleep," she said, having regained her dignity. She turned her gaze from the beautiful youth.

Waking, she felt warm, as if she were sleeping in the sun on a pinnacle of rock with the whole world spreading out around her. But her cheek rested against chill metal; she opened her eyes knowing once more where she was.

The youth lay beside her, asleep, wing outstretched across them both. She started to speak but remained silent. She felt she should be angry, but the closeness was too pleasurable. Guilt sprang up, at allowing this child to retain desire for the love of one about to die, but still the old one did not move. She lay beneath the caressing wing, seeking to recapture her dreams. But the youth shifted, and the old one found herself looking into dark, gold-flecked, startled eyes.

The youth pulled away. "I am sorry. I meant only to warm you, not to . . ."

"I . . . found it pleasant, after so long in this cold metal. I thank thee."

The youth gazed at her, realizing gradually what she had said, then lay down and gently enfolded her again.

"Thou art a fool. Thou dost seek pain."

The youth rested against her, head on her shoulder.

"I will only call thee 'thee,'" she said.

"All right."

The flying chamber enclosed half the levels of a segment two twelfths of the habitation wide. Its floor and its side walls were transparent to space.

The old one and the youth stood on a brilliant path of stars. On one side of them, the sails rippled as they changed position to hold the ship on course. They obscured a point of light only slightly brighter than the stars that formed its background: the sun of the home planet, the star this ship and a thousand like it had abandoned. On the other side, a second star flared bright, and even the old one could see the changing phases of the spheres that circled it.

The youth stared out at the illuminated edge of their destination. "Will you be happy there?"

"I'll be happy to see the sky and the land again."

"A blue sky, without stars . . . I think that will be very empty."

"We became used to this ship," the old one said. "We can

go back again as easily." She turned, spread her wings, ran a few steps, and lifted herself into the air. The takeoff felt clumsy, but the flying was more graceful.

She glided, spiraling upward on the gravity gradient. To fly higher with less and less effort had been strange and exciting; now she only wished for a way to test her strength to the breaking point. Her distance perception had weakened with time, but she knew the dimensions of the chamber by kinesthetic sense and memory: long enough to let one glide, but not soar, wide enough to let one stroke slowly from one side to the next, but not tax one's muscles with speed, deep enough to let one swoop, but not dive.

At the top of the chamber, she slid through the narrow space between ceiling and walking bridge; she heard the youth, behind her, falter, then plunge through. The old one had laughed when they built the crossing, but there were those who could not cross the chamber without the bridge, and that she did not find amusing.

Sound guided her. Sometimes she wished to plug her ears and fly oblivious to the echoes that marked boundaries. She had considered dying that way, soaring with senses half crippled until she crashed against the thick tapestry of stars and blessed the sailship with her blood. But she wanted to touch the earth again; so she continued to live.

She grew tired; her bones would ache when she had rested. She dipped her wings and slipped toward the floor, stretching to combat the rising end of the gradient. She landed; her wings drooped around her. The youth touched down and approached her. "I am tired."

She appreciated the concession to her dignity. "I, too."

The days passed; the youth stayed with her. They flew together, and they sailed the long-deserted ion boats in the whirlpools of converging stellar winds. At first fearful, the youth gained confidence as the old one demonstrated the handling of the sails. The old one recalled other, half-forgotten voyages with other, long-dead youths. Her companion's growing pleasure made her briefly glad that her dream of dying properly, veiled and soaring, had kept her from taking one of the boats and sailing until the air ran out or some accident befell her.

When the features of the new world could be discerned, the old one made the long walk to the navigation room. Her eyes no longer let her feel the stars, and so she did not navigate, yet though the young people could guide the ship as well as her generation had, she felt uneasy leaving her fate in the hands of others. From the doorway, she pushed off gently and floated to the center of the chamber. A few young adults drifted inside the transparent hemisphere, talking, half dozing, watching the relationships between ship, planet, primary, and stars. The navigation room did not rotate; directions were by convention. Streaked with clouds, glinting with oceans, the crescent world loomed above them; below, the ship's main body spun, a reflective expanse spotted with dark ports and the transparent segment of the flying chamber.

"Hello, grandmother."

"Hello, grandchild." She should call him "grandson," she thought, but she was accustomed to the other, though this child of her first child, already youngermated, had long been adult. She felt once more that she should choose a graceful way to die.

Nearby, two people conferred about a few twelfths of a second of arc and altered the tension on the main sail lines. Like a concave sheet of water, the sail rippled and began to fold.

"It seems the engines will not be necessary." They had begun the turn already; the stars were shifting around them.

He shrugged, only his shoulders, not his wings. "Perhaps just a little." He gazed at her for a long time without speaking. "Grandmother, you know the planet is smaller than we thought."

She looked up at the white-misted, half-shadowed globe. "Not a great deal, surely."

"Considerably. It's much denser for its mass than our world was. The surface gravity will be higher."

"How much?"

"Enough that our people would be uncomfortable."

The conditional, by its implications, frightened her. "Our people are weak," she said. "Have the council suggest they move to the first level."

"No one would, grandmother." Though he never flew, he sounded sad.

"You are saying we will not land?"

"How can we? No one could live."

"No one?"

"You are old, grandmother."

"And tired of sailing. I want to fly again."

"No one could fly on that world."

"How can you say? You don't even fly in the chamber."

He stared down at the shimmering, half-folded sails. "I fly with them. Those are all the wings our people need."

The old one flexed her wing-fingers; the membranes opened, closed, opened. "Is that what everyone believes?"

"It's true. The sails have carried us for two generations. Why should we abandon them now?"

"How can we depend on them so heavily? Grandson, we came onto this ship to test ourselves, and you're saying we will avoid the test."

"The ambitions and needs of a people can change."

"And the instincts?"

She knew what his answer would be before he did. "Even those, I think."

The old one looked out over space. She could not navigate, but she could evaluate their trajectory. It was never meant to be converted into an orbit. The ship would swing around the planet, catapult past it, and sail on.

"We felt trapped by a whole world," the old one said. "How can our children be satisfied on this uninteresting construct?"

"Please try to understand. Try to accept the benefits of our security." He touched her hand, very gently, his claws retracted. "I'm sorry."

She turned away from him, forced by the lack of gravity to use clumsy swimming motions. She returned to the low regions of the habitation, feeling almost physically wounded by the decision not to land. The ship could sustain her life no longer.

The youth was in her room. "Shall we fly?"

She hunched in the corner near the window. "There is no reason to fly."

"What's happened?" The youth crouched beside her.

"Thou must leave me and forget me. I will be gone by morning."

"But I'm coming."

She took the youth's hand, extending her silver claws against the patterned black and tan fur. "No one else is landing. Thou wouldst be left alone."

The youth understood her plans. "Stay on the ship." The tone was beyond pleading.

"It doesn't matter what I do. If I stay, I will die, and thou wilt feel grief. If I leave, thou wilt feel the same grief. But if I allow thee to come, I will steal thy life."

"It's my life."

"Ah," she said sadly, "thou art so young."

The old one brought out a flask of warm red wine. As the sky spun and tumbled beside them, she and the youth shared the thick, salty liquid, forgetting their sorrows as the intoxicant went to their heads. The youth stroked the old one's cheek and throat and body. "Will you do one thing for me before you leave?"

"What dost thou wish?"

"Lie with me. Help me make the change."

With the wine, she found herself half amused by the youth's persistence and naiveté. "That is something thou shouldst do with thy mate."

"I have to change soon, and there's no one else I want to court."

"Thou dost seek loneliness."

"Will you help me?"

"I told thee my decision when thou asked to stay."

The youth seemed about to protest again, but remained silent. The old one considered the easy capitulation, but the strangeness slipped from her as she drank more wine. Stroking her silver claws against her companion's patterned temple, she allowed her vision to unfocus among the swirls of tan, but she did not sleep.

When she had set herself for her journey, she slipped away. She felt some regret when the youth did not stir, but she did not want another argument; she did not want to be cruel again. As she neared the craft bay, excitement overcame disappointment; this was her first adventure in many years.

She saw no one, for the bay was on the same level as her room. She entered a small power craft, sealed it, and gave orders to the bay. The machinery worked smoothly, despite lack of use or care. The old one could understand the young people's implicit trust in the ship; her generation had built seldom, but very well. The air gone, she opened the hatch. The craft fell out into space.

Her feeling for the workings of the power craft returned. Without numbers or formulae she set its course; her vision was not so bad that she could not navigate in harbors.

Following gravity, she soon could feel the difference between this world and the home planet; not, she thought, too much. She crossed the terminator into daylight, where swirls of cloud swept by beneath her. She anticipated rain, cool on her face and wings, pushed in rivulets down her body by the speed of her flight. Without the old one's conscious direction, her wing fingers opened slightly, closed, opened.

She watched the stars as her motion made them rise. Refraction gave her the approximate density of the air: not, she thought, too low.

The ship dipped into the outer atmosphere. Its stubby wings slowed it; decelerating, it approached the planet's surface, fighting the differences of this world, which yielded, finally, to the old one's determination. She looked for a place to land.

The world seemed very young; for a long while she saw only thick jungles and marshes. Finally, between mountain ranges that blocked the clouds, she found a desert. It was alien in color and form, but the sand glittered with mica like the sand of home. She landed the ship among high dunes.

The possibility had always existed that the air, the life, the very elements would be lethal. She broke the door's seal; air hissed sharply. She breathed fresh air for the first time in two generations. It was thin, but it had more oxygen than she was used to, and made her light-headed. The smells teased her to identify them. She climbed to the warm sand, and slowly, slowly, spread her wings to the gentle wind.

Though the land pulled at her, she felt she could overcome it. Extending her wings to their limits, she ran against the breeze. She lifted, but not enough; her feet brushed the ground, and she was forced to stop.

The wind blew brown sand and mica flakes against her feet and drooping wingtips. "Be patient to bury me," she said. "You owe me more than a grave."

She started up the steep face of a nearby dune. The sand tumbled grain over grain in tiny avalanches from her footsteps. She was used to feeling lighter as she rose; here, she only grew more tired. She approached the knife-edged crest, where sunlight sparkled from each sand crystal. The delicate construct collapsed past her, pouring sand into her face. She had to stop and blink until her eyes were clear of grit, but she had kept her footing. She stood at the broken summit of the dune, with the sail-like crests that remained stretched up and out to either side. Far above the desert floor, the wind blew stronger. She looked down, laughed, spread her wings, and leaped.

The thin air dropped her; she struggled; her feet brushed the sand, but her straining wings held her and she angled toward the sky, less steeply than of old, but upward. She caught an updraft and followed it, spiraling in a wide arc, soaring past the shadowed hills of sand. This flight was less secure than those of her memories; she felt intoxicated by more than the air. She tried a shallow dive and almost lost control, but pulled herself back into the sky. She was not quite ready to give life up. She no longer felt old, but ageless.

Motion below caught her attention. She banked and glided over the tiny figure. It scuttled away when her shadow touched it, but it seemed incapable of enough speed to make a chase exhilarating. Swooping with some caution, she skimmed the ground, snatched up the animal in her hand-fingers, and soared again. Thrashing, the scaly beast cried out gutturally. The old one inspected it. It had a sharp but not unpleasant odor, one of the mysterious scents of the air. She was not hungry, but she considered killing and eating the creature. It smelled like something built of familiar components of life, though along a completely alien pattern. She was curious to know if her system could tolerate it, and she wondered what color its blood was, but her people's tradition and instinct was to kill lower animals only for food. She released the cold beast where she had found it and she soared away.

The old one climbed into the air for one final flight. She felt deep sorrow that the young ones would not stop here.

At first, she thought she was imagining the soft, keening whine, but it grew louder, higher, until she recognized the shriek of a power craft. It came into view, flying very fast, too fast—but it struggled, slowed, leveled, and it was safe. It circled toward the old one's craft. She followed.

From the air, she watched the youth step out into the sand. She landed nearby.

"Why didst thou come? I will not go back."

The youth showed her ankle bands and multicolored funeral veils. "Let me attend your death. At least let me do that."

"That is a great deal."

"Will you allow it?"

"Thou hast exposed thyself to great danger. Canst thou get back?"

"If I want to."

"Thou must. There is nothing here for thee."

"Let me decide that!" The youth's outburst faltered. "Why . . . why do you pretend to care so much about me?"

"I—" she had no answer. Her concern was no pretense, but she realized that her actions and her words had been contradictory. She had changed, perhaps as much as the young ones, keeping the old disregard for death to herself, applying the new conservation of life to others. "I do care," she said. "I do care about you."

And the youth caught his breath at her use of the adult form of address. "I've hoped for so long you might say that," he said. "I've wanted your love for such a long time . . ."

"You will only have it for a little while."

"That is enough."

They embraced. The old one folded her wings over him, and they sank down into the warm sand. For the first time, they touched with love and passion. As the sun struck the sharp mountains and turned the desert maroon, the old one stroked the youth and caressed his face, holding him as he began the change. The exterior alterations would be slight. The old one felt her lover's temperature rising, as his metabolism accelerated to trigger the hormonal changes.

"I feel very weak," the youth whispered.

"That is usual. It passes."

He relaxed within her wings.

The sun set, the land grew dim; the moons, full, rose in tandem. The stars formed a thick veil above the fliers. They lay quietly together, the old one stroking her lover to ease the tension in his muscles, helping maintain his necessary fever with the insulation of her wings. The desert grew cool with the darkness; sounds moved and scents waxed and waned with the awakening of nocturnal creatures. The world seemd more alien at night.

"Are you there?" His eyes were wide open, but the pupils were narrow slits, and the tendons in his neck stood out, strained.

"Of course."

"I didn't know it would hurt . . . I'm glad you're here . . ."

"We all survive the passage," she said gently. But something about this world or the changing one himself made this transition difficult.

She held him all night while he muttered and thrashed, oblivious to her presence. As dawn approached, he fell into a deep sleep, and the old one felt equally exhausted. The sun dimmed the veil of stars and warmed the fliers; the creatures that had crept around them during darkness returned to their hiding places. The old one left her lover and began to climb a dune.

When she returned, the new adult was awakening. She landed behind him; he heard her and turned. His expression changed from grief to joy.

"How do you feel?"

He rubbed his hands down the back of his neck. "I don't know. I feel . . . new."

She sat on her heels beside him. "I was hungry afterward," she said. She held up a squirming pair of the reptiles. "But I didn't have to wonder if the food would kill me." She slashed one creature's throat. The blood was brilliant yellow, its taste as sharp as the smell. She sampled the flesh: it was succulent and strong after the mushy, flavorless meat on the ship. "It's good." She offered him a piece of the meat she held. "I feel you can eat it safely." He regarded it a moment, but took the second beast and bit through its scales and skin. It convulsed once and died.

"A clean kill," she said.

He smiled at her, and they feasted.

He stood and spread his wings, catching a soft hot breeze. "We *can* fly here," the old one said.

He ran a few steps and launched himself into the air. She watched him climb, astonished and delighted that he needed no assistance. He seemed unsure of distances and angles, unsteady on turns and altitude changes, but that would have improved if he had had the time. She heard him laugh with joy; he called to her.

Wishing she were still strong, she climbed the dune again and joined him. All that day they flew together; she taught him to hunt, and they fed each other; they landed and lay together in the sand.

Twilight approached.

The old one ached in every bone. She had imagined, as the

air supported her, that she might somehow escape her age, but the ground dragged at her, and she trembled.

"It's time," she said.

Her lover started as if she had struck him. He started to protest, but stopped, and slipped his wings around her. "I will attend you."

He walked with her up the dune, carrying the veils. At the top, he fastened the bands around her fingers and ankles. The old one spread her wings and fell into the air. She flew toward the mountains of sunrise until darkness engulfed her and the stars seemed so close that she might pull them across her shoulders. Her lover flew near.

"What will you do?"

"I'll go back to the ship."

"That's good."

"I may be able to persuade a few to return with me."

She thought of his loneliness, if he were refused and returned nonetheless, but she said nothing of that. "I respect your decision."

She climbed higher, until the air grew perceptibly thinner, but she could not fly high enough for cosmic rays to burst against her retinas. She took comfort in the clear sky and in flying, and plucked a veil from her companion. After that, he slipped them into the bands, staying near enough for danger. She felt the cold creeping in; the veils drifted about her like snow. "Goodbye, my love," she said. "Do not grieve for me."

Her senses were dimmed; she could barely hear him. "I have no regrets, but I will grieve."

The old one stretched out her stiffening wings and flew on.

He followed her until he knew she was dead, then dropped back. She would continue to some secret grave; he wished to remember her as she had been that day.

He glided alone over the desert and in the treacherous currents of mountains' flanks, impressing the world on his mind so he could describe its beauties. At dawn, he returned to his craft. A breeze scattered tiny crystals against his ankles.

He dropped to his knees and thrust his fingers into the bright, warming sand. Scooping up a handful, he wrapped it in the last silver funeral veil and carried it with him when he departed.

The End's Beginning

Through long captivity, I learned to mimic the humans' speech, but not to understand the thoughts behind it. How could anyone learn to understand the ways of those who spend their lives seeking such desperate independence? Though they have forced me to be like them, still I cannot understand. I would have to be mad to desire such solitude, and I am not yet mad.

They have made me mute and almost blind. They left me my eyes, but eyes are less than useless in this cold dark heavy sea. I still can taste and smell. Many different particles drift among the gentle salt flavors that encircle evolution: sharp diatoms, bright edible crustacean sparks (so welcome after many seasons obscured by battered chunks of fish-flesh sharp with ice), the bitter taint of the water that seeps from the humans' land (in the sea the great ones sing fading songs that tell of unfouled oceans, but the great ones are dying, murdered; their songs will die with them and no one will remember the taste of clean sea), and the gritty sediment washed toward me from a wide rainswollen river. The sediment is what blinds my sight. The men have muted my voice so I cannot call for help, and thus they have almost blinded my ears.

No longer can I sing against the tides. The men attached a

machine to me that emits an ugly squeak. Though the metallic sound mixes and melds erratically with the din that fills the ocean, it is sufficient for navigation (they tested this quite carefully). But the beauty is gone from my home. Even the stones are opaque.

I break the surface to breathe. It is dark, and the water sparkles in the moonlight. I slow to look around, for it has been a long time since I have seen the ocean or the sky. I rest with my back and eyes above the warm caressing water. But soon the men realize I have stopped, and they send a signal that forces me onward. I cannot resist it. I do not even have the satisfaction of trying, failing, to overcome pain. There is no pain, only compulsion as inescapable as the glass and concrete walls that held me prisoner.

While I was going nearly mad from solitude, I dreamed of being freed and swimming out into the wide sweet ocean. My mate would come with our people, and we would sing and leap and copulate and rejoice in my freedom. But I cannot call, I cannot sing. There is no freedom or rejoicing.

And my mate will never find me, but will wait and search in vain near the human-built where they imprisoned me. No one could know that the men put wet smelly things all around me (I thought they were trying to cover my skin as they cover their own) and put me in a box and put the box in one of their metal creatures. (The humans have a terrible need to put things inside things, to overcome the inevitable randomness of life. People know better.) The metal creature rose up in the air and took me from the Middle Ocean to the Wide Ocean, and that is where I am now, swimming along the sun's track to reach the Sunset Land. When I reach it, I will die.

My body has stopped aching from the way the men cut it. I am healed, but I still can feel the scar. The heavy weight of metal inside me disturbs my balance. They do not understand how much it hurts that I can no longer play. I cannot sing, I cannot leap. The men must have no art at all.

I hear the faint pulses of a whale's song, nearly obliterated by the harsh scream and chatter of the men's water machines. This song is fading and distorted; it has carried perhaps halfway across the Wide Ocean. It is useless for information, but it is an illusion of companionship. For the next few hours, whenever the cacophony becomes too painful or the single sound of my navigation devices bores me to distraction, I will be able to seek and find the low long tones of the great one's singing. In other days it could have told its stories from halfway around the world.

Now when the great ones are not singing about the taste of the sea they sing of its sounds. A hundred years ago a song sung at midnight would reach a place in full daylight, though by the time the song traveled that far the destination would be in darkness and the source in day. The natural sounds of the sea were no impediment to the songs, which slipped through choruses of grunts and bubbles, splashes and cries, even the chatter of smaller people, my own kind. The whales were never parted from each other, no matter how far they separated. Now they are solitary, lonely creatures who cannot learn fear.

I swim, I swim. The men's signal will not let me rest. There is a schedule. Schedules are for men and machines, not for people. But now I am a machine, or little better. What else is a machine but a creature with no will?

The machine inside me is cold.

If I could find my people I could tell them—even mute, I could tell them by sight and motion—to stop me. Perhaps if they held me back long enough the humans would abandon me.

I might still have to die . . . but the men will kill me with the machine when I reach the end of my journey. Nothing would keep them from destroying me if I could not finish the mission. Destroying me would be safer for the men, who would think I had been captured by their enemies. If my kind stopped me and the machine exploded, I would not be the only one to die. So I must cease hoping to find anyone to help me.

I hear the low grumble of a killer whale, a sound that is almost the only thing we ever feared. But it is not searching, simply lounging in the midnight sea. It must know I am here, but it is not hungry now. The men call it killer whale but that species has no taste for human flesh, only for small people.

I do not wish to do the men's will. If the loss were only my life I could accept it, I think, if there were any reason I could understand. But my life's end will be a signal for the men to begin killing each other. They no longer kill each other only. This time when they begin the killing they will kill the world as well.

They have been practicing destruction on small southern islands. When they stop practicing they will send their machines to explode on the earth like storms, and the dust from them will spread over land and sea alike, poisoning everything. We who die quickly will be the fortunate ones.

If I could sing, I would taunt the killer whale and it would kill me. But I cannot attract its attention and the men will not let me deviate far enough from my path to tease it, nip its flanks, provoke it to fury.

The men's command urges me on. I will tire sooner than I would have before I was imprisoned, but I have not yet reached my limits. The moon disappears behind a cloud and the sea turns black and bright in patches. The moon's light overpowered the glow of luminescent plankton, but in the darkness they stream in glimmering streaks against the water. I pass beneath them, swim up and leap through them. I fling drops of glowing spray in all directions. I come down flat, clumsily. I have forgotten my balance again.

I wonder if there are others like me, swimming toward the men's human enemies, trying to imagine the wish to kill a member of one's own species. Or am I the only one directed across the sunless sea? Have I the lonely duty of beginning the destruction?

If there are others, we all have similar fears. I wonder if any of us will be clever or lucky enough to discover a way to stop.

The clouds that covered the moon are thick and ominous. I can see the scatter of rain across the ocean's smooth swells. Now the rain is upon me, and I slow as much as I dare. I love to float just beneath the surface and feel the raindrops on my back.

Fresh and salt water mix in a delicious pattern of textures on my skin. But the effect only occurs when I stand still. The signal forces me to continue; the patterns disappear. I can feel only the seawater stroking my sides and back as I swim on.

A dull throb grows louder. It is the sound of a ship's engines, almost in my path. At first I cannot see it, but finally its lights appear on the horizon as I propel myself toward it. Could this be my destination? I thought I was being sent to a harbor, so I had hoped for a few more hours of life.

Now I can see the ship clearly. It is a fishing boat.

Perhaps it will stop me. The humans' way to hunt fishes is to find a place where people are feeding and herd us into their nets. The fish flee before us. We are a convenient marker, very useful to the humans, but when the nets close in there is no way for us to escape. We are captured and we drown. Many of us have been murdered this way; the men kill our youngest, those whose inexperience leaves them vulnerable to panic. The nets give a cruel death.

I swim straight at the trawler, staying near the surface. If the nets are out they are invisible at this distance; the men's sound-maker will not form a sensitive enough picture to show them to me.

How strange to think that men will prevent me from carrying out the task given me by other men . . .

I can smell and taste the cold metal hull and the hot-metal hot-oil of the propellors and engines. And now I can even hear the murky curtain of fish-nets, spread like great wings, sweeping the sea as they approach. I have avoided them so many times before . . .

In a few moments my life will end. My people may be safe for a short time after I die—yet I want to live. I must give up my life, but I will not do it happily, nor even bravely. The nets will close around me and panic with them, and I will thrash and struggle and silently cry out as the ropes and wires cut into me.

The nets are just before me. I touch them, and the hard mesh scrapes my skin.

Suddenly my body wrenches away, turning too swiftly, convulsed by the signal. Unwillingly I dive and turn, circle the ship and fishing nets, and flee.

How can the men know so much about what is going on this far out in the ocean? Can they know where every ship is, and where each creature swims?

I move onward with powerful involuntary strokes of my tail, frightened to realize how close a control the men have over me, yet relieved to have even a few more minutes.

But there is no joy left in me. The men have given me a terrible gift that will be paid for in the lives of people. Even if the men do not begin to kill each other and the world because of my actions, if I finish this task all the airbreathers in the sea will be under more suspicion. Already the undersea machines kill us if we come too close. We have learned to avoid them, but we cannot avoid every human machine. There are too many of them, and our foolish young ones court pleasure and death riding their bowwaves.

The taste of land grows stronger now, and the water is much shallower. The metal sounds that guide me echo loudly, quickly. The water is thick with the waste of humans and their creatures. People never visit this bay anymore.

Driven onward, my whole body quivers with weariness and fear. I am only a presence within it, able to guide myself around the worst islands of trash and poison, but little more. If I could shut off my hearing as I can close my eyes I would, and know nothing more until the end.

I am the only living creature in a desert world.

As I round a point of land the cry and groan of machinery washes over me, a wave of sound opposing the waves of the sea. I am swimming into a harbor full of ships and other things important to men. I surface, breathe the heavy air, listen to the air-borne sounds. The lights are bright before me.

I dive again. That is another compulsion the men have put into me, to stay beneath the surface as much as possible. They would have given me gills if they could.

This maze of shapes and echoes is not a place people would come of their own free will, though with my own voice I would not be so confused. Each note would tell me something new about my surroundings.

A shape is coming toward me.

These men have discovered me. They realize I am a creature of the other men, and they are sending a weapon to kill me. I surge forward, seeking to outrun it.

Of a sudden I cease fleeing. This is what I have sought: death by some other means than the plan of the men who captured me.

The shape comes closer and I swim as slowly as I am able. I do not want to die.

The shape does not move like a machine.

And now I can see it, through the darkness and the murk. This is no man-weapon.

If I were free I could never swim so calmly onward, waiting for the shark. Its ancestors slaughtered mine when people decided to return to the sea. We in turn learned how to kill the only creatures we ever hated.

Better the killer whale, the nets, the weapons of men. I can smell the cold beast now. It will writhe in a frenzy at the first taste of my blood. It will kill me with whatever its tiny brain grasps as joy, for it knows my people are its only challenge in the sea. Except the men. And there is no defense for people or for sharks against the men.

The shark will stop me, but I cannot stop the men from killing themselves. When they have suicided, when their poisons have murdered all the people, the shark will remain, as it has remained for millions of years, as it will remain until the end of the world.

This is the end's beginning.

Screwtop

Hot and wet from the fine, steamy rain, Kylis sat on her heels at the top of the drilling pit and waited for the second-duty shift to end. She rubbed at a streak of the thick red mud that had spattered her legs and her white boots when she walked across the compound. Redsun's huge dim star altered colors; white became a sort of pinkish gray. But among the forest's black foliage and against the Pit's clay, white uniforms stood out and made prisoners easier for the guards to see.

A few other people waited with Kylis at the south end of the deep slash in the earth. Like them, she crouched unsheltered from the rain, strands of wet hair plastered to her cheeks, watching for friends she had not seen in forty days.

Below lay two completed generator domes; above them rose the immense delicate cooling towers, and the antenna beaming power along the relay system to North Continent. Fences and guards protected the finished installations from the prisoners. Kylis and the rest worked only on clearing the fern forest, extending the Pit, drilling a third steam well—the dirty, dangerous jobs.

Paralleling the distant wall of volcanoes in the east, the drill pit extended northward. Its far end was invisible, obscured by the rain and by clouds of acrid smoke that billowed from the trash piles. The Pit was being lengthened again to follow the fault line where drilling was most efficient. Another strip of frond forest had been destroyed, and its huge primitive ferns now lay in blackened heaps. The stalks never burned completely, but until the coals died a bank of irritating smoke and sticky ash would hang over the prison camp. The fine rain sizzled into steam when it fell on glowing embers.

Kylis started at the long shrill siren that ended the second shift. For an instant she was afraid the hallucinations had returned, but the normal sounds of the prison responded to the signal. The faraway roar of bulldozers ceased; the high whine of the drill slipped down in pitch and finally stopped. People left their machines, threw down their tools, and straggled toward the trail. They passed beneath the guards' towers, watched and counted by the Lizard's crew. One by one and in occasional pairs they started up the steep slope of clay and debris and volcanic ash, picking their way around gullies and across muddy rivulets. Screwtop seemed very quiet now, almost peaceful, with no noise but the hum of turbines in the two geothermal power plants, and the rhythmic clatter of the pumps that kept the drill pit unflooded.

Kylis could not yet see Jason. She frowned. He and Gryf, who was on the third shift, had both been all right when she got off duty. She was sure of that, for news of accidents traveled instantaneously between working crews. But Kylis had been alone, sleeping much of the time, in the nine hours since the end of her shift. Anything could happen in nine hours. She tried to reassure herself about her friends' safety, because the pattern and rhythm of the work just ended had been too normal to follow a really bad accident.

She could not put aside her anxiety, and knew she would not until she had seen and spoken to and touched both Gryf and Jason. She still found herself surprised that she could care so much about two other human beings. Her past life had depended on complete independence and self-sufficiency.

Below, Gryf would be standing in the group of prisoners near the drilling rig. She tried to make him out, but the only person she could distinguish at this distance was the guard captain, called by everyone—when he was out of earshot— the Lizard, for his clean-shaven face and head gave him a smoothly impervious reptilian appearance. He was standing alone, facing the prisoners, giving orders. He wore black, as if in defiance of the heat, as a symbol of his superiority over everyone else in the camp. Even so, he was conspicuous now only because he was separated from the others. Gryf was conspicuous in any crowd, but the rig was too far away for Kylis to identify even Gryf's astonishing ebony and tan calico-patterned skin. The first time she had seen him, his first day at Screwtop, she had stared at him so long that he noticed and laughed at her. It was not a ridiculing laugh, but an understanding one. Gryf laughed at himself, too, sometimes, and often at the people who had made him what he was.

Gryf was the first tetraparental Kylis had ever seen or heard of, and even among tetras Gryf was unusual. Of his four biological parents, it happened that two of them were dark, and two fair. Gryf had been planned to be a uniform light brown, only his hair, perhaps, varicolored. Genes for hair color did not blend like those for skin. But the sets of sperm and ova had been matched wrong, so the mixture of two embryos forming Gryf made him his strange paisley pattern. He still had all the selectable intellectual gifts of his various parents. Those qualities, not his skin, were important.

New tetraparentals were special; the life of each was fully planned. Gryf was part of a team, and it was inconceivable to the government of Redsun and to the other tetras that after all the work of making him, after all the training and preparation, he would refuse his duty. When he did, he was sent for punishment to Redsun's strictest prison. If he changed his mind, he could at a word return to the tetras' secluded retreat. He had been at Screwtop half a year and he had not said that word.

Kylis was no Redsun native; she was oblivious to the others' awe of Gryf. She was curious about him. Neither because of nor in spite of the pattern of his skin, he was beautiful. Kylis wondered how his hair would feel, the locks half black and wiry, half blond and fine.

He was assigned to a nearby crew. Kylis saw immediately that he had been given hard and dirty jobs, not the most dangerous ones but those most tiring. The guards' task was not to kill him but to make life so unpleasant that he would return to the tetras.

Kylis waited to speak to him until she would not risk discipline for either of them. Without seeming to, the Lizard was watching Gryf closely, padding by every so often in his stealthy, silent way, his close-set eyes heavy-lidded, the direction of his gaze impossible to determine. But eventually his duties took him to another part of the camp, and Kylis left her own work to tell Gryf the tricks experience had taught her to make the labor a little easier.

Their first night together was Gryf's first night at Screwtop. When the shift ended, it seemed natural to walk back to the prisoners' shelters together. They were too tired to do much more than sleep, but the companionship was a comfort and the potential for more existed. They lay facing each other in the darkness. Starlight shone through a break in the clouds and glinted from the blond locks of Gryf's hair.

"I may never be let out of here," Gryf said. He was not asking for sympathy, but telling her his future as best he knew it. He had a pleasant, musical voice. Kylis realized these were the first words she heard him say. But she remembered his thanking her for her advice—and recalled that he had thanked her with his smile and a nod and the look in his eyes.

"I'm in for a long time," Kylis said. "I don't think there's that much difference between us." Screwtop could kill either of them the next day or the day before release.

Kylis reached up and touched Gryf's hair. It was stiff and matted with sweat. He took her hand and kissed her grimy palm. From then on they stayed together, growing closer but never speaking of a future outside the prison.

Several sets later Jason arrived and changed everything.

Kylis brought herself back to the present. She knew Gryf was below somewhere, though she could not make him out in the blotch of dirty white. She had been on the last shift during a previous set and she knew the schedule. The prisoners still working would not be exposed to much more danger today. Instead, they would have the dullest and most exhausting job of the period. During the last shift before the free day, once every forty days, all the equipment was cleaned and inspected. Anything done wrong was done over; the shift could drag on long past its normal end. Kylis hoped that would not happen this time.

At the bottom of the slope, Jason emerged from the bright cancer of machinery. He was muddy and grease-spattered, gold-flecked with bleached hair. He was very large and very fair, and even on Redsun where the light had little ultraviolet he sunburned easily. Though he had been working from dusk to midmorning his legs were horizontally striped with sunburn, darkest at the top of his thighs and lightest just below his knees, marking the different levels to which he had pulled the cuffs of his boots. Right now they were folded all the way down.

He glanced up and saw Kylis. His carriage changed; he straightened and waved. His blond beard was bristly and uncombed and his hair was plastered down with sweat. The waistband of his shorts was red with mud spattered onto his body and washed down by perspiration and rain. As he came closer she saw that he was thinner, and that the lines around his eyes had deepened. They had been lines of thought and laughter; now they were of fatigue and exposure. He hurried toward her, slipping on the clay, and she realized he, too, had been worried.

He heard I was in sensory deprivation, she thought, and he was afraid for me. She stood motionless for a few seconds. She was not quite used to him yet; his easy acceptance of her and his concern seemed innocent and admirable compared to the persistent distrust Kylis had felt toward him for so long. She started forward to meet him.

He stopped and held out his hands. She touched him, and he came forward, almost trembling, holding himself taut against exhaustion. His pose collapsed. Bending down, he rested his forehead on her shoulder. She put her hands on his back, very gently.

"Was it bad?" His voice was naturally low but now it was rough and hoarse. He had probably been directing his crew, shouting above the roar of machinery for eighteen hours.

"Bad enough," Kylis said. "I've been glad of the work since."

Still leaning against her, he shook his head.

"I'm okay now. I've quit hallucinating," she said, hoping it was true. "And you? Are you all right?" She could feel his breath on her damp shoulder.

"Yes. Now. Thanks to Gryf."

Jason had started this set on first day shift, which began at midnight and ended in the afternoon. Its members worked through the hottest part of the day when they were most tired. Halfway through his third work period Jason had collapsed. He was delirious and dehydrated, sunburned even through his shirt. The sun drained him. Gryf, just getting off when Jason fell, had worked through his own sleep period to finish Jason's shift. For them to switch shifts, Gryf had worked almost two of Redsun's days, straight. When Kylis heard about that, she could not see how anyone could do it, even Gryf.

Gryf had broken the rules, but no one had made Jason go back to his original shift. The Lizard must never have said anything about it. Kylis could imagine him standing in shadow, watching, while Gryf waited for a confrontation that never came. It was something the Lizard would do.

Jason's shoulders were scarred where blisters had formed in the sun, but Kylis saw that they had healed cleanly. She put her arm around Jason's waist to support him. "Come on. I found a place to sleep." They were both sticky with sweat and the heat.

"Okay." They crossed the barren mud where all the vegetation had been stripped away so the machines could pass. Before they turned off the path they drew rations from the mechanical dispenser near the prisoners' quarters. The tasteless bars dropped through a slot, two each. There were times in Kylis' life when she had not eaten well, but she had seldom eaten anything as boring as prison rations. Jason put one of his bars into his belt pouch.

"When are you going to give that up?"

Jason nibbled a corner of his second ration bar. "I'm not." His grin made the statement almost a joke. He saved part of his food against what Kylis thought ludicrous plans of escape. When he had saved enough supplies, he was going to hike out through the marsh.

"You don't have to save anything today." She slipped her tag back into the slot and kept reinserting it until the extra points were used and a small pile of ration bars lay in the hopper.

"They forgot to void my card for the time I was in the deprivation box," Kylis said. In sensory deprivation, one of the prison's punishments for mistakes, she had been fed intravenously. She gave Jason the extra food. He thanked her and put it in his belt pouch. Together they crossed the bare clay and entered the forest.

Jason had been at Screwtop only three sets. He was losing weight quickly here, for he was a big-boned man with little fat to burn. Kylis hoped his family would discover where he was and ransom him soon. And she hoped they would find him before he tried to run away, though she had stopped trying to argue him out of the dream. The marsh was impassable except by hovercraft. There were no solid paths through it, and people claimed it held undiscovered animals that would crush a boat or raft. Kylis neither believed nor disbelieved in the animals; she was certain only that a few prisoners had tried to escape during her time at Screwtop, and the guards had not even bothered to look for them. Redsun was not a place where the authorities allowed escape toward freedom, only toward death. The naked volcanoes cut off escape to the north and east with their barren lava escarpments and billowing clouds of poison gas; the marsh barred west and south. Screwtop was an economical prison, requiring fences only to protect the guards' quarters and the power domes, not to enclose the captives. And even if Jason could escape alive, he could never get off Redsun. He did not have Kylis' experience at traveling undetected.

The fern forest's shadows closed in around them, and they walked between the towering blackish-red stalks and lacy fronds. The foliage was heavy with huge droplets formed slowly by the misty rain. Kylis brushed past a leaf and the water cascaded down her side, making a faint track in the ashes and mud on her skin. She had washed herself when she got off duty, but staying clean was impossible at Screwtop.

They reached the sleeping place she had discovered. Several clumps of ferns had grown together and died, the stems falling over to make a conical shelter. Kylis pulled aside a handful of withered fronds and showed Jason in. Outside it looked like nothing but a pile of dead plants.

"It isn't even damp," he said, surprised. "And it's almost cool in here." He sat down on the carpet of dead moss and ferns and leaned back smiling. "I don't see how you found it. I never would have looked in here."

Kylis sat beside him. A few hours ago she had slept the soundest sleep she had had in Screwtop. The shade alleviated the heat, and the fronds kept the misty rain from drifting inside and collecting. Best of all, it was quiet.

"I thought you and Gryf would like it."

"Have you seen him?"

"Only across the compound. He looked all right."

Jason said aloud what Kylis feared. "The Lizard must have had a reason for letting him take my shift. To make it harder on him." He too was worried, and Kylis could see he felt guilty. "I shouldn't have let him do it," he said.

"Have you ever tried to stop him from doing something he thinks he should?"

Jason smiled. "No. I don't think I want to." He let himself sink further down in the moss. "Gods," he said, drawing out the word. "It's good to see you."

"It's been lonely," Kylis said, with the quiet sort of wonder she felt every time she realized that she did care enough to miss someone. Loneliness was more painful now, but she was not lonely all the time. She did not know how to feel about her newly discovered pleasure in the company of Gryf and Jason. Sometimes it frightened her. They had broached her defenses of solitude and suspicion, and at times she felt exposed and vulnerable. She trusted them, but there were even more betrayers at Screwtop than there were outside.

"I didn't give you those extra rations so you could save them all," she said. "I gave them to you so you'd stop starving yourself for one day at least."

"We could all get out of here," he said, "if we saved just a little more food." Even at midmorning, beneath the ferns, it was almost too dark to make out his features, but Kylis knew he was not joking. She said nothing. Jason thought the prisoners who fled into the marsh were still alive there; he thought he could join them and be helped. Kylis thought they were all dead. Jason believed escape on foot possible, and Kylis believed it death. Jason was an optimist, and Kylis was experienced.

"All right," Jason said. "I'll eat one more. In a while." He lay down flat and put his hands behind his head.

"How was your shift?" Kylis asked.

"Too much fresh meat."

Kylis grinned. Jason was talking like a veteran, hardened and disdainful of new prisoners, the fresh meat, who had not yet learned the ways of Screwtop.

"We only got a couple new people," she said. "You must have had almost the whole bunch."

"It would have been tolerable if three of them hadn't been assigned to the drilling rig."

"Did you lose any?"

"No. By some miracle."

"We were fresh once too. Gryf's the only one I ever saw who didn't start out doing really stupid things."

"Was I really that fresh?"

She did not want to hurt his feelings or even tease him.

"I was, wasn't I?"

"Jason . . . I'm sorry, but you were the freshest I ever saw. I didn't think you had any chance at all. Only Gryf did."

"I hardly remember anything about the first set, except how much time he spent helping me."

"I know," Kylis said. Jason had needed a great deal of help. Kylis had forgiven him for being the cause of her first real taste of loneliness, but she could not quite forget it.

"Gods—this last set," Jason said. "I didn't know how bad it was alone." Then he smiled. "I used to think I was a solitary person." Where Kylis was contemptuous of her discovered weaknesses, Jason was amused at and interested in his. "What did you do before Gryf came?"

"Before Gryf came, I didn't know how bad it was alone, either," she said rather roughly. "You'd better get some sleep."

He smiled. "You're right. Good morning." He fell asleep instantly.

Relaxed, he looked tireder. His hair had grown long enough to tie back, but it had escaped from its knot and curled in tangled, dirty tendrils around his face. Jason hated being dirty, but working with the drill left little energy for extras, like bathing. He would never really adjust to Screwtop as Gryf and Kylis had. His first day here, Gryf had kept him from being killed or crippled at least twice. Kylis had been working on the same shift but a different crew, driving one of the bulldozers and clearing another section of forest. The drill could not be set up among the giant ferns, because the ground itself would not stand much stress. Beneath a layer of humus was clay, so wet that in response to pressure it turned semiliquid, almost like quicksand. The crews had to strip off the vegetation and the layers of clay and volcanic ash until bedrock lay exposed. Kylis drove the dozer back and forth, cutting through ferns in a much wider path than the power plants themselves would have required. She had to make room for the excavated earth, which was piled well back from the Pit's edges. Even so the slopes sometimes collapsed in mudslides.

At the end of the day of Jason's arrival, the siren went off and Kylis drove the dozer to the old end of the Pit and into the recharging stall. Gryf was waiting for her, and a big fair man was with him, sitting slumped on the ground with his head between his knees and his hands limp on the ground. Kylis hardly noticed him. She took Gryf's hand, to walk with him back to the shelters, but he quietly stopped her and helped the other man to his feet. The new prisoner's expression was blank with exhaustion; in the dawn light he looked deathly pale. Hardly anyone on Redsun was as fair as he, even in the north. Kylis supposed he was from off-world, but he did not have the shoulder tattoo that would have made her trust him instantly. But Gryf was half carrying the big clumsy man, so she supported him on the other side.

Together she and Gryf got him to their shelter. He neither ate nor drank nor even spoke, but collapsed on the hard lumpy platform and fell asleep. Gryf watched him with a troubled expression.

"Who is that?" Kylis did not bother to hide the note of contempt in her voice.

Gryf told her the man's name, which was long and complicated and contained a lot of double vowels. She never remembered it all, even now. "He says to call him Jason."

"Did you know him before?" She was willing to help Gryf save an old friend, though she did not quite see how they would do it. In one day he had spent himself completely.

"No," Gryf said. "But I read his work. I never thought I'd get to meet him."

The undisguised awe in Gryf's voice hurt Kylis, not so much because she was jealous as because it reminded her how limited her own skills were. The admiration in the faces of drunks and children in spaceport bazaars, which Kylis had experienced, was nothing compared to Gryf's feeling for the accomplishments of this man.

"Is he in here for writing a book?"

"No, thank gods—they don't know who he is. They think he's a transient. He travels under his personal name instead of his family name. They are making him work for his passage home."

"How long?"

"Six sets."

"Oh, Gryf."

"He must live and be released."

"If he's important, why hasn't anybody ransomed him?"

"His family doesn't know where he is. They would have to be contacted in secret. If the government finds out who he is, they will never let him go. His books are smuggled in."

Kylis shook her head.

"He affected my life, Kylis. He helped me understand the idea of freedom. And personal responsibility. The things you have known all your life from your own experience."

"You mean you wouldn't be here except for him."

"I never thought of it that way, but you are right."

"Look at him, Gryf. This place will grind him up."

Gryf stared somberly at Jason, who slept so heavily he hardly seemed to breathe. "He should not be here. He's a person who should not be hurt."

"We should?"

"He's different."

Kylis did not say Jason would be hurt at Screwtop. Gryf knew that well enough.

Jason had been hurt, and he had changed. What Gryf had responded to in his work was a pure idealism and innocence that could not exist in captivity. Kylis had been afraid Jason would fight the prison by arming himself with its qualities; she was afraid of what that would do to Gryf. But Jason had survived by growing more mature, by retaining his humor, not by becoming brutal. Kylis had never read a word he had written, but the longer she knew him, the more she liked and admired him.

Now she left him sleeping among the ferns. She had slept as much as she wanted to for the moment. She knew from experience that she had to time her sleeping carefully on the day off. In the timeless environment of space, where she had spent most of her life, Kylis' natural circadian rhythm was about twenty-three hours. A standard day of twenty-four did not bother her, but Redsun's twenty-seven hour rotation made her uncomfortable. She could not afford to sleep too much or too little and return to work exhausted and inattentive. At Screwtop inattention was worth punishment at best, and at worst, death.

She was no longer tired, but she was hungry for anything besides the tasteless prison rations. The vegetation on Redsun, afflicted with a low mutation rate, had not evolved very far. The plants were not yet complex enough to produce fruiting bodies. Some of the stalks and roots, though, were edible.

On Redsun, there were no flowers.

Kylis headed deeper into the shadows of the rain forest. Away from the clearings people had made, the primitive plants reached great heights. Kylis wandered among them, her feet sinking into the soft moist humus. Her footprints remained distinct. She turned and looked back. Only a few paces behind her, seeping water had already formed small pools in the deeper marks of her bootheels.

She wished she and Gryf and Jason had been on the same shift. As it was, half of their precious free time would be spent sleeping and readjusting their time schedules. When Gryf finally got off, they would have less than one day together, even before he rested. Sometimes Kylis felt that the single free day in every forty was more a punishment than if the prisoners had been forced to work their sentences straight through. The brief respite allowed them to remember just how much they hated Screwtop, and just how impossible it was to escape.

Since she could not be with both her friends, she preferred complete solitude. For Kylis it was almost instinctive to make certain no one could follow her. Unfolding the cuffs of her boots, she protected her legs to halfway up her thighs. She did not seal the boots to her shorts because of the heat.

The floor of the forest dipped and rose gently, forming wide hollows where the rain collected. Kylis stepped into one of the huge shallow pools and waded across it, walking slowly, feeling ahead with her toe before she put her foot down firmly. The mist and shadows, the reddish sunlight, and the glassy surface created illusions that concealed occasional deep pits. Where the water lay still and calm, microscopic parasites crawled out of the earth and swarmed. They normally reproduced inside small fishes and primitive amphibians, but they were not particular about their host. They would invade a human body through a cut or abrasion, causing agonizing muscle lesions. Sometimes they traveled slowly to the brain. The forest was no place to fall into a water hole.

Avoiding one deep spot, Kylis reached the far bank and stepped out onto a slick outcropping of rock where her footprints would not show. Where the stone ended and she reentered the frond forest, the ground was higher and less sodden, although the misty rain still fell continuously.

The ferns thinned, the ground rose steeply, and Kylis began to climb. At the top of the hill the air stirred, and the vegetation was not so thick. Kylis found some edible shoots, picked them, and peeled them carefully. The pulp was spicy and crunchy. The juice, pungent and sour, trickled down her throat. She picked a few more stalks and tied the small bundle to her belt. Those that were sporing she was careful not to disturb. Edible plants no longer grew near camp; in fact, nothing edible grew close enough to Screwtop to reach on any but the free day.

Redsun traveled upright in its circular orbit; it had no seasons. The plants had no sun-determined clock by which to synchronize their reproduction, so a few branches of any one plant or a few plants of any one species would spore while the rest remained asexual. A few days later a different random set would begin. It was not a very efficient method of spreading traits through the gene pool, but it had sufficed until people came along and destroyed fertile plants as well as spored-out ones. Kylis, who had noticed in her wanderings that evolution ceased at the point when human beings arrived and began to make their changes, tried not to cause that kind of damage.

A flash of white, a movement, caught the edge of her vision. She froze, wishing the hallucinations away but certain they had come back. White was not a natural color in the frond forest, not even the muddy pink that passed for white under Redsun's enormous star. But no strange fantasy creatures paraded around her; she heard no furious imaginary sounds. Her feet remained firmly on the ground, the warm fine rain hung around her, the ferns drooped with their burden of droplets. Slowly Kylis turned until she faced the direction of the motion. She was not alone.

She moved quietly forward until she could look through the black foliage. What she had seen was the uniform of Screwtop, white boots, white shorts, white shirt for anyone with a reason to wear it. One of the other prisoners sat on a rock, looking out across the forest, toward the swamp. Tears rolled slowly down her face, though she made no sound. Miria.

Feeling only a little guilty about invading her privacy, Kylis watched her, as she had been watching her for some time. Kylis thought Miria was a survivor, someone who would leave Screwtop without being broken. She kept to herself; she had no partners. Kylis had admired her tremendous capacity for work. She was taller than Kylis, bigger, potentially stronger, but clearly unaccustomed to great physical labor. For a while she had worn her shirt tied up under her breasts, but like most others she had discarded it because of the heat.

Miria survived in the camp without using other people or allowing herself to be used. Except when given a direct order, she acted as if the guards simply did not exist, in effect defying them without giving them a reasonable excuse to punish her. They did not always wait for reasonable excuses. Miria received somewhat more than her share of pain, but her dignity remained intact.

Kylis retreated a couple of steps, then came noisily out of the forest, giving Miria a few seconds to wipe away her tears if she wanted to. But when Kylis stopped, pretending to be surprised at finding another person so near, Miria simply turned toward her.

"Hello, Kylis."

Kylis went closer. "Is anything wrong?" That was such a

silly question that she added, "I mean, is there anything I can do?"

Miria's smile erased the lines of tension in her forehead and revealed laugh lines Kylis had never noticed before. "No," Miria said. "Nothing anyone can do. But thank you."

"I guess I'd better go."

"Please don't," Miria said quickly. "I'm so tired of being alone—" She cut herself off and turned away, as if she were sorry to have revealed so much of herself. Kylis knew how she felt. She sat down nearby.

Miria looked out again over the forest. The fronds were a soft reddish black. The marsh trees were harsher, darker, interspersed with gray patches of water. Beyond the marsh, over the horizon, lay an ocean that covered all of Redsun except the large inhabited North Continent and the tiny South Continent where the prison camp lay.

Kylis could see the ugly scar of the pits where the crews were still drilling, but Miria had her back half turned and she gazed only at unspoiled forest.

"It could all be so beautiful," Miria said.

"Do you really think so?" Kylis thought it ugly—the black foliage, the dim light, the day too long, the heat, no animals except insects that did not swim or crawl. Redsun was the most nearly intolerable planet she had ever been on.

"Yes. Don't you?"

"No. I don't see any way I ever could."

"It's sometimes hard, I know," Miria said. "Sometimes, when I'm tiredest, I even feel the same. But the world's so rich and so strange—don't you see the challenge?"

"I only want to leave it," Kylis said.

Miria looked at her for a moment, then nodded. "You're not from Redsun, are you?"

Kylis shook her head.

"No, there's no reason for you to have the same feelings as someone born here."

This was a side of Miria that Kylis had never seen, one of quiet but intense dedication to a world whose rulers had imprisoned her. Despite her liking for Miria, Kylis was confused. "How can you feel that way when they've sent you here? I hate them, I hate this place—"

"Were you wrongly arrested?" Miria asked with sympathy.

"They could have just deported me. That's what usually happens."

"Sometimes injustice is done," Miria said sadly. "I know

that. I wish it wouldn't happen. But I deserve to be here, and I know that too. When my sentence is completed, I'll be forgiven."

More than once Kylis had thought of staying on some world and trying to live the way other people did, even of accepting punishment, if necessary, but what had always stopped her was the doubt that forgiveness was often, or ever, fully given. Redsun seemed an unlikely place to find amnesty.

"What did you do?"

Kylis felt Miria tense and wished she had not asked. Not asking questions about the past was one of the few tacit rules among the prisoners.

"I'm sorry . . . it's not that I wouldn't tell you, but I just cannot talk about it."

Kylis sat in silence for a few minutes, scuffing the toe of her boot along the rock like an anxious child and rubbing the silver tattoo on the point of her left shoulder. The pigment caused irritation and slight scarring. The intricate design had not hurt for a long time, nor even itched, but she could feel the delicate lines. Rubbing them was a habit. Even though the tattoo represented a life to which she would probably never return, it was soothing.

"What's that?" Miria asked. Abruptly she grimaced. "I'm sorry, I'm doing just what I asked you not to do."

"It doesn't matter," Kylis said. "I don't mind. It's a spaceport rat tattoo. You get it when the other rats accept you." Despite everything, she was proud of the mark.

"What's a spaceport rat?"

That Miria was unfamiliar with the rats did not surprise Kylis. Few Redsun people had heard of them. On almost every other world Kylis ever visited, the rats were, if not exactly esteemed, at least admired. Some places she had been actively worshiped. Even where she was officially unwelcome, the popular regard was high enough to prevent the kind of entrapment Redsun had started.

"I used to be one. It's what everybody calls people who sneak on board starships and live in them and in spaceports. We travel all over."

"That sounds . . . interesting," Miria said. "But didn't it bother you to steal like that?"

A year before, Kylis would have laughed at the question, even knowing, as she did, that Miria was quite sincere. But recently Kylis had begun to wonder: Might something be more important than outwitting spaceport security guards? While she was wondering she came to Redsun, so she never had a chance to find out.

"I started when I was ten," Kylis said to Miria. "So I didn't think of it like that."

"You sneaked onto a starship when you were only ten?"

"Yes."

"All by yourself?"

"Until the others start to recognize you, no one will help you much. It's possible. And I thought it was my only chance to get away from where I was."

"You must have been in a terrible place."

"It's hard to remember if it was really as bad as I think. I can remember my parents, but never smiling, only yelling at each other and hitting me."

Miria shook her head. "That's terrible, to be driven away by your own people—to have nowhere to grow up . . . Did you ever go back?"

"I don't think so."

"What?"

"I can't remember much about where I was born. I always thought I'd recognize the spaceport, but there might have been more than one, so maybe I have been back and maybe I haven't. The thing is, I can't remember what they called the planet. Maybe I never knew."

"I cannot imagine it—not to know who you are or where you come from or even who your parents were."

"I know *that*," Kylis said.

"You could find out about the world. Fingerprints or ship records or regression—"

"I guess I could. If I ever wanted to. Sometime I might even do it, if I ever get out of here."

"I'm sorry we stopped you. Really. It's just that we feel that everyone who can should contribute a fair share."

Kylis still found it hard to believe that after being sent to Screwtop Miria would include herself in Redsun's collective conscience, but she had said "we." Kylis only thought of authorities as "they."

She shrugged. "Spaceport rats know they can get caught. It doesn't happen too often and usually you hear that you should avoid the place."

"I wish you had."

"We take the chance." She touched the silver tattoo again.

"You don't get one of these until you've proved you can be trusted. So when places use informers against us, we usually know who they are."

"But on Redsun you were betrayed?"

"I never expected them to use a child," Kylis said bitterly.

"A child!"

"This little kid sneaked on my ship. He did a decent job of it, and he reminded me of me. He was only ten or eleven, and he was all beat up. I guess we aren't so suspicious of kids because most of us started at the same age." Kylis glanced at Miria and saw that she was staring at her, horrified.

"They used a child? And injured him, just to catch you?"

"Does that really surprise you?"

"Yes," Miria said.

"Miria, half the people who were killed during the last set weren't more than five or six years older than the boy who turned me in. Most of the people being sent here now are that age. What could they possibly have done terrible enough to get them sent here?"

"I don't know," Miria said softly without looking up. "We need the power generators. Someone has to drill the steam wells. Some of us will die in the work. But you're right about the young people. I've been thinking about . . . other things. I had not noticed." She said that as if she had committed a crime, or more exactly a sin, by not noticing. "And the child . . ." Her voice trailed off and she smiled sadly at Kylis. "How old are you?"

"I don't know. Maybe twenty."

Miria raised one eyebrow. "Twenty? Older in experience, but not that old in time. You should not be here."

"But I am. I'll survive it."

"I think you will. And what then?"

"Gryf and Jason and I have plans."

"On Redsun?"

"Gods, no."

"Kylis," Miria said carefully, "you do not know much about tetraparentals, do you?"

"How much do I need to know?"

"I was born here. I used to . . . to work for them. Their whole purpose is their intelligence. Normal people like you and me bore them. They cannot tolerate us for long."

"Miria, stop it!"

"Your friend will only cause you pain. Give him up. Put him away from you. Urge him to go home."

"No! He knows I'm an ordinary person. We know what we're going to do."

"It makes no difference," Miria said with abrupt coldness. "He will not be allowed to leave Redsun."

Kylis felt the blood drain from her face. No one had ever said that so directly and brutally before. "They can't keep him. How long will they make him stay here before they realize they can't break him?"

"He is important. He owes Redsun his existence."

"But he's a person with his own dreams. They can't make him a slave!"

"His research team is worthless without him."

"I don't care," Kylis said.

"*You*—" Miria cut herself off. Her voice became much gentler. "They will try to persuade him to follow their plans. He may decide to do as they ask."

"I wouldn't feel any obligation to the people who run things on Redsun even if I lived here. Why should he be loyal to them? Why should you? What did they ever do but send you here? What will they let you do when you get out? Anything decent or just more dirty, murderous jobs like this one?" She realized she was shouting, and Miria looked stunned.

"I don't know," Miria said. "I don't know, Kylis. Please stop saying such dangerous things." She was terrified and shaken, much more upset than when she had been crying.

Kylis moved nearer and took her hand. "I'm sorry, Miria, I didn't mean to hurt you or say anything that could get you in trouble." She paused, wondering how far Miria's fear of Redsun's government might take her from her loyalty.

"Miria," she said on impulse, "have you ever thought of partnering with anybody?"

Miria hesitated so long that Kylis thought she would not answer. Kylis wondered if she had intruded on Miria's past again.

"No," Miria finally siad. "Never."

"Would you?"

"Think about it? Or do it?"

"Both. Partner with me and Gryf and Jason. Not just here, but when we get out."

"No," Miria said. "No, I couldn't." She sounded frightened again.

"Because we want to leave Redsun?"

"Other reasons."

"Would you just think about it?"

Miria shook her head.

"I know you don't usually live in groups on Redsun," Kylis said. "But where I was born, a lot of people did, even though my parents were alone. I remember, before I ran away, my friends were never afraid to go home like I was. Jason spent all his life in a group family, and he says it's a lot easier to get along." She was skipping over her own occasional doubts that any world could be as pleasant as the one Jason described. Whatever it was like, it had to be better than her own former existence of constant hiding and constant uncertainty; it had to be better than what Gryf told her of Redsun, with its emphasis on loyalty to the government at the expense of any family structure too big to move instantly at the whim or order of the rulers.

Miria did not respond.

"Anyway, three people aren't enough—we thought we'd find others after we got out. But I think—"

"Gryf doesn't—" Miria interrupted Kylis, then stopped herself and started over. "They don't know you were going to ask me?"

"Not exactly, but they both know you," Kylis said defensively. She thought Miria might be afraid Kylis' partners would refuse her. Kylis knew they would not but could not put how she knew into proper words.

The rain had blurred away the marks of tears on Miria's cheeks, and now she smiled and squeezed Kylis' hand. "Thank you, Kylis," she said. "I wish I could accept. I can't, but not for the reasons you think. You'll find someone better." She started up, but Kylis stopped her.

"No, you stay here. This is your place." Kylis stood. "If you change your mind, just say. All right?"

"I won't change my mind."

"I wish you wouldn't be so sure." Reluctantly, she started away.

"Kylis?"

"Yes?"

"Please don't tell anyone you asked me this."

"Not even Gryf and Jason?"

"No one. Please."

"All right," Kylis said unwillingly.

Kylis left Miria on the stony hillside. She glanced back once before entering the forest. Miria was sitting on the stone again, hunched forward, her forearms on her knees. Now she was looking down at the huge slash of clay and trash heaps, the complicated delicate cooling towers that condensed the generators' steam, the high impervious antenna beaming power north toward the cities.

When Kylis reached the sleeping place, the sun was high. Beneath the dead fern trees it was still almost cool. She crept in quietly and sat down near Jason without waking him. He lay sprawled in dry moss, breathing deeply, solid and real. As if he could feel her watching him, he half opened his eyes.

Kylis lay down and drew her hand up his side, feeling bones that had become more prominent, dry and flaking sunburned skin, and the scabs of cuts and scratches. He was bruised as though the guards had beaten him, perhaps because of his occasional amusement at things so odd that his reaction seemed insolence. But for now, she would not notice his new scars, and he would not notice hers.

"Are you awake?"

He laughed softly. "I think so."

"Do you want to go back to sleep?"

He reached out and touched her face. "I'm not that tired."

Kylis smiled and leaned over to kiss him. The hairs of his short beard were soft and stiff against her lips and tongue. For a while she and Jason could ignore the heat.

Lying beside Jason, not quite touching because the afternoon was growing hot, Kylis only dozed while Jason again slept soundly. She sat up and pulled on her shorts and boots, brushed a lock of Jason's sunstreaked hair from his damp forehead, and slipped outside. A couple of hours of Gryf's work shift remained, so Kylis headed toward the guards' enclosure and the hovercraft dock.

Beyond the drill-pit clearing, the forest extended for a short distance westward. The ground continued to fall, growing wetter and wetter, changing perceptibly into marsh. The enclosure, a hemispherical electrified fence completely covering the guards' residence domes, was built at the juncture of relatively solid land and shallow, standing water. It protected the hovercraft ramp, and it was invulnerable. She had tried to get through it. She had even tried to dig beneath it. Digging under a fence or cutting through one was something no spaceport rat would do, short of desperation. After her first few days at Screwtop, Kylis had been desperate. She had not believed she could survive her sentence in the prison. So, late that night, she crept over to the electrified fence and began to dig. At dawn she had not reached the bottom of the fence supports, and the ground was wet enough to start carrying electricity to her in small warning tingles.

Her shift would begin soon; guards would be coming in and going out, and she would be caught if she did not stop. She planned to cover over the hole she had dug and hope it was not discovered.

She was lying flat on the ground, digging a narrow deep hole with a flat rock and both hands, smeared all over with the red clay, her fingernails ripped past the quick. She reached down for one last handful of dirt, and grabbed a trap wire.

The current swept through her, contracting every muscle in her body. It lasted only an instant. She lay quivering, almost insensible, conscious enough to be glad the wire had been set to stun, not kill. She tried to get up and run, but she could not move properly. She began to shudder again. Her muscles were overstimulated, incapable of distinguishing a real signal. She ached all over, so badly that she could not even guess if the sudden clench of muscles had broken any bones.

A light shone toward her. She heard footsteps as the guard approached to investigate the alarm the trap wire had set off. The sound thundered through her ears, as though the electric current had heightened all her senses, toward pain. The footsteps stopped; the light beam blinded her, then left her face. Her dazzled vision blurred the figure standing over her, but she knew it was the Lizard. It occurred to her, in a vague, slow-motion thought, that she did not know his real name. (She learned later that no one else did either.) He dragged Kylis to her feet and held her upright, glaring at her, his face taut with anger and his eyes narrow.

"Now you know we're not as easy to cheat as starship owners," he said. His voice was low and raspy, softly hoarse. He let her go and she collapsed again. "You're on probation. Don't make any more mistakes. And don't be late for duty."

The other guards followed him away. They did not even bother to fill in the hole she had dug.

Kylis had staggered through that workday; she survived it, and the next, and the next, until she knew that the work itself would not kill her. She did not try to dig beneath the fence again, but she still watched the hovercraft when it arrived.

By the time she reached her place of concealment on the bank above the fence, the hovercraft had already climbed the ramp and settled. The gate was locked behind it. Kylis watched the new prisoners being unloaded. The cargo bay door swung open. The people staggered out on deck and down the gangway, disoriented by the long journey in heat and darkness. One of the prisoners stumbled and fell to his knees, retching.

Kylis remembered how she had felt after so many hours in the pitch-dark hold. Even talking was impossible, for the engines were on the other side of the hold's interior bulkhead and the fans were immediately below. She was too keyed up to go into a trance, and a trance would be dangerous while she was crowded in with so many people.

The noise was what Kylis remembered most about coming to Screwtop—incessant, penetrating noise, the high whine of the engines and the roar of the fans. She had been half deaf for days afterward. The compartment was small. Despite the heat the prisoners could not avoid sitting and leaning against each other, and as soon as the engines started the temperature began to rise. By the time the hovercraft reached the prison, the hold was thick with the stench of human misery. Kylis hardly noticed when the craft's sickening swaying ceased. When the hatch opened and red light spilled in, faintly dissipating the blackness, Kylis looked up with all the others, and, like all the others, blinked like a frightened animal.

The guards had no sympathy for cramped muscles or nausea. Their shouted commands faded like faraway echoes through Kylis' abused hearing. She pushed herself up, using the wall as support. Her legs and feet were asleep. They began regaining sensation, and she felt as if she were walking on tiny knives. She hobbled out, but at the bottom of the gangway she, too, had stumbled. A guard's curse and the prod of his club brought her to her feet in a fury, fists clenched, but she quelled her violent temper instantly. The guard watched with a smile, waiting. But Kylis had been to Earth, where one of the few animals left outside the game preserves and zoos was the possum. She had learned its lesson well.

Now she crouched on the bank and watched the new prisoners realize, as she had, that the end of the trip did not end the terrible heat. Screwtop was almost on the equator of Redsun, and the heat and humidity never lessened. Even the rain was lukewarm.

The guards prodded the captives into a compact group and turned hoses on them, spraying off filth and sweat. Afterward the new people plodded through the mud to the processing dome. Kylis watched each one pass through the doorway. She had never defined what she looked for when she watched the new arrivals, but whatever it was, she did not find it today. Even more of them were terribly young, and they all had the look of hopelessness that would make them nothing more than fresh meat, new bodies for the work to use up. Screwtop would grind them down and throw them away. They would die of disease or exhaustion or carelessness. Kylis did not see in one of them the spark of defiance that might get them through their sentences intact in body or spirit. But sometimes the spark only came out later, exposed by the real adversity of the work.

The hatch swung shut and the hovercraft's engines roared to full power. No one at all had been taken on board for release on North Continent.

The boat quivered on its skirts and floated back down the ramp, through the entrance, onto the glassy gray surface of the water. The gate sparked shut. Kylis was vaguely disappointed, for the landing was no different from any she had seen since she was brought to Screwtop herself. There was no way to get on board the boat. The familiar admission still annoyed her. For a spaceport rat, admitting defeat to the safeguards of an earthbound vehicle was humiliating. She could not even think of a way to get herself out of Screwtop, much less herself and Gryf and Jason. She was afraid that if she did not find some chance of escape, Jason might really try to flee through the swamp.

She ran her fingers through her short black hair and shook her head, flinging out the misty rain that gathered in huge drops and slipped down her face and neck and back. The heat and the rain—she hated both.

In an hour or two the evening rain would fall in solid sheets, washing the mist away. But an hour after that the faint infuriating droplets would begin again. They seemed never to fall, but to hang in the air and collect on skin, on hair, beneath trees, inside shelters.

Kylis grabbed an overhanging plant and stripped off a few of its red-black fronds, flinging them to the ground in anger.

She stood up, but suddenly crouched down in hiding again. Below, Miria walked up to the fence, placed her hand against the palm lock, and waited, glancing over her shoulder as if making certain she was alone. As the gate swung open and Miria, a prisoner, walked alone and free into the guards' enclosure, Kylis felt her knees grow weak. Miria stopped at a dome, and the door opened for her. Kylis thought she could see the Lizard in the dimness beyond.

Almost the only thing this could mean was that Miria was a spy. Kylis began to tremble in fear and anger, fear of what Miria could tell the Lizard that would help him increase the pressure on Gryf, anger at herself for trusting Miria. She had made another mistake in judgment like the one that had imprisoned her, and this time the consequences could be much worse.

She sat in the mud and the rain trying to think, until she realized that Gryf would be off work in only a few minutes. She did not even have time to wake Jason.

When Kylis turned her back on the guards' domes, Miria had not yet come out.

Kylis was a few minutes late reaching the drill pit. The third shift had already ended; all the prisoners were out and drifting away. Gryf was nowhere around, and he was nothing if not conspicuous. She began to worry, because Gryf was frequently first out, never last—he did not seem to tire. Certainly he would wait for her.

She stood indecisively, worried. Maybe he wanted something in the shelter, she thought.

She did not believe that for a moment. She glanced back toward the bottom of the Pit.

Everything happened at once. She forgot about Miria, Lizard, the prison. She cried out for Jason, knowing her voice would not carry that far. She ran downhill, fighting the clay that sucked at her feet. Two people she knew slightly trudged up the hill—Troi, skeletal, sharp-featured, sardonic, and Chuzo, squarely built and withdrawn. Both were very young; both were aging quickly here.

They supported Gryf between them.

Ash and grease disguised the pattern of his paisley skin. Kylis knew he was alive only because no one at Screwtop would spend any energy on someone who was dead. When she was closer, she could see the ends of deep slashes made by the whip where it had curled around his body. Blood had dried in narrow streaks on his sides. His wrists were abraded where he had been tied for the punishment.

"Oh, Gryf—"

Hearing her, Gryf raised his head. She felt great relief. Troi and Chuzo stopped when Kylis reached them.

"The Lizard ordered it himself," Troi said bitterly. Screw-top held few amenities, but people were seldom flogged on the last day of the shift.

"Why?"

"I don't know. I was too far away. Anything. Nothing. What reason do they ever have?"

Kylis quieted her anger for the moment. She took over for Chuzo. "Thank you," she said, quite formally.

Troi stayed where he was. "Get him to the top, anyway," he said in his gruff manner.

"Gryf? Can you make it?"

He tightened his hand on her shoulder. They started up the steep path. When they finally reached the top, the immense sun had set. The sky was pink and scarlet in the west, and the volcanoes eastward glowed blood red.

"Thanks," Kylis said again. Chuzo hesitated, but Troi nodded and left. After a moment Chuzo followed him.

Gryf leaned heavily on her, but she could support him. She tried to turn toward the shelters and their meager stock of medical supplies, but he resisted weakly and guided her toward the waterfall. If he wanted to go there first, he must think his wounds had been contaminated.

"Gods," Kylis whispered. Clumsily, they hurried. She wished Jason had heard her, for with him they could have gone faster. It was her fault he was not there. She could not hold Gryf up alone without hurting his back.

Gryf managed a smile, just perceptible, telling her, I hurt but I am strong.

Yes, Kylis thought, stronger than Jason, stronger than me. We'll survive.

They continued.

"Kylis! Gryf!"

Gryf stopped. Kylis let him, with relief. Jason splashed toward them.

Gryf's knees buckled. Kylis strained to keep him out of the mud, away from more parasites. Jason reached them and picked Gryf up.

"Could you hear me?" Kylis asked.

"No," Jason said. "I woke up and came looking. Where are you taking him?"

"To the overflow pipe."

Jason needed no explanation of the dangers of infection. He carried Gryf toward the waterfall, swearing softly.

The cooling towers from the steam wells produced the only safe water the prisoners had for bathing. It spewed from a pipe to a concrete platform and spilled from there to the ground, forming a muddy pool that spread into the forest. The water was too hot for anyone to go directly beneath the cascade. Jason stopped in knee-deep hot water. They were all standing in heavy spray.

Jason held Gryf against his chest while Kylis splashed water on Gryf's back from her cupped hands. She washed him as gently as she could and still be safe. She found no parasites and none of their eggs. The water swept away mud and sweat, turning Jason gold and bright pink and Kylis auburn and Gryf all shades of dark brown and tan.

Kylis cursed the Lizard. He knew he would look bad in the eyes of the tetra committee if Gryf were crushed or bled to death or went home with everything but his brain. But he would look worse if he could not force Gryf to go home at all.

Gryf's eyelids flickered. His eyes were bright blue, flecked irregularly with black.

"How do you feel?"

He smiled, but he had been hurt—she could see the memory of pain. They had touched his spirit. He looked away from her and made Jason let him turn. He staggered. His knees would not support him, which seemed to surprise him. Jason held him up, and Gryf took the last thin flake of antiseptic soap from Kylis' hand.

"What's the matter?" she asked.

Gryf turned her around. For a moment his touch was painful, then she felt the sharp sting of soap on raw flesh. Gryf showed her his hand, which glittered with a mass of tiny, fragile eggs like mica flakes. Gryf used up her soap scrubbing her side, and Jason got out what soap he had left.

"This cut's pretty deep but it's clean now. You must have fallen and smashed a nest."

"I don't remember—" She had a kinesthetic memory, from running down into the Pit. "Yes, I do . . ." It hit her then, a quick shock of the fear of what might have been—agony, paralysis, senility—if Gryf had not noticed, if the eggs had healed beneath her skin and hatched. Kylis shuddered.

They returned to the compound, supporting Gryf between them. The wall-less, stilt-legged shelters were almost deserted.

Jason climbed the slanted ladder to their shelter backward,

leaning against it for stability while he helped Gryf. The steps were slick with yellow lichen. Kylis chinned herself onto the platform. In their floor locker she had to paw through little stacks of Jason's crumbling ration bars before she found their mold poultice and the web box. She had been very hungry, but she had never eaten any of her friend's hoarded food. She would not have had such restraint a year ago.

Jason put Gryf down between the makeshift partitions that marked their section of the shelter. Gryf was pale beneath the pattern of tan and pigment. Kylis almost wished Troi and Chuzo had left him in the Pit. The Lizard might then have been forced to put him in the hospital. She wondered if Troi or Chuzo might be helping the Lizard make Screwtop as hard on Gryf as they could. She did not want to believe that, but she did not want to believe Miria was an informer, either.

Their spider—Kylis thought of it as a spider, though it was a Redsun-evolved creature—skittered up the corner post to a new web. Kylis often imagined the little brown mottled creature hanging above them on her tiny fringed feet, hating them. Yet she was free to crawl down the stilt and into the jungle, or to spin a glider and float away, and she never did. In dreams, Kylis envied her; awake, she named her Stupid. Kylis hoped the web box held enough silk to soothe Gryf's back.

"Hey," Jason said, "this stuff is ready."

"Okay." Kylis took the bowl of greenish mold past. "Gryf?"

He glance up. His eyelashes and eyebrows were black and blond, narrowly striped.

"Hang on, it might hurt."

He nodded.

Jason held Gryf's hands while Kylis applied first the mold, then delicate strips of spider silk. Gryf did not move. Even now he had enough strength to put aside the pain.

When she was done, Jason stroked Gryf's forehead and gave him water. He did not want to eat, even broth, so they kissed him and sat near him, for his reassurance and their own, until he fell asleep. That did not take long. When he was breathing deeply, Jason got up and went to Kylis, carrying the bowl.

"I want to look at the cut."

"Okay," Kylis said, "but don't use all the paste."

The poultice burned coldly, and Jason's hands were cool on

her skin. She sat with her forearms on her drawn-up knees, accepting the pain rather than ignoring it. When he had finished treating her, she took the bowl and daubed the mold on his cuts. She almost told Jason about Miria, but finally decided not to. Kylis had created the problem; she wanted to solve it herself if she could. And, she admitted, she was ashamed of her misjudgment. She could think of no explanation for Miria's actions that would absolve her.

Jason yawned widely.

"Give me your tag and go back to sleep," Kylis said. Since she had been the first to get off work this time, it was her turn to collect their rations. She took Gryf's tag from his belt pouch and jumped from the edge of the platform to the ground.

Kylis approached the ration dispenser cautiously. On Redsun, violent criminals were sent to rehabilitation centers, not to work camps. Kylis was glad of that, though she did not much like to remember the stories of obedient, blank-eyed people coming out of rehab.

Still, some prisoners were confident or foolish or desperate enough to try to overpower others and steal. At Screwtop it was safest to collect neither obligations nor hatreds. Vengeance was much too simple here. The underground society of spaceport rats had not been free of psychopaths; Kylis knew how to defend herself. Here she had never had to resort to more serious measures. If she did, the drill pit was a quick equalizer between a bully and a smaller person. Mistakes could be planned; machines sometimes malfunctioned.

The duty assignments were posted on the ration dispenser. Kylis read them and was astonished and overjoyed to find herself and her friends all on the same shift, the night shift. She hurried back to tell them the news, but Jason was sound asleep, and she did not have the heart to wake him. Gryf had gone.

Kylis threw the rations in the floor locker and sat on the edge of the platform. A scavenger insect crawled across the lumpy floor of fern stalks. Kylis caught it and let it go near Stupid, barricading it until the spider, stalking, left her new web and seized the insect, paralyzed it, wrapped it in silk to store it, and dragged it away. Kylis wondered if their spider ever slept, or if spiders even needed sleep. Then she stole the web.

She grew worried. She knew Gryf could take care of

himself. He always did. He had probably never really reached his limits, but Gryf might overestimate even his strength and endurance. He had rested barely an hour.

Kylis fidgeted for a little while longer. Finally she slid down into the mud again.

Water seeped quickly into new footprints in the battered earth around the shelters; Gryf had left no trail that she could distinguish from the other marks in the clay. She went into the forest, with some knowledge and some intuition of where he might be. Above her, huge insects flitted past, barely brushing clawed wingtips against the ferns. It was dark, and the star path, streaked across the sky like the half-circular support of a globe, gave a dim yellow light through broken clouds.

Kylis was startled and frightened by a tickling of the short hair at the back of her neck. She flinched and turned. Gryf looked down at her, smiling, amused.

"Kylis, my friend, you really needn't worry about me all the time." She was always surprised, when he spoke, to remember how pleasant and calming his voice was.

His eyes were dilated so the iris was only a narrow circle of light and dark striations.

Every few sets, someone died from sucking slime. It grew in the forest, in small patches like purple jellyfish. It was hallucinogenic, and it was poisonous. Kylis had argued with Gryf about his using it, before her sentence in the sensory deprivation chamber showed her what Screwtop was like for Gryf all the time.

"Gryf—"

"Don't reproach me!"

"I won't," Kylis said. "Not anymore."

Her response startled him only for a moment; that it startled him at all revealed how completely drained he really was. He nodded and put his arms around her.

"Now you know," he said, with sympathy and understanding. "How long did they make you stay in the box?"

"Eight days. That's what they said, anyway."

He passed his hand across her hair, just touching it. "My poor friend. It seems so much longer."

"It doesn't matter. It's over for me." She almost believed the hallucinations had stopped, but she wondered if she would ever be certain they never return.

"Do you think the Lizard sentenced you because of me?"

"I don't know. I guess he'd use anything he could if he thought it'd work. Never mind. I'm all right."

"I would have done what they want, but I could not. Can you believe I tried?"

"Do you think I wanted you to?" She touched his face, tracing bone structure with her fingers like someone blind. She could feel the difference between the blond and black hair in his striped eyebrows, but the texture of his skin was smooth. She drew her fingers from his temples to the corners of his jaw, to the tendons of his neck and the tension-knotted muscles of his shoulders. "No one should make friends here," she said.

He smiled, closing his eyes, understanding her irony. "We would lose our souls if we did not."

He turned away abruptly and sat down on a large rock with his head between his knees, struggling against nausea. The new scars did not seem to hurt him. He breathed deeply for some time, then sat up slowly.

"How is Jason?"

"Fine. Recovered. You didn't have to take his shift. Lizard couldn't let him die like that."

"I think the Lizard collects methods of death."

Kylis remembered Miria with a quick shock of returning fear. "Oh, gods, Gryf, what's the use of fighting them?"

Gryf drew her closer. "The use is that you and Jason will not let them destroy you and I believe I am stronger than those who wish to keep me here, and justified in wishing to make my own mistakes rather than theirs." He held out his hand, pale-swirled in the darkness. It was long and fine. Kylis reached out and rubbed it, his wrist, his tense forearm. Gryf relaxed slightly, but Kylis was still afraid. She had never felt frightened before, not like this. But Miria, uncertainty, seeing Gryf hurt, had all combined to make her doubt the possibility of a future.

Gryf was caught and shaken by another spasm of retching. This time he could not suppress it, and it was more severe because he had not eaten. Kylis stood by, unable to do anything but hold his shoulders and hope he would survive the drug this time, as he had all the times before. The dry vomiting was replaced by a fit of coughing. Sweat dripped from his face and down his sides. When the pitch of his coughing rose and his breath grew more ragged, Kylis realized he was sobbing. On her knees beside him, she tried to soothe him. She did not know if he was crying from the sickness, from some vision she would never see, or from despair. She held him until, gradually, he was able to stop.

Sparkles of starlight passed between the clouds, mottling Gryf with a third color. He lay face down on the smooth stone, hands flat against it, cheek pressed to the rock. Kylis knew how he felt, drained, removed, heavy.

"Kylis . . . I never slept before like this . . ."

"I won't go far."

She hoped he heard her. She sat cross-legged on the wide rock beside him, watching slow movements of muscle as he breathed. His roan eyelashes were very long and touched with sweat droplets. The deep welts in his back would leave scars. Kylis' back had similar scars, but she felt that the marks she carried were a brand of shame, while Gryf's meant defiance and pride. She reached toward him, but drew back when her hand's vague shadow touched his face.

When she was certain he was sleeping easily, she left him and went to look nearby for patches of the green antibiotic mold. Their supply was exhausted. It was real medicine, not a superstition. Its active factor was synthesized back north and exported.

Being allowed to walk away from Screwtop, however briefly, made remaining almost endurable, but the privilege had a more important purpose. It was a constant reminder of freedom. The short moment of respite only strengthened the need to get out, and, more important, the need never to come back. Redsun knew how to reinforce obedience.

Kylis wandered, never going very far from Gryf, looking for green mold and finding the rarer purple hallucinogenic slime instead. She tried to deny that it tempted her. She could have taken some to Gryf—she almost did—but in the end she left it under the rocks where it belonged.

"I want to talk to you."

She spun, startled, recognizing the rough voice, fearing it, concealing her fear badly. She did not answer, only looked toward the Lizard.

"Come sit with me," he said. Starlight glinted on his clean fingernails as he gestured to the other end of an immense uprooted fern tree. It sagged but held when he sat on it.

As always, his black protective boots were pulled up and sealed to his black shorts. He was even bigger than Jason, taller, heavier, and though he had allowed his body to go slightly to fat, his face had remained narrow and hard. His clean-shaven scalp and face never tanned or burned, but somehow remained pale, in contrast to his deep-set black eyes. He licked his thin lips quickly with the tip of his tongue.

"What do you want?" She did not approach him.

He leaned forward and leaned his forearms on his knees. "I've been watching you."

She had no answer. He watched everyone. Standing there before him, Kylis was uneasy for reasons that somehow had nothing to do with his capacity for brutality. The Lizard never acted this way. He was direct and abrupt.

"I made a decision when sensory deprivation didn't break you," he said. "That was the last test."

The breeze shifted slightly. Kylis smelled a sharp odor as the Lizard lifted a small pipe to his lips and drew on it deeply. He held his breath and offered the pipe to her.

She wanted some. It was good stuff. She and Gryf and Jason had used the last of theirs at the end of the previous set, the night before they went on different shifts. Kylis was surprised that the Lizard used it at all. She would never have expected him to pare off the corners of his aggression out here. She shook her head.

"No?" He shrugged and put the pipe down, letting it waste, burning unattended. "All right."

She let the silence stretch on, hoping he would forget her and whatever he wanted to say, wander off or get hungry or go to sleep.

"You've got a long time left to stay here," he said.

Again, Kylis had no answer.

"I could make it easier for you."

"You could make it easier for most of us."

"That's not my job." He ignored the contradiction.

"What are you trying to say?"

"I've been looking for someone like you for a long time. You're strong, and you're stubborn." He got up and came toward her, hesitated to glance back at his pipe, but left it where it was. He took a deep breath. He was trying so hard to look sincere that Kylis had an almost overwhelming urge to laugh. She did not, but if she had, it would have been equally a laugh of nervous fear. She realized suddenly, with wonder: The Lizard's as scared as I am.

"Open for me, Kylis."

Incredulity was her first reaction. He would not joke, he

could not, but he might mock her. Or was he asking her an impossibility, knowing she would refuse, so he could offer to let her alone if Gryf would return to the tetras. She kept her voice very calm.

"I can't do that."

"Don't you think I'm serious?"

"How could you be?"

He forced away his scowl, like an inexperienced mime changing expressions. The muscles of his jaw were set. He moved closer, so she had to look up to see his eyes.

"I am."

"But that's not something you ask for," Kylis said. "That's something a family all wants and decides on." She realized he would not understand what she meant.

"*I've* decided. There's only me now." His voice was only a bit too loud.

"Aren't you lonely?" She heard her words, not knowing why she had said them. If the Lizard had been hurt, she would revel in his pain. She could not imagine people who would live with him, unless something terrible had changed him.

"I had a kid—" He cut himself off, scowling, angry for revealing so much.

"Ah," she said involuntarily. She had seen his manner of superficial control over badly suppressed violence before. Screwtop gave the Lizard justifiable opportunities to use his rage. Anywhere else it would burst out whenever he felt safe, against anyone who was defenseless and vulnerable. This was the kind of person who was asking her for a child.

"The board had no right to give him to her instead of me."

He would think that, of course. No right to protect the child? She did not say it.

"Well?"

To comply would be easy. She would probably be allowed to live in the comfort and coolness of the domes, and of course she would get good food. She could forget the dangerous machines and the Lizard's whip. She imagined what it would be like to feel a child quickening within her, and she imagined waiting to give birth to a human being, knowing she must hand it over to the Lizard to raise, all alone, with no other model, no other teacher, only this dreadful, crippled person.

"No," she said.

"You could if you wanted do."

So many things she had discovered about herself here had mocked her; now it was a claim she had once made to Gryf: I would do anything to get out of here.

"Leave it at that," she said quietly. "I don't want to." She backed away.

"I thought you were stubborn and strong. Maybe I made a mistake. Maybe you're just stupid, or crazy like the rest of them."

She tried to think of words he would understand, but always came up against the irreconcilable differences between her perception of the Lizard and what he thought of himself. He would not recognize her description.

"Or you want something more from me. What is it?"

She started to say there was nothing, but hesitated. "All right," she said, afraid her voice would be too shrill. Somehow it sounded perfectly normal. "Tell Gryf's people to set him free. Get Jason a parole and ticket off-world." For a moment she almost allowed herself to hope he had believed her offer was sincere. She was a very good liar.

The Lizard's expression changed. "No. I need them around so you'll do what I say."

"I won't."

"Pick something else."

For an instant's flash Kylis remembered being taunted like this before, when she was very small. Anything but that. Anything but what you really want. She pushed the recollection away.

"There isn't anything else," she said.

"Don't hold out. You can't bribe me to let them go. I'm not a fool."

He needed no officially acceptable reason to hurt her. She knew that. Fear of his kind of power was almost an instinctive reaction for Kylis. But she whispered, "Yes, Lizard, you are," and, half-blind, she turned and fled.

She almost outran him, but he lunged, grabbed her shoulder, pulled her around. "Kylis—"

Standing stiffly, coldly, she looked at his hand. "If that's what you want—"

Even the Lizard was not that twisted. Slowly, he let his hand fall to his side.

"I could force you," he said.

Her gaze met his and did not waver. "Could you?"

"I could drug you."

"For seven sets?" She realized, with a jog of alienness, that she had unconsciously translated the time from standard months to sets of forty days.

"Long enough to mess up your control. Long enough to make you pregnant."

"You couldn't keep me alive that long, drugged down that far. If the drugs didn't kill it, I would. I wouldn't even need to be conscious. I could abort it."

"I don't think you're that good."

"I am. You can't live like I did and not be that good."

"I can put you in the deprivation box until you swear to—"

She laughed bitterly. "And expect me to honor that oath?"

"You'd have children with Gryf and Jason."

This was real, much more than a game for the Lizard to play against Gryf. He wanted her compliance desperately. Kylis was certain of that, as certain as she was that he would use his own dreams to help fulfill his duty to Redsun. Still she could not understand why he felt he had some right to accuse her.

"Not like this," she said. *"With* them—but not *for* one of them. And they wouldn't make themselves fertile, either, if you were a woman and asked one of them to give you a child."

"I'm quitting. I'd take him out of here. I'd give him a good home. Am I asking that much? I'm offering a lot for a little of your time and one ovulation." His voice held the roughness of rising temper.

"You're asking for a human being."

She waited for some reaction, any reaction, but he just stood there, accepting what she said as a simple statement of fact without emotional meaning or moral resonance.

"I'd kill a child before I'd give it to you," she said. "I'd kill myself." She felt herself trembling, though it did not show in her hands or in her voice. She was trembling because what she had said was true.

He reacted not at all. She turned and ran into the darkness, and this time the Lizard did not follow.

When she was sure she was not being watched, she returned to Gryf's rock in the forest. Gryf still slept. He had not moved from the time he fell asleep, but the gray rock around him gleamed with his sweat. Kylis sat down beside him, drew up her knees and wrapped her arms around them, and put her head down. She had never felt as she felt now—unclean by implication, ashamed, diminished—and she could not explain the feeling to herself. She felt a tear slide down her cheek and clenched her teeth in anger. He will not make me cry, she thought. She breathed deeply, slowly, thinking, Control. Slow the heartbeat, turn off the adrenalin, you don't need it now. Relax. Her body, at least, responded. Kylis sat motionless for a long time.

The heavy, moist wind began to blow, bringing low black clouds to cut off the stars. Soon it would be too dark to see.

"Gryf?" Kylis touched his shoulder. He did not move until she shook him gently; then he woke with a start.

"Storm's coming," Kylis said.

In the dimming starlight, a blond lock of Gryf's hair glinted as he rose. Kylis helped him up. Dead ferns rustled at their feet, and the sleeping insects wrapped themselves more closely in their wings.

At the edge of the forest Kylis and Gryf picked their way across a slag heap and reached the trail to the prisoners' area. A faint blue glow emanated from their shelter, where Jason sat hunched over a cold light reading a book he had managed to scrounge. He did not hear them until they climbed the stairs.

"I was beginning to get worried," he said mildly, squinting to see them past the light.

"Gryf was sick."

"You okay now?" Jason asked.

Gryf nodded, and he and Kylis sat down in the circle of bioluminescence that did not waver in the wind. Jason put his book away and got their rations and water bottles from the locker. The stalks Kylis had picked were by now a bit wilted, but she gave them to Gryf anyway. He shared them out. The meal was slightly better and slightly more pleasant than most at Screwtop, but Kylis was not hungry. She was ashamed to tell her friends what had happened.

"What's the matter?" Jason asked suddenly.

"What?" Kylis glanced up at him, then at Gryf. Both were watching her with concern.

"You look upset."

"I'm okay." She leaned back gradually as she spoke, so her face was no longer in the light. "I'm tired, I guess." She searched for words to put into the silence. "I'm so tired I almost forgot to tell you we're all on night shift."

That was good enough news to change the subject and take her friends' attention from her. It was even good enough news to cheer her.

Later they returned to the hiding place in the forest and slept, lying close with Gryf in the middle. In the distance the sky flashed bright, then darkened. Only a faint mutter reached them, but the lightning revealed heavy clouds and the wind carried the sound closer. Kylis touched Gryf gently, taking comfort in his deep and regular breathing. Lightning scarred the sky again, and seconds later thunder rumbled softly. The wind rustled dry fronds.

Gryf stroked Kylis' tattooed shoulder. He touched her hand and their fingers intertwined.

"I wish you could get out," she whispered. "I wish you would." The lightning flashed again, vivid and close, its thunder simultaneous. Jason started in his sleep. During the brief flare Gryf looked at Kylis, frowning.

It began to rain.

In the morning Kylis woke by reflex, despite the absence of the siren. The whole day was free, but she and her friends had to rest, for the night shift was first on duty.

Gryf was already sitting up. He smiled in his it's-all-right way.

"Let's see," Kylis said.

He turned. The welts were silver-gray down their lengths, even where they crossed. They were uninfected and the ends had begun to heal. Gryf stretched his arms and looked over his shoulder. Kylis watched his face, the fine lines at the corners of his eyes, but he did not flinch. Biocontrol was one thing Kylis had proper training in, and she knew Gryf could not stretch human limits indefinitely. This time, though, he had succeeded.

"How much better are you?" she asked.

He grinned and Kylis laughed in spite of herself. She forced away the thought and worry of the Lizard. Together she and Gryf woke Jason.

But all the rest of the day her apprehension grew. She was certain the Lizard would not accept her refusal easily. Now Kylis had to look twice at the little movements in her peripheral vision, once to make sure they were not hallucinations and again to make sure they were not the Lizard. By evening she was taut with acting out a pose of normality and maintaining an artifical calm, and she was affecting Jason and

Gryf with her agitation. She would not speak of the reason. She could be nearly as stubborn as Gryf.

Kylis was almost relieved when the siren shrieked and they had to return to the installation to gather their rations and the set's allowance of medicinal soap. She had tried being angry, and sullen, and heedless, but under it all she was frightened.

They walked past the guard stations, across the lengthening shadows of afternoon. At the top of the Pit they stopped, looking down. But they could not delay; they descended.

The heat from the unworked day pooled in the center of Screwtop. The sides of the Pit reflected heat; the metal of the machinery radiated it. The effects of temperature and noise combined synergistically.

Kylis and Gryf and Jason were all assigned to the probe crew. Across the Pit, Kylis saw the Lizard watching her with no expression at all. She looked away. Miria was on this shift, too, but Kylis did not see her.

They dragged out the new drill bit and raised it; it hung suspended above the shaft, taller than a person, narrow and dangerous. It frequently seemed to recognize the absurdity of its domestication by weak human beings, and rebelled. At Screwtop it was all too easy to ascribe personality and malevolent intentions to inanimate objects.

Shaft sections lay in racks like giant petals around the stem of the drill, fanning out in rays opposite the bubblecovered works of the first two generators. The hum of turbines spread across the floor of the Pit, through bootsoles, reaching flesh and blood and bone. To Kylis, the vibration seemed to be the anger of the wounded earth, unwillingly giving up the secrets and the energy of its interior, helpless in its resentment.

When this shaft was finished, the temperature at its bottom would approach 800 degrees C. When the crew broke through the caprock and released the pressure, that temperature was enough to turn the water below into superheated steam. It was enough to drive another generator. It was enough, if they did not seal the caprock properly, to kill them all instantly. They would seal it, tap it, and build an air-conditioned bubble over it. Then engineers, heavily protected, would move in and build the machinery. The prisoners, who were not trusted anywhere near the generators, would move farther on to drill another well.

This was a clean way of generating power, and cheap in all but human terms. The wells eventually ran dry and power needs for North Continent grew greater. Redsun had no fossil fuel, few radioactive elements, too many clouds to use the energy of its dim star.

Gryf's job was to guide the shaft sections to the drill. Some concession was made to his value; he was not put on the most dangerous jobs. The command to begin was given, and the small contrived delays and grumblings ceased.

The work turned the prisoners almost into automata. It was monotonous, but not monotonous enough. Complete boredom would have allowed daydreams, but danger hung too close for fantasies. Sweat slid into Kylis' eyes when she was too busy to wipe it away. The world sparkled and stung around her. The night passed slowly. The Lizard watched from a distance, a shade like any other shadow. While he was near, Kylis felt alone and, somehow, obscenely naked.

At midnight the prisoners were allowed to stop for a few minutes to eat. Gryf eased himself down the control tower ladder. At the bottom, Kylis and Jason waited for him. They sat together to eat and swallow salt tablets. The break gave them time to rest against the morning.

Kylis sat on the ground, her back against metal, half asleep, waiting for the bell. The floor of the pit was wet and muddy and littered with broken rock and ash, so she did not lie down. The Lizard had kept his distance all evening. Kylis thought he was unlikely to do anything direct while she was among so many people, though they could do nothing against him.

"Get up."

She started, frightened out of a light doze by the Lizard's voice. He and his people had their backs to her; they moved between her and Gryf and encircled him. He rose, emerging from the shadows like a tortoiseshell cat.

The Lizard looked at him, then at Kylis. "Take him," he said to his people.

"What are you going to do?" Hearing the note of panic in her own voice, Kylis clenched her fists.

"The tetras want him back. They need him. They're getting impatient."

"You're sending him home?" Kylis asked in disbelief.

"Of course," the Lizard said. He looked away from Kylis, at Gryf. "As soon as he's had enough of the deprivation box."

Beside Gryf, Jason stood up. Gryf put his hand on Jason's arm. The Lizard's people were moving nearer, closing in, should the Lizard need aid. A few of the prisoners came closer to see what was happening. Miria was among them. Kylis watched her from shadows, unseen. As the guards led Gryf away, Miria half smiled. Kylis wanted to scream with rage.

"How will they like it if you kill him?" Jason shouted.

"They take that chance," the Lizard said.

"It won't work," Kylis said. The deprivation box would never make Gryf go back to the tetras, and it could not force Kylis to do what the Lizard wanted. Even for Gryf she could not do that.

"Won't it?" The Lizard's voice was heavy and angry.

"Don't do this to him," Kylis said. "Gryf is—just being here is like being in the box. If you put him in a real one—" She was pleading for Gryf; she had never begged for anything in her life. The worst of it was she knew it was useless. She hoped bitterly that Miria was still human enough to understand what her spying had done.

"Shall I take you instead of him?" Without waiting for an answer, laughing at her, the Lizard turned away.

"Yes," Kylis said.

He swung around, astonished.

"You can put me in the box instead of him."

The Lizard sneered at her. "And send the tetras you instead of him? What use do you think you'd be to any of *them?* You could be a pet—you could be a host mother for another little speckled baby!"

Leaning down, scooping up a handful of mud, Kylis took one step toward the Lizard and threw the sticky clay. It caught him in the chest, spattering his black uniform and pale skin. Kylis turned, bending down again. This time the clay was heavy and rocky.

"Kylis!" Jason cried.

"And *you!*" Kylis shouted. She flung the mud and stones at Miria.

As the Lizard's people grabbed her, Kylis saw Miria fall. Under the spotlights the clay was red, but not as red as the blood spurting from Miria's forehead.

The Lizard, scowling, wiping clay from his chin, barely glanced at Miria's unmoving form. He gestured to Kylis.

"Put her where she can't hurt anyone else."

They marched her away, leaving Jason behind, alone.

They put Kylis in a bare cell with one glass wall and a ledge without corners and ventilation that did not temper the heat.

They stripped her and locked her in. The room passively prevented self-injury; even the walls and the window yielded softly to blows.

From inside, she could see the deprivation box. It was the correct shape for a coffin, but larger, and it stood on supports that eliminated the vibration of the generator.

The guards led Gryf into the deprivation room. He, too, was naked, and the guards had hosed him down. He looked around quickly, like a hunted animal alarmed from two sides at once. There was no help, only Kylis, pressed against the window with her fists clenched. Gryf tried to smile, but she could see he was afraid.

As they blindfolded him and worked to prepare him, Kylis remembered the feel of the soft padding packed in around her body, restraining head and arms and legs, preventing all movement and all sensation. First it had been pleasant; the box was dark and silent and gave no sensation of either heat or cold. Tubes and painless needles carried wastes from her body and nourishment in. Kylis had slept for what seemed a very long time, until her body became saturated with sleep. Without any tactile stimulation she grew remote from the physical world, and shrank down as a being to a small spot of consciousness behind the place her eyes had been. She then tried to put herself in a trance, but they had expected that. They prevented it with drugs. Her thoughts had become knit with fantasies, at first such gentle ones that she did not notice. Later they separated themselves from reality and became bizarre and identifiable. Finally they were indistinguishable from a reality too remote to believe in. She remembered the encompassing certainty of madness.

Kylis watched them lock Gryf into the same fate. They turned on the monitors. If he tried to ask to be let out, the subvocalization would be detected and his wish would be granted.

After that no one came near them. Kylis' sentence in the box had been eight days, but the sensory deprivation had overcome her time sense and stretched the time to weeks, months, years. She spent her time now waiting, almost as isolated. At intervals she fell asleep without meaning to, but when she awoke, everything was always the same. She was afraid to think of Gryf, afraid to think what might be happening to Jason alone outside, afraid to think about herself. The hallucinations crept back to haunt her. The glass turned to ice and melted in puddles, and the walls turned to snow clouds and drifted away. Her body would begin to shiver, and then she would realize that the walls were still there, quite real, and she would feel the heat again. She would feel Gryf's touch, and turn to embrace him, but he was never there. She felt herself slipping into a pit of confusion and visions and she could not gather strength or will to pull herself out. Sometimes she cried.

She lay in the cell, felt herself change, and felt her courage dissolve in the sterile whiteness. The floor of the cell cradled her, softly, like a soothing voice telling her she could do what was easiest, anything that would ensure her own survival.

She sat up abruptly, digging her nails into her palms.

If she believed all that, she should yell and beat her fists on the glass until the guards came, beg them to take her to the Lizard, and do what he had asked. If she did that, everything Gryf was going through and everything she had endured would be betrayed. If she decided now to let another person make her decisions for her, or if she lost herself so completely that she could not make them herself, then she had only trivial reasons for what she had done.

Her reasons were not trivial; she could not force herself to believe they were, not for Gryf's sake or Jason's or her own. Gryf had found the strength to gamble coming to Screwtop on the chance of his own freedom; Jason had found the strength to stay alive where by all rights he should have died. Kylis knew she would have to find the same kind of strength to keep her sanity and her control.

She wiped the back of her hand across her eyes, put her right hand on the point of her left shoulder, leaned against the wall, and very slowly relaxed, concentrating on the reality of each individual muscle, the touch of plastic beneath her, the drop of sweat sliding down between her breasts.

When a cool draft of air brushed her legs, she opened her eyes. The Lizard stood in the doorway, looking down at her, a black shape surrounded by concentric rings of color. She had never seen him with such a gentle expression, but she did not return his expectant smile.

"Have you decided?"

Kylis blinked and all the bright colors dispersed, leaving a stark black-clothed figure. His expression hardened as Kylis gradually returned to Redsun's hell and made the connections she needed to answer him. Her fingers were half curled. She turned her hands over and flattened them on the floor.

"You haven't changed . . . you haven't changed me."

The Lizard glared at her, his expression changing to disbelief. Kylis said nothing more. She did not move. The Lizard made a sound of disgust and slammed the door. The cool air stopped.

He did not return, but Kylis did not try to convince herself she had beaten him.

She stared through the window and willed the tetras to come and free her friend. They must keep track of what was done to him. She could not believe they did not realize what such isolation would do to one of their own kind.

She had been staring at the same scene for so long that it took her a moment to realize it had changed. Four guards came in and began to open the sensory deprivation chamber. Kylis leaped up and pressed her hands to the glass. The deprivation chamber swung open. Kylis remembered her own first glimpse of light as the guards had pulled the padding from her eyes and disconnected tubes and needles. Gryf would be trying to focus his black-flecked blue eyes, blinking; his roan eyelashes would brush his cheeks.

The guards lifted him out, and he did not move. His long limbs dangled limp and lifeless. They carried him away.

Kylis sank to the floor and hugged her knees, hiding her face. When the guards came, they had to pull her to her feet and shake and slap her to force her to stand. They led her through their compound and pushed her through the exit, locking the gate behind her. They did not speak.

Kylis stood in the harsh illumination of spotlights for a few blank moments, then walked slowly toward the comforting shadows of night. She had needed darkness for a long time. Everything seemed more than real, with the absurd clarity of shock.

She saw Jason before he heard her; he was a pale patch on the edge of the light, sitting with his knees drawn up and his head down. Kylis was afraid to go to him.

"Kylis?"

She stopped. Jason's voice was rough, almost controlled but breaking. She turned around and saw him peering at her over his folded arms. His eyes were very bright. He pushed himself to his feet.

"I was afraid," he said. "I was afraid they'd take you both, and I didn't want to stay here alone."

"Go away."

"What? Kylis, why?"

"Gryf's dead." Desperation made her cruel. She wanted to

go to him, and mourn with him, but she was afraid she would cause his destruction too. "And Gryf's the only thing that kept us together."

Stunned, Jason said nothing.

"Stay away from me," Kylis said, and walked past him.

"If Gryf is dead, we've got to—"

"No!"

"Are you sure he's dead? What happened?"

"I'm sure." She did not face him.

He put his hands on her shoulders. "We've got to get out of here before they kill us too. We've got to get north and tell people what's going on."

"Crazy!" She pulled free.

"Don't do this to me, Kylis."

His plea sliced through her grief and guilt, and even through her fear for him. She could not stand to hurt him. There was no fault in Jason, and no blame to assign to him. His only flaw was a loyalty she hardly deserved. Kylis looked around her, at the bare earth and the distant machines and the soft black ferns, all so alien. She turned back.

"I'm sorry," she said.

They held each other, but it was not enough comfort. Jason's tears fell cool on her shoulder, but she could not cry.

"There's something more than Gryf and the tetras," Jason said. "Please let me help. Tell me why all this is happening."

She shook her head. "It's dangerous for you to stay with me."

Suddenly he clenched his fingers around her arm. She pulled back, startled, and when she looked up, he scared her. She had never seen cruelty in Jason, but that was how he looked, cruel and filled with hatred.

"Jason—"

"I won't kill him," he said. "I won't . . . let me go—" He looked down and realized he was gripping Kylis' arm. "Oh, gods." He let her go and turned and walked into the forest.

Rubbing the bruise he had left, Kylis slowly looked behind her. What Jason had seen was the Lizard watching them from the gateway of the guards' enclosure. He did not move. Kylis ran.

The thick band of multicolored stars, shining through breaks in the clouds, lighted the way only where the ferns did not close in overhead. Kylis stumbled through the darkness, not even slowing for pools of rainwater. Her legs ached from fighting the suction of wet clay. Suddenly her shoulder rammed a rough stalk and her momentum spun her, flinging her against another. She stopped, gasping for breath, the air burning her throat.

Kylis straightened and looked around, getting her bearings. The stars glittered like sparks in the surface of standing water. She walked more carefully among the ferns. Her footsteps spread ripples out around her and the water sloshed gently from her boots. Only when she reached the shelter of dead ferns did she realize how silly and unnecessary it had been for her to be careful not to fall.

Inside the cool nest she lay down and composed herself. When she finally caught her breath, she began breathing slowly and regularly, counting her heartbeats. Gradually she extended the number of beats for each inhalation, for each exhalation, then she slowed her heart as well. She thought about Gryf, dying deliberately rather than giving his life to those he hated. And she thought about Jason, who would never kill even in vengeance. She was certain of that. If she were gone, he at least would be safe.

She felt the gasp reflex growing stronger and set her perception of it aside. Her breathing had ceased now, and her heartbeat would stop soon. Her thoughts slowed, her memory drifted to more pleasant times. She found herself with Gryf again, kissing him, standing in the clean hot lake, touched by spray from the overflow pipe. She smiled. A bright yellow star glittered through a gap between the ferns. Kylis let her eyes close, shutting out the last light.

Insistent hands shook her. She was dimly aware of them and of a voice calling her name. She concentrated more strongly on dying. A fist pounded her chest and she gasped involuntarily. Someone leaned down and breathed into her mouth, holding her chin up and her head back, forcing air into her lungs. Her heart pounded. Pushing the person away, Kylis sat up angrily and almost fainted.

Miria caught her and made her lie down again. "Thank gods, I found you. I could hear you but then you disappeared."

Kylis did not answer, but only blinked her eyes against the light Miria carried. She tried to be angry at her, but it seemd too futile.

"Kylis!" Miria's voice rose in panic. "Are you there? Can you hear me?"

"Of course I'm here," she said. She felt dizzy. She

wondered why Miria had asked such a silly question. "What do you mean, am I here?"

Miria relaxed and brightened her lantern. "I was afraid I'd come too late." She had a bad scar, pink and new, on her forehead.

"Get away from me. Why couldn't you let us alone?" Kylis knew she would not be able to try to kill herself again for quite a while; she had used up too much strength.

"Gryf's all right," Miria said.

Kylis stared at her. "But I saw— How do you know? You're lying!"

"He's all right, Kylis. I know. Please trust me."

"Trust you! You told the Lizard about Gryf and Jason and me! He never knew before how much he could hurt us! And now he'll go after Jason, too, so I'll—" She stopped.

"The Lizard knew you were together, but I never told him your plans. You honored me with a request to join your family. Do you think your judgment of me was so wrong?"

Kylis sighed. "It wasn't very good about the kid who turned me in." She had to rest and breathe a moment. "I saw you go inside the fence without any guards. And after that, the Lizard—"

"What was he trying to make you do?"

"Have a child and give it to him."

Miria sat back on her heels. "To *Lizard?* Gods." She shook her head in disbelief, in sympathy for Kylis, for anyone, particularly a child who would come under the Lizard's control. The yellow lantern glow glinted from the dark and lighter brown strands of Miria's hair. Kylis suddenly saw the two distinct colors for the first time. The lighter brown was not sun-streaked—it grew that way naturally.

"You're a tetra, aren't you?"

Miria looked up, and Kylis knew she would not lie. "Yes. Anyway," she said sadly, "I used to be."

"They let you go?"

"No!" She ran her hand across her hair and spoke more calmly. "No. I was never like Gryf. I never understood what he wanted, at least until a few days ago. Until you and I talked . . ." She drew in a long breath. "Three years ago I was in an accident. I was foolish. I took chances I had no right to take, and I nearly drowned. I died for several minutes. No oxygen could get to my brain." She looked away, fiddling with the control on the lantern. "I can remember who I used to be, but I'm not her anyone. I cannot do the work I was meant for. I feel so *stupid* . . . I was afraid you'd done that to yourself. I was afraid you'd damaged your brain."

"I'm all right, Miria." Kylis pushed herself up on her elbow, suspicion and anger forgotten for a moment. "They sent you here because you had an accident? I think that's awful."

"They could have—they should have, for what I did. But I'm here to watch Gryf."

"To protect him? And you let them put him in the box?"

"You know enough about Gryf to know . . ." Miria's voice faltered. "I was not here only to be sure he lived. I wanted to force him to go back to his team. I wanted him . . . to make up for my failure."

"Why should he be responsible?"

"Because we're the same."

"Miria, I don't understand."

"He had the same place I did, on a different team. For important projects we make two groups and keep them separate, so they will confirm each other's research or develop alternate lines. Gryf is my trans-brother. That is what we call tetras with the same parents in opposite couples." She rubbed her tawny forearm. "He was never meant to be a trans, of course, but it made no difference for the work. I crippled my team—I felt I had to keep Gryf from crippling his. I felt responsible."

"What's going to happen now?"

"Now . . ." Miria grasped Kylis' hands. "I'm not a tetra anymore, Kylis. I have no vote. But I have a say, and I will do my best to persuade them to set him free."

"Miria, if you can—"

"I may do no better than keep them from sending him back here."

"Why did you change your mind?"

"Because of what you told me. I thought about it all the time Gryf was in deprivation. What I was doing to him to force him to share my loyalties—I almost killed him! I allowed the Lizard to torture him. You knew better than I what that could mean."

"But he's all right—you said he's all right."

"He is," Miria said quickly. "He will be. He overcame the drugs and put himself in a deep trance. I haven't lied. But I had nothing to do with freeing him before he died. I understand now what happened. After two days I realized

Gryf must be let go, but the Lizard would not come out and he would not reply to my messages. He hoped to break you to his will and Gryf to mine. When he could not—finally he was afraid to keep Gryf in there any longer." Her voice was strained. "I've caused you so much pain. I hope some day you will all be together, and happy, and will be able to forgive me."

"Miria, I wish—"

The roar of a plane drowned out her words. Kylis glanced up, startled. In all the time she had been at Screwtop, she had never heard or seen a plane. The North Continent was too far away, and here there was no place to land.

"I've got to go. I shouldn't have left Gryf, but I had to talk to you." Miria helped Kylis to her feet and out of the shelter. Kylis accepted the help gratefully. She felt wobbly.

They waded through shimmering shadows as Miria's light swung on her hip.

"Kylis," Miria said slowly. "I don't know what will happen. I hope I can free Gryf. I will try to help you. And Jason. But the Lizard serves the government well. They may decide he was right and I wrong. Whatever happens will take time, and I may not be able to do anything at all. I don't want to deceive you."

"I understand." Jason was in no less danger now, nor was she. But at least Gryf was safe. For a few moments Kylis could set aside her fear in the joy that he was alive.

They entered the compound's long clearing and reached the path that led toward the prisoners' shelter. Kylis saw the vertical-takeoff plane hanging in midair. It slowly lowered itself, straight down, until it was out of sight behind the bank. Its engines slowed, idling.

"I can't take you to your shelter," Miria said. "I'm sorry—"

"Can I come the rest of the way—just to be sure—?"

"Gryf will already be on the plane, Kylis. You wouldn't be allowed to see him."

"All right," she said reluctantly. "I can get back myself from here."

"Are you sure? Will you be all right?"

Kylis nodded. "For now."

"Yes . . ." Miria shifted her weight back and forth, reluctant to leave her alone but anxious to meet the plane.

"Go *on*," Kylis said.

"Yes. I must . . ." She hesitated a moment more, then

leaned quickly forward and embraced Kylis. "This is such a terrible place," she whispered. "Somehow I'll change it." She turned abruptly and hurried away.

Miria walked silhouetted against the lights and lantern. Kylis watched her go. At least she could hope now. She realized she must find Jason and tell him everything, but most particularly that Gryf was alive and out of the prison. Perhaps to be free. Then he could contact Jason's family—

"Oh, gods," Kylis groaned. "Miria! Miria, wait!" She ran toward the enclosure, stumbling from exhaustion.

She reached the bank above the fence just as Miria put her palm against the lock. The gate swung open.

"Miria!" Kylis cried. She was afraid Miria would not hear her over the engines of the plane, now inside the enslosure. But she cried out once more, sliding down the hill, and Miria turned.

She met Kylis between the bank and the fence, taking her elbow to support her as she struggled for breath.

"Jason's family," Kylis said. "Redsun thinks he's just a transient but he's not. If his people knew he was here, they'd ransom him." She remembered most of Jason's name, his family name, and told it to Miria. "Can you tell them? Just send a message?"

Miria's eyes widened. "Is that who he is?"

Kylis nodded.

"It will have to be done carefully, to keep his identity a secret, but I can do that, Kylis, yes." Then she sobered. "You'll be alone—"

"I'm all right alone. I've always been alone before. I can protect myself, but I can't protect Jason from the Lizard. Will you do it? Will you promise?"

"I promise."

Kylis clasped Miria's hands for an instant and let her go. Miria went inside the enclosure and boarded the plane. The engines screamed, and the aircraft rose, sliding forward like a hovercraft through the gateway. Clear of the fence, it rose higher until it had cleared the height of the marsh plants. It accelerated straight north.

Kylis watched it until it was out of sight. She wished she had seen Gryf, but now she believed Miria; she could believe he was alive.

In the eerie gentle light of dawn, as Kylis started away, the harsh spotlights dimmed one by one.

Only at Night

At night, when I'm here, all the babies lie quiet with their eyes closed. The ones that have eyes.

At night, covered with sheets against the whisper of air in the wards, the children begin to look almost human. I walk between the cribs of deserted newborns and the railed beds of the older ones, sometimes trying not to burst into tears. I touch them, gently, trying to soothe them. Most of them aren't capable of being soothed. They're all waiting to die. Sometimes one awakens and lies there helpless and immobile, staring up. They never cry. I hold them and wonder if they think the dull pinpoints of light on the ceiling are stars.

Tonight most of the children are awake. It might be the heat, which is too much for the air conditioning. I do what I can, touch them, change diapers (I am reprimanded if I use too many), offer water. I wish I weren't here. It's too quiet and the air is too heavy and no one's here to talk to. On other wards someone will awaken and need the reassurance of companionship to go back to sleep. Or I'll whisper a story to a child and he'll correct me if I change a line until we both begin to giggle, try to stop, and just laugh harder. But these children don't need bedtime stories. A record of gibberish would do as well. They don't need me. Maybe if they had always had love they would be able to want it and accept it now, but all they need is food and cleaning and a place out of the rain. To them I'm an automaton, wound up and set to take care of them.

I wish I weren't here at night, but the others have been here longer and choose to come during the day. While drab sunlight seeps in they put the children on the floor to drag themselves around with stumps of limbs, like mindless invertebrates making their first foray onto the land.

I pick a child up, gently, because her skull has never grown together. There is a soft depression at the top of her head, like skin on cooled soup. I sing, more for myself than her. She is deaf.

She is watching me. My voice trails off and she blinks as if disappointed that I've stopped. Do all babies have blue eyes? I know I'm putting my own thoughts and sadnesses and fears into her gaze. She does not think; she can't. None of them can. But there's something behind her eyes that's more than complacent blankness. I put her back in her crib and move on.

I wonder if all their parents have forgotten them. They must have. They hardly ever come . . . If I believed that I'd be a fool. Their parents remember them too well, every instant of every day, and that's why they don't come. They've spawned monsters that they're afraid to try to love. They're perfect people who hide their mistakes. If they see their deformed child before it is taken away (I've seen the parents; they can't resist one guilty peek between meshed fingers, as if they were at a freak show), they cry "Oh, God, why me?" and then they leave.

The children are restless. The ones that can move rustle their sheets. Those with limbs wave them. Twisted fingers clutch handsful of air and discard it again. I know I shouldn't be afraid, but it's very strange.

One of the larger children (I can only think of him as a large child) is strong and dully mean. Sometimes he has to be restrained with soft straps and buckles so he won't hurt himself or us. I hear him begin to beat his head against the backboard, over and over. I run down the ward. He's supposed to have an injection every night to make him sleep; they don't want me to have to handle him alone. I gave him a name because his parents didn't. He's perfectly formed and beautiful, but he has no mind and no control over bladder or bowels. I call to him, *Peter!* but he doesn't stop. He doesn't know me; he has never seen me. I take his arm and tell him gently to sit still and I try to pull him away from the backboard. His head hits again and I see his eyes when his hair flops away. They are blue . . . the same clear blue . . .

My voice rises and I try to soften it. He'll feel my panic like an animal and know I'm afraid. I drop the railing and take his shoulders. He's taller than I, and heavier by half. His expression when he sleeps is peaceful, but now he pulls his lips back from his teeth—the light sparks from them and blinds me. I feel tears running down my cheeks like molten ore.

He hits me. The force throws me back against another bed; I hit my head and slide to the floor. I can't get up; though I try I have as little control over my body as the children. I feel blood from my cut lip flowing out to mix with tears, and a sticky dampness spreads from the dull pain where a bed rail cut my scalp. I try to rise again and almost faint. I lie still.

I hear a clang and the sliding of sheets. I strain my eyes and see Peter crawling out of his bed. He has never been taught to walk. He seems to be coming toward me and I'm afraid again, but he ignores me and flounders to the aisle between the rows of beds. He moves farther into my field of vision. I can see the other children coming and I hear the sides of cribs clanking down. I must be dreaming. The noises rise. I clench my teeth for the pain, but unlike a pinch it doesn't wake me up. I know that if I could move, or scream, or make any noise at all, this would stop. If I didn't think that I would doubt my sanity.

The children gather around Peter.

My hearing is distorted and I feel very far away. I can hear them talking but I can't make out any words. They look like a war council of ancient veterans, come to display their war wounds: missing hands and feet and ears and noses, twisted bodies, seal flippers and crab-skins, deep scars that twinge before storms. They look so absurd that I'd laugh if I could. It would be the first time I ever laughed here.

They look very angry and their voices are shrill. One of them shakes a fist of seven fingers grown together.

I wish it were day. Then I could hope for a nurse on a coffee break or a doctor on rounds or even one of the infrequent parents on pilgrimage to purge their guilt with fifteen minutes, and pity, and finally flight.

I think the children are there for a long time, but I can't really tell. I'm dizzy. My hip and shoulder hurt where they're pressed against the floor. My physical incapacity gives my imagination too much freedom: the children are plotting against me. When the doctors and the other nurses come in the morning they will find me hanging, crucified, against the wall. I will wear a crown of needles and catheters. I will be nude and bleeding, but in three days I will not rise. If they can make plans of revolt or revenge, surely they can see that I am not the one to hate. I try to ridicule myself for taking dreams and fancies seriously, but I'm not sure now that it's all a dream. It seems very real. I'm frightened, and I'm trembling.

They seem to be done talking. The council roils and breaks and moves toward me. As if I could stop them with my eyes I watch them crawl and drool on the floor. I brace myself . . . but they fragment their united front and crawl away. A few of them look at me. Peter touches my hand before he clambers up into bed. I lie here, and slowly everything becomes quiet again.

In the morning I'm asleep and the nurses easily wake me. I can move. I have a cut on my head and blood and a bruise on my chin. There's a lot of blood on the floor, but I only have a dull headache and orders to get some stitches. I remember what happened last night. I decide not to say anything, because they'll think I'm crazy. Peter is lying on his back in his bed-cage, gabbling dully like a grotesque newborn. Everything else is in order. The other nurses ask me if I'm all right. I tell them I had a nightmare while I was unconscious and they cluck in sympathy. One of them offers to take my shift, the inconvenient, lonely one, at least until I'm better. I'm going to pretend I don't notice it when she begins to regret her generosity.

They smile and the head nurse tells me to take some time off and rest until my scalp has healed. I thank her. After I go home I'll have to decide whether to come back or not . . . If I do I'll come at night. The parents only visit in the daytime.

Recourse, Inc.

BESET BY FORM LETTERS FOR BILLS YOU'VE ALREADY PAID?
HARANGUED ABOUT ORDERS YOU NEVER SENT FOR OR
RECEIVED?
THREATENED BY COLLECTION AGENCIES WHO HAVE YOU
MIXED UP WITH THE DEADHEAD DOWN THE STREET?

Contact:
RECOURSE, INC.

We are funded by a private foundation, and we are on your
side. We will write threatening letters to the unscrupulous
companies who dun you for payments you do not owe, and
who refuse to acknowledge your communications. We will
send letters of complaint in your behalf to people who are in a
position to make life uncomfortable for impersonal or
fraudulent organizations. We will, if necessary, represent you
in a court of law. We use dunning tactics with the best of
them. We guarantee satisfaction.

Humptulips 98000
January 29

Dear People,

I need help. I bought a zygomat with my brand new Sovereign credit card, #1839485729384, in January of last year. It was a really nice one and it cost $99.98 plus 5 percent sales tax. But when I got the bill, it was for $199.98 plus 5 percent sales tax. I paid them everything except the extra hundred and five dollars and wrote them a letter and asked them to fix their records. They sent me another bill in February, for the whole $199.98 plus 5 percent sales tax plus a 1.5 percent late charge. That was $213.13. I wrote them and explained that I'd already paid the bill. I thought that would do it, but I got another bill in March, with another 1.5 percent late charge. That was $216.33. I decided to ignore the bills for a while, but they kept on coming. By last September they said I owed $240.69, and they were starting to send me those form letter that said they understood if I was having some kind of financial difficulty, but they couldn't help me if I wouldn't tell them what was wrong. I wrote them back and said I'd been trying to tell them what was wrong. They were wrong! They didn't send me a bill that month, but they didn't fix the account, either. I thought it might take them a little longer to get straightened out, so I didn't do anything. But then in November, a bill for $247.96 came, and another letter, a nasty one this time, and I was really getting worried, so I sent them the canceled check to show them that I'd paid. The next month, the check came through again, and all my other checks for the month bounced, because the credit card company had cashed my check again, and the bank didn't notice. This time I wrote them a really nasty letter, and one to the bank, too. But they ignored it, and the bank sent me a letter that said they were very sorry, but my account was overdrawn by $87.43, and I had better get them some money quick. I did, as soon as I could, as soon as I got my paycheck, and I figured then that the credit card company would leave me alone, and maybe it was worth it. But just now I've got another bill from them, this time it's for $254.46, and they're threatening to turn me over to a collection agency, and they didn't even apply the money they got from the second check. Please help me, I haven't got another $250 to get them off my back with.

And the zygomat broke yesterday.

Sincerely,
Hedley Satsop

Dr. Francis Takeoka
January 29

Ms. Galena Carbury
Attorney-at-Law
Recourse, Inc.

Dear Lennie,

I've recommended you to a fellow I've been treating recently. Hedley's been having some trouble with this credit card company. He's in the right—they owe him money, in fact—but they're harassing the hell out of him. He's quite a nice guy, but he's just never really learned to function in modern society. He even finds it embarrassing to admit he needs psychiatric help, as if most of us didn't these days. I've been treating him for depression (confidential information between shrink and shyster), and if they keep after him he's going to go right back under. I'm sure he could get it straightened out eventually, and it might even do him some good to do it himself, but it's going to do him even more harm if it isn't fixed *soon* —and that, I don't think he can do. I feel particularly responsible because I urged him to get a few credit cards in the first place, so he could see that he could handle them. I'd appreciate it if you'd take some time out from your law practice and spend it on your hobby, and if you'd use the fastest tactics in that flamboyant bag of tricks of yours.

Frank

Galena Carbury
RECOURSE, INC.
31 January

Dear Frank,

Heard from your client today. Will do. All (legal) measures. (She parenthesized for the benefit of the bugs.)

Lennie

Galena Carbury
RECOURSE, INC.
31 January

Dear M. Satsop,

A carbon of our first letter to Sovereign Credit is enclosed. You'll receive copies of all the correspondence we have with them. We are delighted to have you as a client. It's quite obvious that Sovereign has made a serious error, and should refund your money with interest. We hope to have their apology for you very soon.

> Sincerely,
> Galena Carbury
> Attorney-at-Law for Recourse, Inc.

By Certified Mail:

> RECOURSE, INC.
> 31 January

B.X. Fornick
Sovereign Credit
Teaneck 07000

Dear M. Fornick,

It has been brought to our attention that you are unfairly dunning M. Hedley Satsop, of Humptulips 98000, Sovereign Credit Card #1839485729384, for a bill he had already paid. In point of fact, due to his trusting nature and to your lack of integrity and the shoddy quality of your service, he has paid his bill twice. In addition, you have failed to credit either of his payments to this erroneous and inflated bill. Your doing so would not provide a satisfactory conclusion to this situation, but at least it would relieve M. Satsop of these dunning form letters.

I have appended a summary of the situation, which may be properly reconciled by your sending my client a check for $99.98 plus 5 percent sales tax, and an apology.

I hope to hear within the week that this matter has been remedied.

> Sincerely,
> Galena Carbury
> Attorney-at-Law for Recourse, Inc.

Delivered by Hand:

> The Hideout
> 1 Feb.

Dear Lennie,

How the hell are you? Congratulations on your new degree. Send a note by Eaglepaws and tell us how you're doing. And what. Congratulations on those cases you won. (We do get a little news out here.)

Where did you find S.O.? He's working out fine, despite his little quirks. We put up with his, he puts up with ours. Did you hear his latest escapade? He's really earning his nickname. Instead of just watching that dreadful old sci-fi show he's addicted to when we're crashing in some town, he's rigged this huge mother antenna to pull in those 485th reruns wherever we are.

But enough! At least he can break phone-codes to computers fairly well—that's what he spends the rest of his time doing, finding the phone lines nearest the current hideout, tapping them, and calling up computers. He says companies are getting very good at keeping people like him out; he says that unless you find a random-number generator that really isn't random, your chances of getting to the important programs in a reasonable amount of time are very low. I suppose you will know what that means. He's getting a little twitchy from lack of computer time, but I can't help that.

I'm mad at J. C.—he got his oil-eaters to breed with *E. coli* (won't everything? But these are "delicate"), they inherited an anaerobic capacity, and he destroyed them. Damn—I am getting tired of oil wells in Puget Sound.

Come back if you get tired of civilization. And we are here if you need us for anything a classy lawyer isn't allowed to do.

Lucifer

Delivered by Hand:
Dear Lucifer,

Thank gods J. C. has a highly developed moral sense. I shudder to think of the havoc you could wreak with an amoral scientist working with you. Think things out, my friend. All the people on this shaky old world do not have your independence from electricity and petrochemicals.

You tempt me to come back—the city is a strain, and sometimes I wonder if being a lawyer isn't as futile these days as being an environmental guerrilla. But for now, I'll stay.

Lennie

By Registered Mail:

RECOURSE, INC.
6 February

B. X. Fornick
Sovereign Credit
Teaneck 07000
Dear M. Fornick,

It has been one week since we wrote you about M. Hedley Satsop, of Humptulips 98000, SCC #1839485729384, and we have not yet received your reply. I presume this is due to some oversight on your part. Sometimes we make little mistakes, or our secretarial pool goes on strike, or our records become confused. If there is some good reason why you cannot clear M. Satsop's account, and refund him his $99.98 plus 5 percent tax by the end of the week, please be sure to contact me and I will attempt to arrange a short extension.

> Sincerely,
> Galena Carbury
> Attorney-at-Law for Recourse, Inc.

> *Humptulips 98000*
> *February 12*

Dear Galena Carbury,
   I've gotten your carbons and your notes, and I really appreciate your help, but I just got another bill, and this time it's for $258.30, and it's from a collection agency. Is there any way you can make them leave me alone? I know you're trying, but I'm really getting worried.

> *Sincerely,*
> *Hedley Satsop*

> RECOURSE, INC.
> 14 February

Dear Hedley Satsop,
   Sovereign Credit seems to be slightly more thick-headed than normal. I expected to hear from them by today, but as I didn't, I've written them again. A copy of the letter is enclosed. Courage.

> Sincerely,
> Galena Carbury

By Special Delivery:

> RECOURSE, INC.
> 14 February

B. X. Fornick
Sovereign Credit
Teaneck 07000
Dear M. Fornick,
   Again, I have not heard from you in the time allowed, I regret that you have not attempted to contact me about your

little problem, because these things can frequently be worked out; after all, my company has no wish to be vengeful, especially today of all days. However, since you choose not to avail yourself of our aid, or to communicate with us at all, we regret that it has become necessary to take more drastic measures to obtain compensation for M. Hedley Satsop. Consequently, we are sending copies of this correspondence to M. Satsop's congresspeople, to the Attorney General of 98000, to the North American Consumer Protection Agency, and to the Business Information Service. We greatly regret that this has become necessary, as we much prefer to conduct business in a friendly manner.

Sincerely,
Galena Carbury
Attorney-at-Law for Recourse, Inc.

Business Information Service
98000

Dear M. Carbury,

Thank you for your letter. We are adding it to our file on Sovereign Credit. As you may be aware, we have no legal authority, and our effectiveness is limited by voluntary cooperation of business and the threat of unfavorable publicity. A great deal of unfavorable publicity about Sovereign Credit has already been disseminated; we regret your client did not contact our office before his association with this company. Our actions are further hampered by the fact that our 07000 branch was unaccountably evicted from its offices.

Sincerely,
Ralph Gollophon

Office of the Attorney General
98000

Dear M. Carbury,

Thank you for your letter. We are starting a file on the Sovereign Credit Company. As you may know, our authority extends only as far as the 98000 borders, and our effectiveness depends on the cooperation of the agencies of other regions. As you may also know, 07000 has formed its own region, from which most mail order and many credit agencies operate. We have written the authorities repeatedly, but have been unable to establish communications with them.

If we can be any further help to you, please contact us again.

Sincerely,
Elaine Lumsden
Assistant Attorney General

North American Consumer
Protection Agency

Dear M. Carbury,

Secretary Haslip has asked me to answer your letter. We are always anxious to be of aid in legitimate difficulties. Naturally, our office is extremely busy. As the company in question is licensed by the North American government and so therefore is presumably a reputable firm, our role is naturally limited to an informational one. We are preparing a file on the matter, and if the situation appeared to warrant it, for example if we were to receive a significant number of additional complaints, we would consider enquiring into the case.

Sincerely,
Oliver Pascua
Assistant to the Director, NACPA

North American Senate
11th Session

Dear M. Carbury,

Senator Amrip has requested that I answer your letters. As you may know, he is exceedingly busy. We are adding your client's case to our file for The Committee To Investigate The Practices of Credit-Card Agencies. This Committee was formed during the ninth NA Legislative session, and has made great progress in the time since. We expect to have a full report by the thirteenth session. At that time, recommendations will be made on the subject of procedures for complaint and on the possible structures for a Bureau to investigate such complaints. As soon as the mechanisms are in order, we will contact you further on behalf of your client.

Best,
Artemistra Armitage
Assistant to Calvin C. Amrip, NA Senator

TELEGRAM:

B. X. FORNICK: CONGRESSIONAL INVESTIGATION IN PROGRESS. CLASS ACTION SUIT IN PREPARATION. CIVILIZED CONCLUSION PREFERRED.—GALENA CARBURY, COUNSEL FOR HEDLEY SATSOP.

By Registered Mail:

Federal Circuit Court
Class Action Division

FORMAL ANNOUNCEMENT
OF CLASS ACTION SUIT

Complainant: Hedley Satsop & others
Counsel: Galena Carbury
Defendant: Sovereign Credit, Teaneck 07000
Under Federal Law BJ543–3825–532–9600, this is to announce release of defendant's registered client list, ordered by subpoena, for notification of suit to other parties.
Copies: B. X. Fornick

NOTIFICATION TO CLIENTS OF
SOVEREIGN CREDIT:

A CLASS ACTION SUIT HAS BEEN FILED ON BEHALF OF ALL CLIENTS OF SOVEREIGN CREDIT.

CHARGES: FRAUDULENT BILLING
FALSIFICATION OF CREDIT
INFORMATION
DEFAMATION OF CHARACTER
HARASSMENT

DAMAGES ASKED: COMPENSATORY: $99.98 +
5 PERCENT SALES TAX
punitory: $50,000,000
COPY: B. X. FORNICK

SOVEREIGN CREDIT
TEANECK 07000

DEAR *M. Satsop*

UH-OH—OUR COMPUTER HAS DONE IT AGAIN!!

IT HAS COME TO OUR ATTENTION THAT A SLIGHT ERROR HAS OCCURRED IN YOUR, *M. Satsop*, ACCOUNT. WE ARE IN THE PROCESS OF RECTIFYING THAT ERROR. WE APPRECIATE THE CHANCE TO INFORM YOU, *M. Satsop*, THAT WE HANDLE OVER 2,585,352 ACCOUNTS EACH YEAR AND SELDOM MAKE AN ERROR.

IT TAKES TIME TO ALTER COMPUTER RECORDS. PLEASE ALLOW SEVERAL WEEKS FOR OUR CORRECTIONS TO TAKE EFFECT ON YOUR, *M. Satsop*, ACCOUNT.

> YOUR FRIEND IN SERVICE,
> B. X. FORNICK
> SOVEREIGN CREDIT

> RECOURSE, INC.
> 1 March

Dear Hedley,

Well, I guess this is the best we can do for the moment; usually I managed to get a letter from a real person, and an apology. If you *don't* get your refund within a few weeks, be sure to write me again. I don't know about you, but *I* haven't gotten my full measure of satisfaction out of the mighty Sovereign Credit. (And I'm most interested in region 07000, which appears to have had its local government options taken over—I've heard of company towns, but this is ridiculous.)

Besides, anybody who treats people like machines and then blames human error on the computer deserves something more than what they've gotten so far.

You may get one or two more notes from the collection agency; you can ignore them with impunity, build a bonfire with them, stick pins in them, whatever you want. They should start leaving you alone shortly. I'll leave the suit in the works as leverage until after we're sure everything's cleared up. It's up to you whether to continue it or not afterwards.

> Sincerely,
> Galena

Delivered by Hand:

> The Hideout
> 2 March

Dear Lennie,

Did you hear about our latest bit of business? The other side of the peninsula some guys have a clear-cut license, so we went over and played Sasquatch. Big fake feet for tracks and everything. (We'd've let them alone, but the mess they left—!) Anyway, we scared them good (so much for the age of reason), and now there are forty-three biologists from the

University running around looking for it, and some guy named Sandusky or something claiming to have met it. Got anything for us to do yet?

Lucifer

Delivered by Hand:

3 March

Dear Luc,

Can't think of a thing; the law office bustles busily and the Recourse case has come to a mildly felicitous conclusion. Thanks, though. Take care.

Lennie

Humptulips 98000
March 8

Dear Galena,

Well, I got another bill from the collection agency, but I'm ignoring it, just like you said. Well, actually, I'm sending it to you just in case anything needs to be done about it. I don't think I want to continue the suit, I don't understand that kind of thing and I just want to be done with it and forget it. Thanks for your help, very much. Maybe we can have lunch sometime when I'm over in town? By the way, most people call me Hank. It's better than "Hedley," anyway.

Sincerely,
Hank

CREDIT REPOSITORY

Hedley Satsop Humptulips 98000
#1839485729384

WE REPRESENT: *Sovereign Credit*

AN OUNCE OF PREVENTION IS WORTH A POUND OF CURE!! THIS PHRASE IS TERRIBLY TRUE, TODAY IN OUR AGE OF COMPUTERS. JUST AS A RANDOM EXAMPLE, LET ME INFORM YOU THAT YOUR INDEBTMENT TO OUR CLIENT IS NOW DELINQUENT. PREVENT YOUR NAME BEING LISTED WITH A CREDIT BUREAU. SIMPLY MAIL YOUR CHECK FOR $288.37 NOW. YOUR PROMPT RESPONSE MAY EVENTUALLY REINSTATE YOUR GOOD CREDIT!

SINCERELY,
DIRK S. LAURANCE, DIRECTOR
CREDIT REPOSITORY

7 March

Dear Hank,

Glad to see you for lunch sometime. That Repository form has been getting more and more offensive for a long time; they must be approaching some kind of hyperbolic limit by now. They shouldn't bother you anymore.

And my friends call me Lennie. Which is better than "Galena." My father made his money in lead, and probably thought it was a pretty word. I've never been amused.

Best,
Lennie

Dear Lennie,

I got another bill and ignored it, and I kept expecting a refund check, but it hasn't come. And I've tried to get a loan from my bank and they won't give it to me. They say I've got a bad credit rating. I'm really scared. What do I do?

Hank

5 April

Dear Hank,

Relax. What has happened is that they sold your account to a collection agency—standard procedure, unfortunately—before they corrected their records, and they're too dense to clear that up without being told. So I'll tell them.

Lennie

RECOURSE, INC.
5 April

B. X. Fornick
Sovereign Credit
Teaneck 07000
M. Fornick:

How very encouraging, to have the attention of a real human being. A basic part of your education has been neglected if no one ever told you that computers do not thrive on special delivery mail.

Your criminal irresponsibility has caused the continued harassment of my client, Mr. Hedley Satsop, by your subsidiary collection agency.

Far from withdrawing the suit I have filed against you (as I intended after you promised to correct your errors), I am increasing the damages asked by a factor of four. If this situation continues, I will be forced to turn over my information to the federal prosecutor, and this would very likely result in charges being filed against you for criminal negligence as well as falsification of credit information, which is a very serious charge.

> Sincerely,
> Galena Carbury
> Attorney-at-Law for Recourse, Inc.

> Sovereign Credit
> April 15

Dear M. Carbury,

Please remain patient. You may not realize that the complexities of our operations make changing our records an extremely tedious and time-consuming affair. Computer-banks are not something to be trifled with. We must make very certain, before we finally alter any bit of data, that the new information is as valid and sound as the old. You would be astonished, I am sure, at how many people attempt to insert erroneous and mistaken data into my computers' memories. I must, for the safety of our Nation's economy, make absolutely certain both that the new information is accurate and precise, and that the sources and subject are responsible, trustworthy, and loyal people.

> I remain,
> B. X. Fornick

> RECOURSE, INC.
> 17 April

Dear M. Fornick,

You are making me very angry. I have, in writing, your admission that through your own haphazard procedures you have erroneously harassed my client. You owe him a considerable sum of money, yet he is the one who is being harassed by your bills and by your collection agency. You have attempted to ruin his credit rating and his good reputation (two quite separate qualities which people like you, over the last two decades, have attempted to make synonymous). You have caused him a great deal of mental anguish. And now you have the insolence to write this unbelievably patronizing letter inferring that your information is correct, that the admitted and provable truth is wrong, that my client is not

Air Mail Special Delivery, Deliver to Addressee Only:

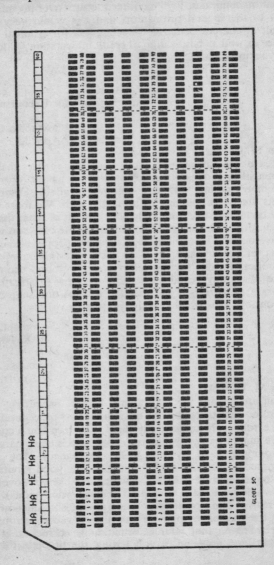

"responsible, trustworthy, and loyal" (although I cannot imagine what the last has to do with the matter at hand), and that in fact a recognized and respected member of the International Bar Association may be lying to you.

My client expects his refund and an apology before the end of the week.

Sincerely,
Galena Carbury

P.S. In the future, you really must not try to pretend, to someone with a degree in computer law in particular, that it is difficult *or* time-consuming to correct records.

April 20

Dear Lennie,

They're trying to garnishee my salary, and my boss is really mad. He wants to fire me, even though I've been working here for fifteen years. He doesn't want to worry about the extra paperwork, he says. And I never told you before, but I've been seeing a psychiatrist the last year or so, he's really helped me, but my boss doesn't like that either. I'm getting scared again. What am I going to do?

Hank

22 April

Dear Hank,

Don't do anything, my friend. I'm doing it.

Lennie

By Special Delivery:

Dr. Francis Takeoka
April 22

Dear Lennie,

Hey, kid, can you get these jerks off Hedley's back? They've started calling him at work, and even coming around the shop. He's on the edge of another breakdown. Haven't you got anything faster in that bag of tricks?

Frank

22 April

Dear Frank,

Keep Hank going another week. Keep reminding him of the suit I've filed—no, it won't solve the problem directly (though we will collect; I'm going to make sure of *that* now), but they can continue to harass him until we get a settlement, maybe two or three years, unless I got a court order, which will still take three weeks to a month. (His case wouldn't be considered "critical" enough for quick action. These days you even have to line up to drag a judge out of bed.) But my bag of tricks isn't empty, and it's time for drastic measures.

Lennie

Delivered by Hand:

22 April

Dear Luc,
Somehow, Eaglepaws always turns up at just the right time. I hate to admit it, but I need some help. Notes appended. Turn S. O. loose on Sovereign's computer and have him make it call off the dogs. My client is pretty frail, mentally, so *this is an emergency*.

Lennie

Delivered by Hand:

23 April

Dear Lennie,
S. O. is sleeping. He was up all night trying to break into their line and it did not work. He says he can do it eventually, but it might take a week or a month or ten years. We have another plan but we need some money.

Lucifer

Delivered by Hand:

23 April

Dear Luc,
Cash enclosed. *Be careful*.

Lennie

Delivered by Hand:

The Hideout
1 May

Dear Lennie,
The enemy is ours. I guess I'll let you stay legit if you keep me well supplied with this kind of amusing game.
Since we couldn't whistle our way into Sovereign's computer, what S. O. and I did was, we went over to Teaneck and

sonared them. But they are like the frigging FBI to electronic surveillance and bugging. Our mikes couldn't hear through their walls; we couldn't resonate them; they didn't even have any windows. We almost thought we'd have to give up.

Then I got one of my customary brilliant ideas.

We waited until dark, and then I did a very unfashionable thing.

I broke in.

S. O. got real sweaty between the time I narco'd the guard and when I got the door open, but once we got to the machines he was like an otter in an abalone field. (Not being able to get computer time is the only thing besides his nickname he doesn't like about the hideout.) We did what you told us to; by now your client ought to have his refund check ($99.98 plus 5 percent sales tax plus 5 percent interest . . . uh . . . per month . . . you know, I never was very good at remembering how banks work). While I hunt-and-pecked a very apologetic letter to your client and a call-off-the-dogs letter to Credit Repository, S. O. told all the computers that your man was ok, and also appropriated a couple hours free machine time. Then we abscent.

I don't think you'll have to worry about them catching on to you. I did some selective additional refunding, and they may even want to settle out of court as fast as possible—to hold off having to show anybody their records. Because, see, their chief red-tape-breeder, the good M. Fornick, is pretty busy right now, trying to explain a certain $237,000 shortage in Sovereign's accounts.

Lucifer

April 30

Dear Lennie,

I got a letter today, air mail special delivery, with a check from Sovereign Credit. I don't know how you did it, but I thank you so much I can't even tell you.

There's just one other thing. The same day I bought my zygomat, I bought a parasang too, with one of the other credit cards my doctor told me I should get. I forgot all about that because the parasang was no good and I took it back a whole year ago. I can't find the receipt I got when I returned it, and yesterday they sent me a bill for $349.95 . . .

The Genius Freaks

Darting into a lighted spot in a dim pool—

Being born—well, Lais remembered it, a gentle transition from warm liquid to warm air, an abrupt rise in the pitch of sounds, the careful touch of hands, shock of the first breath. She had never told anyone that her easy passage had lacked some quality, perhaps a rite that would have made her truly human. Somewhere was a woman who had been spared the pain of Lais' birth, everywhere were people who had caused pain, and, causing, experienced it, paying a debt that Lais did not owe. Sleeping curled in fetal position in the dark gave her no comfort: the womb she was formed in had seemed a prison from the time she was aware of it. Yet the Institute refused to grow its fetuses in the light. The Institute administrators were normal and had been born normally. If they had ever been prenatally aware, the memory had been obliterated or forgotten. They could not understand the frustration of the Institute Fellows, or perhaps the thought of fishlike little creatures peering out, watching, learning, was too much even for them to bear.

Lais' quiet impatience with an increasingly cramped world was only relieved by her birth, and by light, which freed a sense she had felt was missing but could not quite imagine.

Having reasoned that something like birth must occur, she was much calmer under restraint than she had been only a little earlier. When she first realized she was trapped, when she first grew large enough to touch both horizons of her sphere, she had been intelligent but wild, suspicious and easily angered. She had thrashed, seeking escape; nothing noticed her brief frenzy. The walls were spongy-surfaced, hard beneath; they yielded slightly, yet held her. They implied something beyond the darkness, and allowed her to imagine it. All her senses were inside the prison, so she imagined being turned inside out to be freed from her tether. She expected pain.

As she waited, she sometimes wished she were still a lower primate, small and stupid enough to accept the warm salty liquid as the universe. Even then, as she kicked and paddled with clumsy hands and feet, missing the strong propulsion of her vanished tail, she was changing. That was when she first thought that the spectrum of her senses might lack a vital part. Her environment was still more alien now than it had been when she was a lithe amphibian, barely conscious, long-tailed and free in an immense world. Earlier than that, her memories were kinetic impressions, of gills pumping, heart fluttering, the low, periodic vibration that never changed.

—the silver-speckled black fish settled in a shadow at Lais' feet, motionless but seeming to ripple beneath the mist and the disturbed surface of the water. Lais hunched down in her thick coat. The layered branches of a gnarled tree protected her from the sleet, but not from the wind. She shivered. Overhead, the vapor rising from the pool condensed in huge drops on the undersides of dark green needles, and fell again. The tree smelled cool and tart. Beyond her shelter, the shapes of sculpture and small gardens rose and flowed between low buildings and sleet-cratered puddles that reflected intermittent lights. Except for Lais and the fishes, the flagstone mall was deserted. People had left their marks, bits of paper not yet picked up, sodden; placards and posters the haranguers had abandoned in the rain, leaning against each other like dead trees. Lais let her gaze pass quickly over them, trying not to see the words; in the dim light, she could almost pretend she could not read them.

If she left this place she could walk downtown for perhaps half an hour in the warmed, well-lit night, before an agent saw her smoothing people and chased her out, or had her held and checked. That she could not afford. She stayed where she was. She pulled her coat over her knees and put her head down. Staying outside was her own choice. The dump nearby would give her one of the transients' beds, but out here the cold numbed her, a free anesthetic that otherwise she might be driven to buy in more destructive form.

A scuffing through slush on the flagstones roused her. Lais crawled stiffly from beneath the tree. Pain clamped on her spine before she could straighten. She leaned against the garden's retaining wall, breathing the thin air in shallow cut-off gasps. The man was almost opposite her when she moved into the mall. "Hey, you got any spare change?"

Startled, a little scared, he peered down at her through the rain. His face was smooth, without character, the set and seemingly plasticized face of a thousand betrayers, a face she would not live to share. He had nothing to be frightened of but mercifully rapid senility and a painless death that could be over a century away. His life span would be ten times hers.

"You're dressed well to want money."

She moved closer to him, so close that she had to conceal her own uneasiness. She needed, if anything, more distance around her than other people, but she understood the need and controlled it. The man succumbed to it, and moved away from her until gradually, as they talked, she backed him against the wall. He was odorless, a complete olfactory blank, firmly scrubbed and deodorized at mouth and armpits and feet and groin, as clean as his genes. Even his clothes had no smell. Lais hadn't bathed in days, and her clothes were filthy; her damp coat smelled familiarly of wool, and she herself smelled like a warm wet female animal with fur. She built up an image of herself preying on others. It amused her, because they had been preying on her all her life.

"Some people are more generous," she said, as if someone had given her the coat. Wisps of hair clung in damp streaks across her forehead and at her neck.

"Why don't you sign up for Aid?"

She laughed once, sharply, and didn't answer, turned her back on him and guessed two steps before he called her. It was one. "Do you need a place to sleep?"

She made her expression one of disdain. "I don't do that, man."

Cold rain beading on his face did not prevent his flush:

embarrassment mixed with indignation. "Come now, I didn't mean—"

She knew he didn't mean—

"Look, if you don't want to give me anything forget it." She stressed "give" just enough.

He blew out his breath and dug in his pockets. He held out a crumpled bill that she looked at with contempt, but she took it first. "Gods, a whole guilder. Thanks a lot." The insolence of her mock gratitude upset him more than derision. She walked away, thinking that she had the advantage, that she was leaving him speechless and confused.

"Do you like hurting people?"

She faced him. He had no expression, only that smooth, unlived-in look. She watched his eyes for a moment. They, at least, were still alive.

"How old are you?"

He frowned abruptly. "Fifty."

"Then you can't understand."

"And how old are you? Eighteen? It isn't that much difference."

No, she thought, the difference is the hundred years that you've got left, and the self-righteous hate you'd give me if you knew what I was. She almost answered him honestly, but she couldn't get the words out. "It is to me," she said, with bitterness. Only fifty. He was the right age to have had his life disrupted by the revolt, and if he did not hate her kind, he would still fear them. Deep feelings were no longer so easily erased by the passage of time.

He seemed about to speak again, but he was too close; she had misjudged him and he had already stepped outside her estimation of him. Her mistakes disturbed her; there was no excuse for them, not this soon. She turned to flee and slipped to her hands and knees in the slush. She struggled to her feet and ran.

Around a corner she had to stop. Even a month earlier she would not have noticed the minor exertion; now it exhausted her. The Institute could at least have chosen a clean way to murder its Fellows. Except that clean deaths would be quick, and too frequently embarrassing.

The wind at Lais' back was rising. On a radial street leading toward the central landing pad, it seemed much colder. Sleet melted on her face and slid under her collar. Going to the terminal, she risked being recognized, but she did not think the Institute could have traced her here yet. At the terminal she would be able to smooth a few more people, and maybe they would give her enough for her to buy a ticket off this mountain and off this world. If she could hide herself well enough, take herself far enough, the Institute would never be sure she was dead.

Halfway between the mall and the landing terminal, she had to stop and rest. The café she entered was physically warm but spiritually cold, utilitarian and mechanical. Its emotional sterility was familiar. Recently she had come to recognize it, but she saw no chance of replacing the void in herself with anything of greater meaning. She had changed a great deal during the last few months, but she had very little time left for changes.

The faint scents of half a dozen kinds of smoke lingered among the odors of automatic, packaged food. Lais slid into an empty booth. Across the room three people sat together, obviously taking pleasure in each other's company. For a moment she considered going to their table and insinuating herself into the group, acting pleasant at first but then increasingly irrational.

She was disgusted by her fantasies. Briefly, she thought she might be able to believe she was insane. Even the possibility would be comforting. If she could believe what she had been taught, that Institute geniuses were prone to instability, she could believe all the other lies. If she could believe the lies, the Institute could remain a philanthropic organization. If she could believe in the Institute, if she was mad, then she was not dying.

She wondered what they would do if she walked over and told them who and what she was. Lais had no experience with normal humans her own age. They might not even care, they might grin and say "so what?" and move over to make room for her. They might pull back, very subtly, of course, and turn her away, if their people had taught them that the freaks might revolt again. That was the usual reaction. Worst, they might stare at her for a moment, look at each other, and decide silently among themselves to forgive her and tolerate her. She had seen that reaction among the normals who worked at the Institute, those who needed any shaky superiority they could grasp, who made themselves the judges of deeds punished half a century before.

A lighted menu on the wall offered substantial meals, but despite her hunger she was nauseated by the mixed smells of meat and sweet syrup. The menu changed a guilder and offered up utensils and a covered bowl of soup. She resented the necessity of spending even this little, because she had almost enough to go one more hard-to-trace world-step away. The sum she had and the sum she needed: they were such pitiful amounts, pocket money of other days.

For a moment she wished she were back at the Institute with the rest of the freaks, being catered to by pleasant human beings. Only for a moment. She would not be at the Institute but hidden in their isolated hospital; those pleasant human beings would be pretending to cure her while sucking up the last fruits of her mind and all the information her body could give them. All they would really care about would be what error in procedure had allowed such a mistake to be brought to term in their well-monitored artificial wombs. Fellows were not supposed to begin to die until they were thirty, though that would be denied. Nothing had warned the Institute that Lais would die fifteen years too early; nothing but the explanation and perhaps not even that, could tell them if any of her colleagues would die fifteen or fifty years too late, given time by a faulty biologic clock to develop into something the Institute could no longer control, let alone understand. Their days would be terror and their sleep nightmare over that possibility.

And her people, the other Fellows, would hardly notice she was gone: that brought a pang of guilt. People she had known had left abruptly, and she had become so used to the excuses that she had ceased to ask about them. Had she ever asked? There were so many worlds, such great distances, so many possibilities: mobility seemed limitless. Lais had never spent as much as a year in a single outpost, and seldom saw acquaintances after transient project collaborations or casual sexual encounters. She had no emotional ties, no one to go to for help and trust, no one who knew her well enough to judge her sane against contrary evidence. Fellows were solitary specialists in fields too esoteric to discuss without the inducement of certain intellectual interaction. The lack of communication had never bothered Lais then, but now it seemed barbarous, and almost inconceivable.

Clear soup took the chill away and let minor discomforts intrude. The thick coat was too warm, but she wore it like a shield. Her hair and clothes were damp, and the heavy material of her pants began to itch as it grew warmer. Her face felt oily.

Trivialities disappeared. She had continued the research she had started before she was forced to run. She was crippled and slowed by having to do the scut-work in her mind. She needed a computer, but she could not afford to line one. It was frustrating, of course, exhausting, certainly, but necessary. It was what Lais did.

A hesitant touch on her shoulder awakened her. She did not remember falling asleep—perhaps she had not slept: the data she had been considering lay organized in her mind, a new synthesis—but she was lying on her side on the padded bench with her head pillowed on her arms.

"I'm really sorry. Mr. Kiviat says you have to leave."

"Tell him to tell me himself," she said.

"Please, miz."

She opened her eyes. She had never seen an old person before; she could not help but stare, she could not speak for a moment. His face was deeply lined and what little hair he had was stringy, yellow-white, shading at his cheeks into two days' growth of gray stubble. He was terrified, put in the middle with no directions, afraid to try anything he might think of by himself. His pale, sunken eyes shifted back and forth, seeking guidance. The thin chain around his throat carried a child's identity tag. Pity touched her and she smiled, without humor but with understanding.

"Never mind," she said. "It's all right. I'll go." His relief was a physical thing.

Groggy with sleep she stood up and started out. She stumbled, and the malignant pain crawled up her spine where eroded edges of bone ground together. She froze, knowing that was useless. The black windows and the shiny beads of icy snow turned scarlet. She heard herself fall, but she did not feel the impact.

She was unconscious for perhaps a second; she came to calmly recording that this was the first time the pain had actually made her faint.

"You okay, miz?"

The old man knelt at her side, hands half extended as if to help her, but trembling, afraid. Two months ago Lais would not have been able to imagine what it would be like to exist in perpetual fear.

"I just—" Even speaking hurt, and her voice shocked her with its weakness. She finished in a whisper. "—have to rest for a little while." She felt stupid lying on the floor, observed by the machines, but the humiliation was less than that of the few endless days at the hospital being poked and biopsied and sampled like an experiment in the culture of a recalcitrant tissue. By then she had known that the treatments were a charade, and that only the tests were important. She pushed herself up on her elbows, and the old man helped her sit.

"I have . . . I mean . . . my room . . . I'm not supposed to . . ." His seamed face was scarlet. It showed emotion much more readily than the dead faces of sustained folk, perhaps because he aged and they did not, perhaps because they were no longer capable of deep feeling.

"Thank you," she said.

He had to support her. His room was in the same building, reached by a web of dirty corridors. The room was white plastic and scrupulously clean, almost bare. The bluish shimmering cube of a trid moved and muttered the corner.

The old man took her to a broken sandbed and stood uncertainly by her. "Is there anything . . . do you need . . . ?" Rusty words learned by rote long before, never used. Lais shook her head. She took off her coat, and he hurried to help her. She lay down. The bed was hard: air was meant to flow through granules and give the illusion of floating, but the jets had stopped and the tiny beads were packed down at the bottom, mobile and slippery only beneath the cover. It was softer than the street. The light was bright, but not intolerable. She threw her arm across her eyes.

Something awakened her: she lay taut, disoriented. The illumination was like late twilight. She heard her name again and turned. Over her shoulder she saw the old man crouched on a stool in front of the trid, peering into the bluish space of it, staring at a silent miniature of Lais. She did not have to listen to know what the voice was saying: they had traced her to Highport; they were telling the residents that she was here and that she was mad, a poor pitiful unstable genius, paranoid and frightened, needing compassion and aid. But not dangerous. Certainly not dangerous. Soothing words assured people that aggression had been eliminated from the chromosomes of the freaks (that was a lie, and impossible, but as good as truth). The voice said that there were only a few Fellows, who all confined themselves to research. Lais stopped listening. She allowed early memories to seep out and affect her. The old man crouched before his trid and stared at the picture. She pushed the twisted blanket away. The old man did not move. At the foot of the bed, Lais reached out until her fingers almost brushed his collar. Beneath it lay the strong thin links of his identity necklace. She could reach out, twist it into his throat, and remove him as a threat. No one would notice he was gone. No one would care. A primitive anthropoid, poised between civilization and savagery, urged her on. ____

When he recognized her, he would straighten. His throat would be exposed. Lais could feel tendons beneath her hands. She glanced down, to those hands outstretched like claws, taut, trembling, alien, She drew them back, still staring. She hesitated, then lay down on the bed again. Her hands lay passive, hers once more, pale and blue-veined, with torn, dirty fingernails.

The old man did not turn around.

They showed pictures of how she might look if she were trying to disguise herself, in dark or medium skin tones, no hair, long hair, curly hair, hair with color. The brown almost had it: anonymous. And she had changed in ways more subtle than disguise. The arrogance was attenuated, and the invincible assurance gone; the self-confidence remained—it was all she had—but it was tempered, and more mature. She had learned to doubt, rather than simply to question.

The estranged face in the trid, despite its arrogance, was not cruel but gentle, and that quality she had not been able to change.

It had taken them two months to trace her. They could not have followed her credit number, for she had stopped using it before they could cancel it. They would have known only how far she could get before her cash ran out. She had gotten farther, of course, but they had probably expected that.

Since they knew where she was, now was almost identical to later, and now it was still light outside. As she allowed herself to sleep again, she tried to imagine not recognizing a picture of someone she had met. She failed.

Lais woke up struggling from a nightmare in which the blue images of the trid attacked and overwhelmed her, and her computers would not come to her aid. The old man pulled his hands from her shoulders abruptly and guiltily when he realized she was awake. The windowless room was stuffy. Lais was damp all over with feverish sweat. Her head ached, and her knees were sore.

"I'm sorry, miz, I was afraid you'd hurt yourself." He must

have been rebuffed and denigrated all his life, to be so afraid of touching another human being.

"It's all right," she said. She seemed always to be saying that to him. Her mental clock buzzed and jumped to catch up with reality: twelve hours since the trid woke her up.

The old man sat quietly, perhaps waiting for orders. He did not take his gaze from her, but his surveillance was of a stange and anxious childlike quality, without recognition. It seemed not to have occurred to him that his stray might be the Institute fugitive. He seemed to live in two spheres of reality. When she looked at his eyes, he put his head down and hunched his shoulders. His hands lay limp and half-curled in his lap. "I didn't know what to do. They yell at me when I ask stupid questions." No bitterness, just acceptance of the judgment that any question he could ask must be stupid.

She forced back her own useless flare of anger. To awaken hate in him would be cruel. "You did the right thing," she said. She would have said the same words if he had innocently betrayed her. Two other lines of possible reality converged in her mind: herself of two months or a year before, somehow unchanged by exile and disillusionment, and an old man who called Aid for the sick girl in his room. She would have told him exactly what she thought without regard for his feelings; she would have looked on him not with compassion but with the kind of impersonal pity that is almost disdain. But they would have been more similar in one quality: neither of them would have recognized the isolation of their lives.

"Are you hungry?"

"No." That was easier than trying to explain why she was, but could not eat. He accepted it without question or surprise, and still seemed to wait for her orders. She realized that she could stay and he would never dare complain— perhaps not wish to—nor dare tell anyone she was here. If he had been one of the plastic people she might have used him, but he was not, and she could not: full circle.

His hands moved in his lap, nervous.

"What's wrong?" She was careful to say it gently.

As an apology, he said, "Miz, I have to work."

"You don't need my permission," she said, trying to keep her tone from sounding like a reprimand.

He got up, stood uncertainly in the center of his room, wanting to speak, not knowing the right words. "Maybe later you'll be hungry." He fled.

She unwrapped herself from the blanket and massaged her knees. She wandered uneasily around the room, feeling trapped and alien.

One station on the trid bounced down all news. She came on at the quarter hour. The hope that they had only traced her to this world evaporated as she listened to the bulletin: the broadcast was satellite-transmitted; unless they had known, they would not have said she was in Highport and risked missing her in another city. They kept saying she was crazy, in the politest possible terms. They could never say that the malignancy was not in her mind but in her body. No one got cancer anymore. People who related their birth dates to the skies of old Earth did not even call themselves Moon children if they were born under the Crab. All the normals had been clean-gened, to strip even the potential for cancer from their chromosomes. Only a few of them, and now Lais, knew that the potential had been put back into the Institute Fellows, as punishment and control.

They used even this announcement to remind the people how important the Fellows were, how many advances they had made, how many benefits they had provided. Before, Lais had never known that that sort of constant persuasion was necessary. Perhaps, in fact, it wasn't. Perhaps they only thought it was, so they continued it, afraid to stop the constant reinforcement, probing, breaking old scars.

She turned off the trid. There was a small alcove of a bathroom off the old man's quarters; there was no pool, only a shower. She stripped and took off the dark wig. If there had been a blower she would have washed her clothes, but there were only a couple of worn towels. She turned on the shower and slumped under it with water running through her bright, colorless, startling hair, over her shoulders and breasts and back. Her bones were etched out at ribs and hips, and her muscles made a clear chart of anatomy. Her knees were black and purple; she bruised very easily now.

She left before the old man returned. Trying to thank him would embarrass him and force him to search for words he did not possess. If she waited she might lose her courage and stay; if she waited she might convince herself that she did not need to run again to defy the Institute. If she waited they might trace her to him. It would not matter to them nor help their search if they questioned him, but it would confuse and hurt him. She felt strangely protective toward him, perhaps as he had felt toward her, as if people responded to help-lessness in ways that had nothing to do with their capacity to think.

Outside it was dark again—could be still dark, for all the sun Lais had seen. But the sleet had stopped and it was a midnight-blue morning, cold and clear, and even the city's sky-glow could not dim the stars. People strolled alone or in groups on the softly lit mall, or sat on the bronze or stone flanks of the sculptures of prehistoric beasts. Lais stayed in shadows and at edges. No frozen-young faces blanched on seeing her; no one sidled toward the nearest cmu booth to call the security agents. Many of the people, by their clothes and languages, were transients who had no reason to be interested in local news.

The haranguers were back after the rain: preachers for bizarre religions, recruiters for little outwoods colonies, proponents of strange social ideals. Lais could ignore them all, except the ones who preached against her. She could feel the age about them: they remembered. Only a few kept that much hate, enough to stand on walls and cry that the freaks were a danger and a curse. Lais crept by them on the opposite side of the path, as if they could know what she was just by looking. Their voices followed her.

Drained, she stopped and entered one of the frequent cmu booths. The door closed over the sounds. She needed to rest. The money she had scrounged and smoothed could buy no ticket now past the watchers in the port. She used it instead to open lines to the city's computers, and they returned to her the power of machines. Their lure was too great, measured against the delay. The problem lay so clear in her mind that the programs needing to be run sprang out full-grown. She did a minute's worth of exploration and put a block on the lines so she could not be cut off as soon as her money ran out. It should hold long enough. Into the wells she inserted the data cubes she had carried around for two months. Working submerged her; reality dissolved.

Later, while waiting for more important output, Lais almost idly probed for vulnerability in the city programs, seeking to construct for herself a self-erasing escape route. The safeguards were intricate, but hidden flaws leaped out at Lais and the defenses fell, laying the manager programs open to her abilities. It was hardly more difficult than blocking the lines. At that moment she could have put glitches in the city's services and untraceable bugs in its programs. She could see a thousand ways to cause disruption for mere annoyance; she could detour garbage service and destroy commercial records and mismatch mail codes and reroute the traffic, and there were a thousand times a thousand ways to disrupt things destructively, to turn a community of a million people into the ruined inhabitants of a chaotic war zone. Entropy was all on her side. Yet when the city was stretched out vulnerable before her, the momentary eagerness to destroy left her. The fact that she could have done it seemed to be enough. Taking vengeance on the plastic people would have been senseless, and very much like experimenting with mice or rabbits or lower primates, small furry stupid beasts that accept the pain and degradation with frightened resignation in their wide deep eyes, not knowing *why*. The emotional isolation that might have allowed her to tamper with the city was shattered in her own experience and existence as a laboratory animal, knowing, but not really understanding why.

She slammed at the terminal to close down the holes she had made in the city's defenses, and touched it more gently to complete her work. She used an hour of computer time in less than an hour of real time.

The results came chuckling out: first one, then a second world ecosystem map in fluorescent colors, shading through the spectrum from violet for concrete through blue and green and yellow for high to low certainty to orange and red for theoretical projections. The control map was mostly blue, very little red: it looked good. Its data had been nothing but a sample of ordinary dirt, analyzed down to its isotopes, from the grounds of the outpost, where Lais had been working when she got sick. The map showed the smooth flow of natural evolution, spotted here and there with the quick jumps and twists and bare spots and rootless branches of alien human occupation. Its accuracy was extraordinary. Lais had not thought herself still capable of elation, but she was smiling involuntarily, and for a few moments she forgot about pain and exhaustion.

The second map had less blue and more red, but it seemed unified and logical. Its data had been a bit of a drone sample from an unexplored world, and it showed that the programs were very likely doing what they were supposed to do: deduce the structure and relationships of a world's living things.

Lais' past research had produced results that could hardly be understood, much less used, by normals. It would be extended and built on by her own kind, eventually, not in her lifetime, or perhaps not even in the lifetime that should have belonged to her. This time she had set out to discover the limits of theory applied to minimal data, and the applications were not only obvious but of great potential benefit. When the hounds tracked her, they would find her last programs, and they would be used. Lais shrugged. If she had wanted to be vindictive, she would have tried not to finish, but her mind and her curiosity and her need for knowledge were not things she could flick on and off at will, to produce results like handsful of cookies.

The screen blinked. Her time had run out long since, and the computer was beginning to cut out the obstructions she had put in its billing mechanism. But they held for the moment, and the computer began obediently to print out the data blocks after the map and the programs. She reached to turn it off, then drew her hand back.

Among crystal structures and mass spectrum plots a DNA sequence zipped by, almost unnoticed, almost unnoticeable, but it caught her attention. She thought it was from the drone sample. She brought it back and put it on the screen. The city computers had all the wrong library programs, and who bothered to translate DNA anymore anyway? She picked a place that looked right and did it by memory; for Lais it was like typing. AUG, adenine, uracil, guanine. Start: methionine. Life is the same all over. The computer built a chain of amino acids like a string of popbeads. 2D valiantly masqueraded as 3D. Lais threw in entropy and let the chain fold up. When it was done she doubled and redoubled it and added a copy of its DNA. The screen flickered again; the openings she had made in the computer's safeguards were beginning to close, and alarms would be sounding.

The pieces on the screen began the process of self-aggregation, and when they were done she had a luminous green reproduction, a couple of million times real size, of something that existed on the borders of life. It was a virus, that was obvious. She could not stay and translate the whole genome and look for equivalents for the enzymes it would need. She did not have to. It felt, to all her experience, and memory, and intuition, like a tumor virus. She glanced at the printout again, and realized with slow shock, free-fall sensation, that this was from the control data.

There were any number of explanations. Someone could have been using the virus as a carrier in genetic surgery, replacing its dangerous parts with genes that it could insert into a chromosome. They did not grow freaks at that outpost, but they might have made the virus stocks that the freaks were infected with when they were no more than one-cell zygotes. Someone could have been careless with their sterile technique, especially if they had not been told what the virus was used for and how dangerous it was.

The looming green virus particle, as absurd and obscene that size as the magnified head of a fly, dimmed. The computer was almost through the block. Lais had been in the company of machines so long that they seemed to have as much personality as people; this one muttered and grumbled at her for stealing its time. It lumbered to stop her, a hippopotamus playing crocodile.

Lais had dug the virus up outside in the dirt, free, by chance, and there was a lot of it. If it were infectious—and it seemed complete—it could be infecting people at and around the outpost, not very many, but some, integrating itself into their chromosomes, eradicating the effects of clean-gening. It might wait ten or fifteen or fifty years, or forever, but when injury or radiation or carcinogen induced it out, it would begin to kill. It would be too late to cure people of it then, just as it was for Lais; the old, crippling methods, surgery, radiation, might work for a few, but if the disease were similar to hers, fast-growing, metastasizing, nothing would be much use.

The light on the screen began to go out. She moved quickly and stored the map programs, the maps, the drone data.

She hesitated. In a moment it would be too late. She felt the vengeful animals of memories trying to hold her back. She jabbed with anger at the keyboard, and sent the control data into storage with the rest as the last bright lines faded from the screen.

The data was there, for them to notice and fear, or ignore and pay the price. She would give them that much warning. The normals might find a way to clean-gene people after they were grown; they might even set Fellows to work on the problem, and let them share the benefits. Lais wondered at her own naiveté, that after everything a small part of her still hoped her people might finally be forgiven.

She left it all behind, even the data cubes, and went back out onto the mall.

A hovercar whirred a few streets back; sharp beams from its searchlights touched the edges and corners of buildings.

She walked faster, then ran painfully past firmly shut doors to a piece of sculpture that doubled as a sitting-park. She crawled into the deepest and most enclosed alcove she could reach. Outside she could hear the security car intruding on the pedestrian mall. The sucks passed without suspecting her presence, not recognizing the sculpture as a children's toy, a place to hide and climb and play, a place for transients to sleep in good weather, a place that, tonight, was Lais' alone.

There was a tiny window by her shoulder that cut through a meter of stone to the outside. Moonlight polished a square of the wall that narrowed, crept upward, and vanished as the moon set.

Lais put her head on her knees and focused all her attention on herself, tracing lines of fatigue through her muscles to extrapolate her reserves of stamina, probing at the wells of pain in her body and in her bones. She had become almost accustomed to betrayal by the physical part of herself, but she was still used to relying on her mind. The slight tilt from a fine edge of alertness was too recent for her to accept. Now, forcing herself to be aware of everything she was, she was frightened by the changes to the edge of panic. She closed her eyes and fought it down, wrestling with a feeling like a great gray slug in her stomach and a small brown millipede in her throat. Both of them retreated, temporarily. Tears tickled her cheeks, touched her lips with salt; she scrubbed them away on her rough sleeve.

She felt marginally better. It had occurred to her that she felt light-headed and removed and hallucinatory because of hunger, not because of advancing pathological changes in her brain; that helped. It was another matter of relying on feedback from a faulty instrument. The thought of food was still nauseating. It would be harder to eat the longer she put it off, but, then, perhaps it was too late to matter anymore.

The sitting-park restored her, as it was meant to; for her it was the silence and isolation, the slight respite from cold and the clean twisting lines of it, whatever reasons others had for responding. She would have liked to stay.

She walked a long way toward the edge of the bazaar. Her knees still hurt—it took her a few minutes to remember when she had fallen, and why; it seemed a very long time before—and her legs began to ache. Resting again, she sat on a wall at the edge of the bazaar, at the edge of the mountaintop, looking down over a city of pinpoint lights (holes in the ground to hell? but the lights were gold and silver, not crimson). The lights led in lines down the flanks of the mountain, dendrites from the cell of the city and its nucleus of landing field. She knew she could get out of Highport. She believed she could run so far that they would not catch her until too late; she hoped they would never find her, and she hoped her body would fail her before her mind did, or that she would have courage and presence enough to kill herself if it did not or if the pain grew great enough to break her. All she really had to do was get to the bottom of the mountain, and past the foothills, until she reached lush jungle and great heat and a climate like an incubator, where life processes are faster and scavengers prowl, and the destruction of decomposition is rapid and complete. The jungle would conspire with her to deny the Institute what she considered most precious, knowledge. She slipped off the wall and started down the hill. Before her the sky was changing from midnight blue to gray and scarlet with the dawn.

Aztecs

She gave up her heart quite willingly.

After the operation, Laenea Trevelyan lived through what seemed an immense time of semiconsciousness, drugged so she would not feel the pain, kept almost insensible while her healing began. Those who watched her did not know she would have preferred consciousness and an end to her uncertainty. So she slept, shallowly, drifting toward awareness, driven back, existing in a world of nightmare. Her dulled mind suspected danger but could do nothing to protect her. She had been forced too often to sleep through danger. She would have preferred the pain.

Once Laenea almost woke: she glimpsed the sterile white walls and ceiling; blurrily, slowly recognizing what she saw. The green glow of monitoring screens flowed across her shoulder, over the scratchy sheets. Taped down, needles scraped nerves in her arm. She became aware of sounds, and heard the rhythmic thud of a beating heart.

She tried to cry out in anger and despair. Her left hand was heavy, lethargic, insensitive to her commands, but she moved it. It crawled like a spider to her right wrist and fumbled at the needles and tubes.

Air shushed from the room as the door opened. A gentle

voice and a gentle touch reproved her, increased the flow of sedative, and cruelly returned her to sleep.

A tear slid back from the corner of her eye and trickled into her hair as she reentered her nightmares, accompanied by the counterpoint of a basic human rhythm, the beating of a heart, that she had hoped never to hear again.

Pastel light was Laenea's first assurance that she would live. It gave her no comfort. Intensive care was stark white, astringent in odor, but yellows and greens brightened this private room. The sedative wore off and she knew she would finally be allowed to wake. She did not fight the continuing drowsiness, but depression prevented anticipation of the return of her senses. She wanted only to live within her own mind, ignoring her body, ignoring failure. She did not even know what she would do in the future; perhaps she had none anymore.

Yet the world impinged on her as she grew bored with lying still and sweaty and self-pitying. She had never been able to do simply *nothing*. Stubbornly she kept her eyes closed, but she could not avoid the sounds, the vibrations, for they went through her body in waves, like shudders of cold and fear.

This was my chance, she thought. *But I knew I might fail. It could have been worse, or better: I might have died.*

She slid her hand up her body, from her stomach to her ribs, across the adhesive tape and bandages and the tip of the new scar between her breasts, to her throat. Her fingers rested at the corner of her jaw, just above the carotid artery.

She could not feel a pulse.

Pushing herself up abruptly, Laenea ignored sharp twinges of pain. The vibration of a heartbeat continued beneath her palms, but now she could tell that it did not come from her own body.

The amplifier sat on the bedside table, sending out low frequency thuddings in a steady pattern. Laenea felt laughter bubbling up; she knew it would hurt and she did not care. She lifted the speaker: such a small thing, to cause her so much worry. Its cord ripped from the wall as she flung it across the room, and it smashed in the corner with a satisfying clatter.

She threw aside the stiff starched sheets; she rose, staggered, caught herself. Her breathing was coarse from fluid in her lungs. She coughed, caught her breath, coughed again. Time was a mystery, measured only by weakness: she thought the doctors fools, to force sleep into her, risk her to pneumonia, and play recorded hearts, instead of letting her wake and move and adjust to her new condition.

The tile pressed cool against her bare feet. Laenea walked slowly to a warm patch of sunshine, yellow on the butter-cream floor, and gazed out the window. The day was variegated, gray and golden. Clouds moved from the west across the mountains and the Sound while sunlight still spilled over the city. The shadows moved along the water, turning it from shattered silver to slate.

White from the heavy winter snowfall, the Olympic mountains lay between Laenea and the port. The approaching rain hid even the trails of spacecraft escaping the earth, and the bright glints of shuttles returning to their target in the sea. But she would see them soon. She laughed aloud, stretching against the soreness in her chest and the ache of her ribs, throwing back her tangled wavy hair. It tickled the back of her neck, her spine, in the gap between the hospital gown's ties.

Air moved past her as the door opened, as though the room were breathing. Laenea turned and faced the surgeon, a tiny, frail-looking woman with strength like steel wires. The doctor glanced at the shattered amplifier and shook her head.

"Was that necessary?"

"Yes," Laenea said. "For my peace of mind."

"It was here for your peace of mind."

"It has the opposite effect."

"I'll mention that in my report," the surgeon said. "They did it for the first pilots."

The administrators are known for continuing bad advice."

The doctor laughed. "Well, Pilot, soon you can design your own environment."

"When?"

"Soon. I don't mean to be obscure—I only decide if you can leave the hospital, not if you may. The scar tissue needs time to strengthen. Do you want to go already? I cracked your ribs rather thoroughly."

Laenea grinned. "I know." She was strapped up tight and straight, but she could feel each juncture of rib-end and cartilage.

"It will be a few days at least."

"How long has it been?"

"We kept you asleep almost three days."

"It seemed like weeks."

"Well . . . adjusting to all the changes at once could put you in shock."

"I'm an experiment," Laenea said. "All of us are. With experiments, you should experiment."

"Perhaps. But we would prefer to keep you with us." Her hair was short and iron gray, but when she smiled her face was that of a child. She had long, strong fingers, muscles and tendons sharply defined, nails pared short, good hands for doing any job. Laenea reached out, and they touched each others' wrists, quite gently.

"When I heard the heartbeat," Laenea said, "I thought you'd had to put me back to normal."

"It's meant to be a comforting sound."

"No one else ever complained?"

"Not quite so . . . strongly."

They would have been friends, if they had had time. But Laenea was impatient to progress, as she had been since her first transit, in which life passed without her awareness.

"When can I leave?" The hospital was one more place of stasis that she was anxious to escape.

"For now go back to bed. The morning's soon enough to talk about the future."

Laenea turned away without answering. The windows, the walls, the filtered air cut her off from the gray clouds and the city. Rain slipped down the glass. She did not want to sleep anymore.

"Pilot—"

Laenea did not answer.

The doctor sighed. "Do something for me, Pilot."

Laenea shrugged.

"I want you to test your control."

Laenea acquiesced with sullen silence.

"Speed your heart up slowly, and pay attention to the results."

Laenea intensified the firing of the nerve.

"What do you feel?"

"Nothing," Laenea said, though the blood rushed through what had been her pulse points: temples, throat, wrists.

Beside her the surgeon frowned. "Increase a little more, but very slowly."

Laenea obeyed, responding to the abundant supply of oxygen to her brain. Bright lights flashed just behind her vision. Her head hurt in a streak above her right eye to the back of her skull. She felt high and excited. She turned away from the window. "Can't I leave now?"

The surgeon touched her arm at the wrist; Laenea almost laughed aloud at the idea of feeling for *her* pulse. The doctor led her to a chair by the window. "Sit down, Pilot." But Laenea felt she could climb the helix of her dizziness: she felt no need for rest.

"Sit down." The voice was whispery, soft sand slipping across stone. Laenea obeyed.

"Remember the rest of your training, Pilot. Sit back. Relax. Slow the pump. Expand the capillaries. Relax."

Laenea called back her biocontrol. For the first time she was conscious of a presence rather than an absence. Her pulse was gone, but in its place she felt the constant quiet hum of a perfectly balanced rotary machine. It pushed her blood through her body so efficiently that the pressure would destroy her, if she let it. She relaxed and slowed the pump, expanded and contracted the tiny arterial muscles, once, twice, again. The headache, the light-flashes, the ringing in her ears faded and ceased.

She took a deep breath and let it out slowly.

"That's better," the surgeon said. "Don't forget how that feels. You can't go at high speed very long, you'll turn your brain to cheese. You can feel fine for quite a while, you can feel intoxicated. But the hangover is more than I'd care to reckon with." She patted Laenea's hand. "We want to keep you here till we're sure you can regulate the machine. I don't like doing kidney transplants."

Laenea smiled. "I can control it." She began to induce a slow, arhythmic change in the speed of the new pump, in her blood pressure. She found she could do it without thinking, as was necessary to balance the flow. "Can I have the ashes of my heart?"

"Not just yet. Let's be sure, first."

"I'm sure." Somewhere in the winding concrete labyrinth of the hospital, her heart still beat, bathed in warm saline and nutrient solution. As long as it existed, as long as it lived, Laenea would feel threatened in her ambitions. She could not be a pilot and remain a normal human being, with normal human rhythms. Her body still could reject the artificial heart; then she would be made normal again. If she could work at all she would have to remain a crew member, anesthetized and unaware from one end of every journey to the other. She did not think she could stand that any longer. "I'm sure. I won't be back."

Tests and questions and examinations devoured several days in chunks and nibbles. Though she felt strong enough to walk, Laenea was pushed through the halls in a wheelchair. The boredom grew more and more wearing. The pains had faded, and Laenea saw only doctors and attendants and machines: her friends would not come. This was a rite of passage she must survive alone and without guidance.

A day passed in which she did not even see the rain that passed, nor the sunset that was obscured by fog. She asked again when she could leave the hospital, but no one would answer. She allowed herself to become angry, but no one would respond.

Evening, back in her room: Laenea was wide awake. She lay in bed and slid her fingers across her collarbone to the sternum, along the shiny-red line of the tremendous scar. It was still tender, covered with translucent synthetic skin, crossed once just below her breasts with a wide band of adhesive tape to ease her cracked ribs.

The efficient new heart intrigued her. She forced herself consciously to slow its pace, then went through the exercise of constricting and dilating arteries and capillaries. Her bio-control was excellent. It had to be, or she would not have been passed for surgery.

Slowing the pump should have produced a pleasant lethar-gy and eventual sleep, but adrenalin from her anger lingered and she did not want to rest. Nor did she want a sleeping pill: she would take no more drugs. Dreamless drug-sleep was the worst kind of all. Fear built up, undischarged by fantasy, producing a great and formless tension.

The twilight was the texture of gray watered silk, opaque and irregular. The hospital's pastels turned cold and mysteri-ous. Laenea threw off the sheet. She was strong again; she was healed. She had undergone months of training, major surgery, and these final capping days of boredom to free herself completely from biological rhythms. There was no reason in the world why she should sleep, like others, when darkness fell.

A civilized hospital: her clothes were in the closet, not squirreled away in some locked room. She put on black pants, soft leather boots, and a shiny leather vest that laced up the front, leaving her arms and neck bare. The sharp tip of the scar was revealed at her throat and between the laces.

To avoid arguments, she waited until the corridor was deserted. Green paint, meant to be soothing, had gone flat and ugly with age. Her boots were silent on the resilient tile, but in the hollow shaft of the fire stairs the heels clattered against concrete, echoing past her and back. Her legs were tired when she reached bottom. She speeded the flow of blood.

Outside, mist obscured the stars. The moon, just risen, was full and haloed. In the hospital's traffic-eddy, streetlights spread Laenea's shadow out around her like the spokes of a wheel.

A rank of electric cars waited at the corner, tethered like horses in an old movie. She slid her credit key into a lock to release one painted like a turtle, an apt analogy. She got in and drove it toward the waterfront. The little beast rolled slowly along, its motor humming quietly on the flat, straining slightly in low gear on the steep downgrades. Laenea relaxed in the bucket seat and wished she were in a starship, but her imagination would not stretch quite that far. The control stick of a turtle could not become an information and control wall; and the city, while pleasant, was of unrelieved ordinariness compared to the places she had seen. She could not, of course, imagine transit, for it was beyond imagination. Language or mind was insufficient. Transit had never been described.

The waterfront was shabby, dirty, magnetic. Laenea knew that she could find acquaintances nearby, but she did not want to stay in the city. She returned the turtle to a stanchion and retrieved her credit key to halt the tally against her account.

The night had grown cold; she noticed the change peripherally in the form of fog and condensation-slick cobblestones. The public market, ramshackle and shored up, littered here and there with wilted vegetables, was deserted. People passed as shadows.

A man moved up behind her while she was in the dim region between two streetlamps. "Hey," he said, "how about—" His tone was belligerent with inexperience or insecurity or fear. Looking down at him, surprised, Laenea laughed. "Poor fool—" He scuttled away like a crab. After a moment of vague pity and amusement, Laenea forgot him.

She shivered. Her ears were ringing and her chest ached from the cold.

Small shops nestled between bars and cheap restaurants. Laenea entered one for the warmth. It was very dim, darker than the street, high-ceilinged and deep, so narrow she could have touched both side walls by stretching out her arms. She did not. She hunched her shoulders and the ache receded slightly.

"May I help you?"

Like one of the indistinct masses in the back of the shop brought to life, a small ancient man appeared. He was dressed in shabby ill-matched clothes, part of his own wares: Laenea was in a pawnshop or secondhand clothing store. Hung up like trophies, feathers and wide hats and beads covered the walls. Laenea moved farther inside.

"Ah, Pilot," the old man said, "you honor me."

Laenea's delight was childish in its intensity. Only the surgeon had called her "pilot"; to the others in the hospital she had been merely another patient, more troublesome than most.

"It's cold by the water," she said. Some graciousness or apology was due, for she had no intention of buying anything.

"A coat? No, a cloak!" he exclaimed. "A cloak would be set off well by a person of your stature." He turned; his dark from disappeared among the piles and racks of clothes. Laenea saw bright beads and spangles, a quick flash of gold lamé, and wondered uncharitably what dreadful theater costume he would choose. But the garment the small man drew out was dark. He held it up: a long swath of black, lined with scarlet. Laenea had planned to thank him and demur; despite herself she reached out. Velvet-silk outside and smooth satin-silk within caressed her fingers. The cloak had a single shoulder cape and a clasp of carved jet. Though heavy, it draped easily and gracefully. She slung it over her shoulders, and it flowed around her almost to her ankles.

"Exquisite," the shopkeeper said. He beckoned and she approached: a dim and pitted full-length mirror stood against the wall beyond him. Bronze patches marred its irregular silver face where the backing had peeled away. Laenea liked the way the cape looked. She folded its edges so the scarlet lining showed, so her throat and the upper curve of her breasts and the tip of the scar were exposed. She shook back her hair.

"Not quite exquisite," she said, smiling. She was too tall and big-boned for that kind of delicacy. She had a widow's peak and high cheekbones, but her jaw was strong and square. Her face laughed well but would not do for coyness.

"It does not please you." He sounded downcast. Laenea could not quite place his faint accent.

"It does," she said. "I'll take it."

He bowed her toward the front of the shop, and she took out her credit key.

"No, no, Pilot," he said. "Not that."

Laenea raised one eyebrow. A few shops on the waterfront accepted only cash, retaining an illicit flavor in a time when almost any activity was legal. But few even of those select establishments would refuse the credit of a crew member or a pilot. "I have no cash," Laenea said. She had not carried any for years, since once finding in various pockets three coins of metal, one of plastic, one of wood, a pleasingly atavistic animal claw (or excellent duplicate), and a boxed bit of organic matter that would have been forbidden on earth fifty years before. Laenea never expected to revisit at least three of the worlds the currency represented.

"Not cash," he said. "It is yours, Pilot. Only—" He glanced up; he looked her in the eyes for the first time. His eyes were very dark and deep, hopeful, expectant. "Only tell me, what is it like? What do you see?"

She pulled back, surprised. She knew people asked the question often. She had asked it herself, wordlessly after the first few times of silence and patient head-shakings. Pilots never answered. Machines could not answer, pilots could not answer. Or would not. The question was answerable only individually. Laenea felt sorry for the shopkeeper and started to say she had not yet been in transit awake, that she was new, that she had only traveled in the crew, drugged near death to stay alive. But, finally, she could not even say that. It was too easy; it would very nearly be a betrayal. It was an untrue truth. It implied she would tell him if she knew, while she did not know if she could or would. She shook her head, she smiled as gently as she could. "I'm sorry."

He nodded sadly. "I should not have asked . . ."

"That's all right."

"I'm too old, you see. Too old for adventure. I came here so long ago . . . but the time, the time disappeared. I never knew what happened. I've dreamed about it. Bad dreams . . ."

"I understand. I was crew for ten years. We never knew what happened either."

"That would be worse, yes. Over and over again, no time between. But now you know."

"Pilots know," Laenea agreed. She handed him the credit key. Though he still tried to refuse it, she insisted on paying.

Hugging the cloak around her, Laenea stepped out into the fog. She fantasied that the shop would now disappear, like all legendary shops dispensing magic and cloaks of invisibility. But she did not look back, for everyting a few paces away dissolved into grayness. In a small space around each low streetlamp, heat swirled the fog in wisps toward the sky.

The midnight ferry chuttered across the water, riding the waves on its loud cushion of air. Wrapped in her cloak, Laenea was anonymous. After the island stops, she was the only foot passenger left. With the food counters closed, the drivers on the vehicle deck remained in their trucks, napping or drinking coffee from thermoses. Laenea put her feet on the opposite bench, stretched, and gazed out the window into the darkness. Light from the ferry wavered across the tops of long low swells. Laenea could see both the water and her own reflection, very pale. After a while, she dozed.

The spaceport was a huge, floating, artificial island, anchored far from shore. It gleamed in its own lights. The parabolic solar mirrors looked like the multiple compound eyes of a gigantic water insect. Except for the mirrors and the launching towers, the port's surface was nearly flat, few of its components rising more than a story or two. Tall structures would present sail-like faces to the northwest storms.

Beneath the platform, under a vibration-deadening lower layer, under the sea, lay the tripartite city. The roar of shuttles taking off and the scream of their return would drive mad anyone who remained on the surface. Thus the northwest spaceport was far out to sea, away from cities, yet a city in itself, self-protected within the underwater stabilizing shafts.

The ferry climbed a low ramp out of the water and settled onto the loading platform. The hum of electric trucks replaced the growl of huge fans. Laenea moved stiffly down the stairs. She was too tall to sleep comfortably on two-seat benches. Stopping for a moment by the gangway, watching the trucks roll past, she concentrated for a moment and felt the increase in her blood pressure. She could well understand how dangerous it might be, and how easily addictive the higher speed could become, driving her high until like a machine her body was burned out. But for now her energy began returning and the stiffness in her legs and back slowly seeped away.

Except for the trucks, which purred off quickly around the island's perimeters and disappeared, the port was silent so late at night. The passenger shuttle waited empty on its central rail. When Laenea entered, it sensed her, slid its doors shut, and accelerated. A push-button command halted it above Stabilizer Three, which held quarantine, administration, and crew quarters. Laenea was feeling good, warm, and her vision was sparkling bright and clear. She let the velvet cloak flow back across her shoulders, no longer needing its protection. She was alight with the expectation of seeing her friends, in her new avatar.

The elevator led through the center of the stabilizer into the underwater city. Laenea rode it all the way to the bottom of the shaft, one of three that projected into the ocean far below the surface turbulence to hold the platform steady even through the most violent storms. The shafts maintained the island's flotation level as well, pumping sea water in or out of the ballast tanks when a shuttle took off or landed or a ferry crept on board.

The elevator doors opened into the foyer where a spiral staircase reached the lowest level, a bubble at the tip of the main shaft. The lounge was a comfortable cylindrical room, its walls all transparent, gazing out like a continuous eye into the deep sea. Floodlights cast a glow through the cold clear water, picking out the bright speedy forms of fish, large dark predators, scythe-mouthed sharks, the occasional graceful bow of a porpoise, the elegant black-and-white presence of a killer whale. As the radius of visibility increased, the light filtered through bluer and bluer, until finally, in violet, vague shapes eased back and forth with shy curiosity between dim illumination and complete darkness. The lounge, sculpted with plastic foam and carpeted, gave the illusion of being underwater, on the ocean floor itself, a part of the sea. It had not been built originally as a lounge for crew alone, but was taken over by unconscious agreement among the starship people. Outsiders were not rejected, but gently ignored. Feeling unwelcome, they soon departed. Journalists came infrequently, reacting to sensation or disaster. Human pilots had been a sensation, but Laenea was in the second pilot group; the novelty had worn away. She did not mind a bit.

Laenea took off her boots and left them by the stairwell. She recognized one of the other pairs: she would have been hard put not to recognize those boots after seeing them once. The scarlet leather was stupendously shined, embroidered with jewels, and inlaid with tiny liquid crystal-filled discs that changed color with the temperature. Laenea smiled. Crew members made up for the dead time of transit in many different ways; one was to overdo all other aspects of their lives, and the most flamboyant of that group was Minoru.

Walking barefoot in the deep carpet, between the hillocks and hollows of converstion pits, was like walking on the sea floor idealized. Laenea thought that the attraction of the lounge was its relation to the mystery of the sea, for the sea still held mysteries perhaps as deep as any she would encounter in space or in transit. No one but the pilots could even guess at the truth of her assumption, but Laenea had often sat gazing through the shadowed water, dreaming. Soon she too would know; she would not have to imagine any longer.

She moved between small groups of people half-hidden in the recesses of the conversation pits. Near the transparent sea wall she saw Minoru, his black hair braided with scarlet and silver to his waist; tall Alannai hunched down to be closer to the others, the light on her skin like dark opal, glinting in her close-cropped hair like diamond dust; and pale, quiet Ruth, whose sparkling was rare but nova bright. Holding goblets or mugs, they sat sleepily conversing, and Laenea felt the comfort of a familiar scene.

Minoru, facing her, glanced up. She smiled, expecting him to cry out her name and fling out his arms, as he always did, with his ebullient greeting, showing to advantage the fringe and beadwork on his jacket. But he looked at her, straight on, silent, with an expression so blank that only the unlined long-lived youthfulness of his face could have held it. He whispered her name. Ruth looked over her shoulder and smiled tentatively, as though she were afraid. Alannai unbent, and, head and shoulders above the others, raised her glass solemnly to Laenea. "Pilot," she said, and drank, and hunched back down with her elbows on her sharp knees. Laenea stood above them, outside their circle, looking down on three people whom she had kissed goodbye. Crew always said goodbye, for they slept through their voyages without any certainty that they would ever awaken. They lived in the cruel childhood prayer: "If I should die before I wake . . ."

Laenea climbed down to them. The circle opened, but she did not enter it. She was as overwhelmed by uncertainty as her friends.

"Sit with us," Ruth said finally. Alannai and Minoru looked uneasy but did not object. Laenea sat down. The triangle between Ruth and Alannai and Minoru did not alter. Each of them was next to the other; Laenea was beside none of them.

Ruth reached out, but her hand trembled. They all waited, and Laenea tried to think of words to reassure them, to affirm that she had not changed.

But she had changed. She realized the surgeon had cut more than skin and muscle and bone.

"I came . . ." But nothing she felt seemed right to tell them. She would not taunt them with her freedom. She took Ruth's outstretched hand. "I came to say goodbye." She embraced them and kissed them and climbed back to the main level. They had all been friends, but they could accept each other no longer.

The first pilots and crew did not mingle, for the responsibility was great, the tensions greater. But Laenea already cared for Ruth and Minoru and Alannai. Her concern would remain when she watched them sleeping and ferried them from one island of light to the next. She understood why she was perpetuating the separation even less than she understood her friends' reserve.

Conversations ebbed and flowed around her like the tides as she moved throught the lounge. Seeing people she knew, she avoided them, and she did not try to join an unfamiliar group. Her pride far exceeded her loneliness.

She put aside the pain of her rejection. She felt self-contained and self-assured. When she recognized two pilots, sitting together, isolated, she approached them straightforwardly. She had flown with both of them, but never talked at length with either. They would accept her, or they would not: for the moment, she did not care. She flung back the cloak so they would know her, and realized quite suddenly—with a shock of amused surprise at what she had never noticed consciously before—that all pilots dressed as she had dressed.

Laced vest or deeply cut gowns, transparent shirts, halters, all in one way or another revealed the long scar that marked their changes.

Miikala and Ramona-Teresa sat facing each other, elbows on knees, talking together quietly, privately. Even the rhythms of their conversation seemed alien to Laenea, though she could not hear their words. Like other people they communicated as much with their bodies and hands as with speech, but the nods and gestures clashed.

Laenea wondered what pilots talked about. Certainly it could not be the ordinary concerns of ordinary people, the laundry, the shopping, a place to stay, a person, perhaps, to stay with. They would talk about . . . the experiences they alone had; they would talk about what they saw when all others must sleep near death or die.

Human pilots withstood transit better than machine intelligence, but human pilots too were sometimes lost. Miikala and Ramona-Teresa were ten percent of all the pilots who survived from the first generation, ten percent of their own unique, evolving, almost self-contained society. As Laenea stopped on the edge of the pit above them, they fell silent and gazed solemnly up at her.

Ramona-Teresa, a small, heavy-set woman with raven-black hair graying to roan, smiled and lifted her glass. "Pilot!" Miikala, whose eyes were shadowed by heavy brow ridges and an unruly shock of dark brown hair, matched the salute and drank with her.

This toast was a tribute and a welcome, not a farewell. Laenea was a part of the second wave of pilots, one who would follow the original experiment and make it work practically, now that Miikala and Ramona-Teresa and the others had proven time-independence successful by example. Laenea smiled and lowered herself into the pit. Miikala touched her left wrist, Ramona-Teresa her right. Laenea felt, welling up inside her, a bubbling, childish giggle. She could not stop it; it broke free as if filled wth helium like a balloon. "Hello," she said, and even her voice was high. She might have been in an Environment on the sea floor, breathing oxy-helium and speaking Donald Duck. She felt the blood rushing through the veins in her temples and her throat. Miikala was smiling, saying something in a language with as many liquid vowels as his name; she did not understand a word, yet she knew everything he was saying. Ramona-Teresa hugged her. "Welcome, child."

Laenea could not believe that these lofty, eerie people could accept her with such joy. She realized she had hoped, at best, for a cool and condescending greeting not too destructive of her pride. The embarrassing giggle slipped up and out again, but this time she did not try to stifle it. All three pilots laughed together. Laenea felt high, light, dizzy: excitement pumped adrenalin through her body. She was hot and she could feel tiny beads of perspiration gather on her forehead, just at the hairline.

Quite suddenly the constant dull ache in her chest became a wrenching pain, as though her new heart were being ripped from her, like the old. She could not breathe. She hunched forward, struggling for air, oblivious to the pilots and all the beautiful surroundings. Each time she tried to draw in a breath, the pain drove it out again.

Slowly Miikala's easy voice slipped beyond her panic, and Ramona-Teresa's hands steadied her.

"Relax, relax, remember your training . . ."

Yes: decrease the blood flow, open up the arteries, dilate all the tiny capillaries, feel the involuntary muscles responding to voluntary control. Slow the pump. Someone bathed her forehead with a cocktail napkin dipped in gin. Laenea welcomed the coolness and even the odor's bitter tang. The pain dissolved gradually until Ramona-Teresa could ease her back on the sitting shelf, onto the cushioned carpet, out of a protective near-fetal position. The jet fastening of the cloak fell away from her throat and the older pilot loosened the laces of her vest.

"It's all right," Ramona-Teresa said. "The adrenalin works as well as ever. We all have to learn more control of that than they think they need to teach us."

Sitting on his heels beside Laenea, Miikala glanced at the exposed bright scar. "You're out early," he said. "Have they changed the procedure?"

Laenea paled: she had forgotten that her leavetaking of hospitals was something less than official and approved.

"Don't tease her, Miikala," Ramona-Teresa said gruffly. "Or don't you remember how it was when you woke up?"

His heavy eyebrows drew together in a scowl. "I remember."

"Will they make me go back?" Laenea asked. "I'm all right, I just need to get used to it."

"They might try to," Ramona-Teresa said. "They worry so

about the money they spend on us. Perhaps they aren't quite so worried anymore. We do as well on our own as shut up in their ugly hospitals listening to recorded hearts—do they still do that?"

Laenea shuddered. "It worked for you, they told me—but I broke the speaker."

Miikala laughed with delight. "Causing all other machines to make frantic noises like frightened little mice."

"I thought they hadn't done the operation. I wanted to be one of you so long—" Feeling stronger, Laenea pushed herself up. She left her vest open, glad of the cool air against her skin.

"We watched," Miikala said. "We watch you all, but a few are special. We knew you'd come to us. Do you remember this one, Ramona?"

"Yes." She picked up one of the extra glasses, filled it from a shaker, and handed it to Laenea. "You always fought the sleep, my dear. Sometimes I thought you might wake."

"Ahh, Ramona, don't frighten the child."

"Frighten her, this tigress?"

Strangely enough, Laenea was not disturbed by the knowledge that she had been close to waking in transit. She had not, or she would be dead; she would have died quickly of old age, her body bound to normal time and normal space, to the relation between time-dilation and velocity and distance by a billion years of evolution, rhythms planetary, lunar, solar, biological: subatomic, for all Laenea or anyone else knew. She was freed of all that now.

She downed half her drink in a single swallow. The air now felt cold against her bare arms and her breasts, so she wrapped her cloak around her shoulders and waited for the satin to warm against her body.

"When do you get your ship?"

"Not for a month." The time seemed a vast expanse of emptiness. She had finished the study and the training; now only her mortal body kept her earthbound.

"They want you completely healed."

"It's too long—how can they expect me to wait until then?"

"For the need."

"I want to know what happens, I have to find out. When's your next flight?"

"Soon," Ramona-Teresa said.

"Take me with you!"

"No, my dear. It would not be proper."

"Proper! We have to make our own rules, not follow theirs. They don't know what's right for us."

Miikala and Ramona-Teresa looked at each other for a long time. Perhaps they spoke to each other with eyes and expressions, but Laenea could not understand.

"No." Ramona's tone invited no argument.

"At least you can tell me—" She saw at once that she had said the wrong thing. The pilots' expressions closed down in silence. But Laenea did not feel guilt or contrition, only anger.

"It isn't because you can't! You talk about it to each other, I know that now at least. You can't tell me you don't."

"No," Miikala said. "We will not say we never speak of it."

"You're selfish and you're cruel." She stood up, momentarily afraid she might stagger again and have to accept their help. But as Ramona and Miikala nodded at each other, with faint, infuriating smiles, Laenea felt the lightness and the silent bells overtaking her.

"She has the need," one of them said, Laenea did not even know which one. She turned her back on them, climbed out of the conversation pit, and stalked away.

The sitting-place she chose nestled her into a steep slope very close to the sea wall. She could feel the coolness of the glass, as though it, not heat, radiated. Grotesque creatures floated past in the spotlights. Laenea relaxed, letting her smooth pulse wax and wane. She wondered, if she sat in this pleasant place long enough, if she would be able to detect the real tides, if the same drifting plant-creatures passed again and again, swept back and forth before the window of the stabilizer by the forces of sun and moon.

Her privacy was marred only slightly, by one man sleeping or lying unconscious nearby. She did not recognize him, but he must be crew. His dark, close-fitting clothes were unremarkably different enough, in design and fabric, that he might be from another world. He must be new. Earth was the hub of commerce; no ship flew long without orbiting it. New crew members always visited at least once. New crew usually visited every world their ships reached at first, if they had the time for quarantine. Laenea had done the same herself. But the quarantines were so severe and so necessary that she, like most other veterans, eventually remained acclimated to one world, stayed on the ship during other planetfalls, and arranged her pattern to intersect her home as frequently as possible.

The sleeping man was a few years younger than Laenea. She thought he must be as tall as she, but that estimation was difficult. He was one of those uncommon people so beautifully proportioned that from any distance at all their height can only be determined by comparison. Nothing about him was exaggerated or attenuated; he gave the impression of strength, but it was the strength of litheness and agility, not violence. Laenea decided he was neither drunk nor drugged but asleep. His face, though relaxed, showed no dissipation. His hair was dark blond and shaggy, a shade lighter than his heavy mustache. He was far from handsome: his features were regular, distinctive, but without beauty. Below the cheekbones his tanned skin was scarred and pitted, as though from some virulent childhood disease. Some of the outer worlds had not yet conquered their epidemics.

Laenea looked away from the new young man. She stared at the dark water wall at light's-end, letting her vision double and unfocus. She touched her collarbone and slid her fingers to the tip of the smooth scar. Sensation seemed refined across the tissue, as though a wound there would hurt more sharply. Though Laenea was tired and getting hungry she did not force herself to outrun the distractions. For a while her energy should return slowly and naturally. She had pushed herself far enough for one night.

A month would be an eternity; the wait would seem equivalent to all the years she had spent crewing. She was still angry at the other pilots. She felt she had acted like a little puppy, bounding up to them to be welcomed and patted, then, when they grew bored, they had kicked her away as though she had piddled on the floor. And she was angry at herself: she felt a fool and she felt the need to prove herself.

For the first time she appreciated the destruction of time during transit. To sleep for a month: convenient, impossible. She first must deal with her new existence, her new body; then she would deal with a new environment.

Perhaps she dozed. The deep sea admitted no time: the lights pierced the same indigo darkness day or night. Time was the least real of all dimensions to Laenea's people, and she was free of its dictates, isolated from its stabilities.

When she opened her eyes again she had no idea how long they had been closed, a second or an hour.

The time must have been a few minutes, at least; for the young man who had been sleeping was now sitting up, watching her. His eyes were dark blue, black-flecked, a color like the sea. For a moment he did not notice she was awake, then their gazes met and he glanced quickly away, blushing, embarrassed to be caught staring.

"I stared, too," Laenea said.

Startled, he turned slowly back, not quite sure Laenea was speaking to him. "What?"

"When I was a grounder, I stared at crew, and when I was crew I stared at pilots."

"I *am* crew," he said defensively.

"From—?"

"Twilight."

Laenea knew she had been there, a long while before; images of Twilight drifted to her. It was a new world, a dark and mysterious place of hight mountains and black, brooding forests, a young world, its peaks just formed. It was heavily wreathed in clouds that filtered out much of the visible light but admitted the ultraviolet. Twilight: dusk, on that world. Never dawn. No one who had ever visited Twilight would think its dimness heralded anything but night. The people who lived there were strong and solemn, even confronting disaster. On Twilight she had seen grief, death, loss, but never panic or despair.

Laenea introduced herself and offered the young man a place nearer her own. He moved closer, reticent. "I am Radu Dracul," he said.

The name touched a faint note in her memory. She followed it until it grew loud enough to identify. She glanced over Radu Dracul's shoulder, as though looking for someone. "Then—where's Vlad?"

Radu laughed, changing his somber expression for the first time. He had good teeth, and deep smile lines that paralleled the drooping sides of his mustache. "Wherever he is, I hope he stays there."

They smiled together.

"This is your first tour?"

"Is it so obvious I'm a novice?"

"You're alone," she said. "And you were sleeping."

"I don't know anyone here. I was tired," he said, quite reasonably.

"After a while . . ." Laenea nodded toward a nearby group of people, hyper and shrill on sleep repressors and energizers. "You don't sleep when you're on the ground when there are people to talk to, when there are other things to do. You get sick of sleep, you're scared of it."

Radu stared toward the ribald group that stumbled its way toward the elevator. "Do all of us become like them?" He held his low voice emotionless.

"Most."

"The sleeping drugs are bad enough. They're necessary, everyone says. But that—" He shook his head slowly. His forehead was smooth except for two parallel vertical lines that appeared between his eyebrows when he frowned; it was below his cheekbones, to the square-angled corner of his jaw, that his skin was scarred.

"No one will force you," Laenea said. She was tempted to reach out and touch him; she would have liked to stroke his face from temple to chin, and smooth a lock of hair rumpled by sleep. But he was unlike other people she had met, whom she could touch and hug and go to bed with on short acquaintance and mutual whim. Radu had about him something withdrawn and protected, almost mysterious, an invisible wall that would only be strengthened by an attempt to broach it, however gentle. He carried himself, he spoke, defensively.

"But you think I'll choose it myself."

"It doesn't always happen," Laenea said, for she felt he needed reassurance; yet she also felt the need to defend herself and her former colleagues. "We sleep so much in transit, and it's such a dark time, it's so empty . . ."

"Empty? What about the dreams?"

"I never dreamed."

"I always do," he said. "Always."

"I wouldn't have minded transit time so much if I'd ever dreamed."

Understanding drew Radu from his reserve. "I can see how it might be."

Laenea thought of all the conversations she had had with all the other crew she had known. The silent emptiness of their sleep was the single constant of all their experiences. "I don't know anyone else like you. You're very lucky."

A tiny luminous fish nosed up against the sea wall. Laenea reached out and tapped the glass, leading the fish in a simple pattern drawn with her fingertip.

"I'm hungry," she said abruptly. "There's a good restaurant in the Point Stabilizer. Will you come?"

"A restaurant—where people . . . buy food?"

"Yes."

"I am not hungry."

He was a poor liar; he hesitated before the denial, and he did not meet Laenea's glance.

"What's the matter?"

"Nothing." He looked at her again, smiling slightly: that at least was true, that he was not worried.

"Are you going to stay her all night?"

"It isn't night, it's nearly morning."

"A room's more comfortable—you were asleep."

He shrugged; she could see she was making him uneasy. She realized he must not have any money. "Didn't your credit come through? That happens all the time. I think chimpanzees write the bookkeeping programs." She had gone through the red tape and annoyance of emergency credit several times when her transfers were misplaced or miscoded. "All you have to do—"

"The administration made no error in my case."

Laenea waited for him to explain or not, as he wished. Suddenly he grinned, amused at himself but not self-deprecating. He looked even younger than he must be, when he smiled like that. "I'm not used to using money for anything but . . . unnecessaries."

"Luxuries?"

"Yes, things we don't often use on Twilight, things I do not need. But food, a place to sleep—" He shrugged again. "They are always freely given on colonial worlds. When I got to Earth, I forgot to arrange a credit transfer." He was blushing faintly. "I won't forget again. I miss a meal and one night's sleep—I've missed more on Twilight, when I was doing real work. In a few hours I correct my error."

"There's no need to go hungry now," Laenea said. "You can—"

"I respect your customs," Radu said. "But my people never borrow and we never take what is unwillingly given."

Laenea stood up and held out her hand. "I never offer unwillingly. Come along."

His hand was warm and hard, like polished wood.

At the top of the elevator shaft, Laenea and Radu stepped out into the end of the night. It was foggy and luminous, sky and sea blending into uniform gray. No wind revealed the surface of the sea or the limits of the fog, but the air was cold.

Laenea swung the cloak around them both. A light rain, almost invisible, drifted down, beading mistily in tiny brilliant drops on the black velvet and on Radu's hair. He was silver and gold in the artificial light.

"It's like Twilight now," he said. "It rains like this in the winter." He stretched out his arm, with the black velvet draping down like quiescent wings, opened his palm to the rain, and watched the minuscule droplets touch his fingertips. Laenea could tell from the yearning in his voice, the wistfulness, that he was painfully, desperately homesick. She said nothing, for she knew from experience that nothing could be said to help. The pain faded only with time and fondness for other places. Earth as yet had given Radu no cause for fondness. But now he stood gazing into the fog, as though he could see continents, or stars. She slipped her arm around his shoulders in a gesture of comfort.

"We'll walk to the Point." Laenea had been enclosed in testing and training rooms and hospitals as he had been confined in ships and quarantine: she, too, felt the need for fresh air and rain and the ocean's silent words.

The sidewalk edged the port's shore; only a rail separated it from a drop of ten meters to the sea. Incipient waves caressed the metal cliff obliquely, sliding into darkness. Laenea and Radu walked slowly along, matching strides. Every few paces their hips brushed together. Laenea glanced at Radu occasionally and wondered how she could have thought him anything but beautiful. Her heart circled slowly in her breast, low-pitched, relaxing, and her perceptions faded from fever clarity to misty dark and soothing. A veil seemed to surround and protect her. She became aware that Radu was gazing at her, more than she watched him. The cold touched them through the cloak, and they moved closer together; it seemed only sensible for Radu to put his arm around her too, and so they walked, clasped together.

"Real work," Laenea said, musing.

"Yes . . . hard work with hands or minds." He picked up the second possible branch of their previous conversation as though it had never gone in any other direction. "We do the work ourselves. Twilight is too new for machines—they evolved here, and they aren't as adaptable as people."

Laenea, who had endured unpleasant situations in which machines did not perform as intended, understood what he meant. Older methods than automation were more economical on new worlds where the machines had to be designed from the beginning but people only had to learn. Evolution was as good an analogy as any.

"Crewing's work. Maybe it doesn't strain your muscles, but it is work."

"One never gets tired. Physically or mentally. The job has no challenges."

"Aren't the risks enough for you?"

"Not random risks," he said. "It's like gambling."

His background made him a harsh judge, harshest with himself. Laenea felt a tinge of self-contempt in his words, a gray shadow across his independence.

"It isn't slave labor, you know. You could quit and go home."

"I wanted to come—" He cut off the protest. "I thought it would be different."

"I know," Laenea said. "You think it will be exciting, but after a while all that's left is a dull kind of danger."

"I did want to visit other places. To be like—in that I was selfish."

"Ahh, stop. Selfish? No one would do it otherwise."

"Perhaps not. But I had a different vision. I remembered—" Again, he stopped himself in mid-sentence.

"What?"

He shook his head. "Nothing." Laenea had thought his reserve was dissolving, but all his edges hardened again. "We spend most of our time carrying trivial cargoes for trivial reasons to trivial people."

"The trivial cargoes pay for the emergencies."

Radu shook his head. "That isn't right."

"That's the way it's always been."

"On Twilight . . ." He went no further; the guarded tone had disappeared.

"You're drawn back." Laenea said. "More than anyone I've known before. It must be a comfort to love a place so much."

At first he tensed, as if he were afraid she would mock or chide him for weakness, or laugh at him. The tense muscles relaxed slowly. "I feel better, after flights when I dream about home."

The fortunate dreamer: if Laenea had still been crew she would have envied him. "Is it your family you miss?"

"I have no family—I still miss them sometimes, but they're gone."

"I'm sorry."

"You couldn't know," he said quickly, almost too quickly, as though he might have hurt her rather than the other way around. "They were good people, my clan. The epidemic killed them."

Laenea gently tightened her arm around his shoulder in silent comfort.

"I don't know what it is about Twilight that binds us all," Radu said. "I suppose it must be the combination—the challenge and the result. Everything is new. We try to touch the world gently. So many things could go wrong."

He glanced at her, his eyes deep as a mountain lake, his face solemn in its strength, asking without words a question Laenea did not understand.

The air was cold. It entered her lungs and spread through her chest, her belly, arms, legs . . . she imagined that the machine was cold metal, sucking the heat from her as it circled in its silent patterns. Laenea was tired.

"What's that?"

She glanced up. They were near the midpoint of the port's edge, nearing lights shining vaguely through the fog. The amorphous pink glow resolved itself into separate globes and torches. Laenea noticed a high metallic hum. Within two paces the air cleared.

The tall frames of fog-catchers reared up, leading inward to the lights in concentric circles. The long wires, touched by the wind, vibrated musically. The fog, touched by the wires, condensed. Water dripped from wires' tips to the platform. The intermittent sound of heavy drops on metal, like rain, provided irregular rhythm for the faint music.

"Just a party," Laenea said. The singing, glistening wires formed a multilayered curtain, each layer transparent but in combination translucent and shimmering. Laenea moved between them, but Radu, hanging back, slowed her.

"What's the matter?"

"I don't wish to go where I haven't been invited."

"You are invited. We're all invited. Would you stay away from a party at your own house?"

Radu frowned, not understanding. Laenea remembered her own days as a novice of the crew; becoming used to one's new status took time.

"They come here for us," Laenea said. "They come hoping we'll stop and talk to them and eat their food and drink their liquor. Why else come here?" She gestured—it was meant to be a sweeping movement, but she stopped her hand before the apex of its arc, flinching at the strain on her cracked ribs—toward the party, lights and tables, a tasseled pavilion, the fog-catchers, the people in evening costume, servants and machines. "Why else bring all this here? They could be on a tropical island or under the Redwoods. They could be on a mountaintop or on a desert at dawn. But they're here, and I assure you they'll welcome us."

"You know the customs," Radu said, if a little doubtfully.

When they passed the last ring of fog-catchers the temperature began to rise. The warmth was a great relief. Laenea let the damp velvet cape fall away from her shoulders and Radu did the same. A very young man, almost still a boy, smooth-cheeked and wide-eyed, appeared to take the cloak for them. He stared at them both, curious, speechless; he saw the tip of the scar between Laenea's breasts and looked at her in astonishment and admiration. "Pilot . . ." he said. "Welcome, Pilot."

"Thank you. Whose gathering is this?"

The boy, now speechless, glanced over his shoulder and gestured.

Kathell Stafford glided toward them, holding out her hands to Laenea. The white tiger followed.

Gray streaked Kathell's hair, like the silver thread woven into her blue silk gown, but her eyes were as dark and young as ever. Laenea had not seen her in several years, many voyages. They clasped hands, Laenea amazed as always by the delicacy of Kathell's bones. Veins glowed blue beneath her light brown skin. Laenea had no idea how old she was. Except for the streaks of gray, she was just the same.

"My dear, I heard you were in training. You must be very pleased."

"Relieved," Laenea said. "They never know for sure if it will work till afterward."

"Come join us, you and your friend."

"This is Radu Dracul of Twilight."

Kathell greeted him, and Laenea saw Radu relax and grow comfortable in the presence of the tiny self-possessed woman. Even a party on the sidewalk of the world's largest port could be her home, where she made guests welcome.

The others, quick to sense novelty, began to drift nearer, most seeming to have no particular direction in mind. Laenea had seen all the ways of approaching crew or pilots: the shyness or bravado or undisguised awe of children; the unctuous familiarity of some adults; the sophisticated nonchalance of the rich. Then there were the people Laenea seldom met, who looked at her, saw her, across a street or across a room, whose expressions said aloud: *She has walked on other worlds; she has traveled through a place I shall never even approach.* Those people looked, and looked reluctantly away, and returned to their business, allowing Laenea and her kind to proceed unmolested. Some crew members never knew they existed. The most interesting people, the sensitive and intelligent and nonintrusive ones, were those one seldom met.

Kathell was one of the people Laenea would never have met, except that she had young cousins in the crew. Otherwise she was unclassifiable. She was rich, and used her wealth lavishly to entertain her friends, as now, and for her own comfort. But she had more purpose than that. The money she used for play was nothing compared to the totality of her resources. She was a student as well as a patron, and the energy she could give to work provided her with endurance and concentration beyond that of anyone else Laenea had ever met. There was no sycophancy in either direction about their fondness for each other.

Laenea recognized few of the people clustering behind Kathell. She stood looking out at them, down a bit on most, and she almost wished she had led Radu around the fog-catchers instead of between them. She did not feel ready for the effusive greetings due a pilot; she did not feel she had earned them. The guests outshone her in every way, in beauty, in dress, in knowledge, yet they wanted her, they needed her, to touch what was denied them.

She could see the passage of time, one second after another, that quickly, in their faces. Quite suddenly she was overcome by pity.

Kathell introduced people to her. Laenea knew she would not remember one name in ten, but she nodded and smiled. Nearby Radu made polite and appropriate responses. Someone handed Laenea a glass of champagne. People clustered around her, waiting for her to talk. She found that she had no more to say to them than to those she left behind in the crew.

A man came closer, smiling, and shook her head. "I've always wanted to meet an Aztec . . ."

His voice trailed off at Laenea's frown. She did not want to be churlish to a friend's guests, so she put aside her annoyance. "Just 'pilot,' please."

"But Aztecs—"

"The Axtecs sacrificed their captives' hearts," Laenea said. "We don't feel we've made a sacrifice."

She smiled and turned away, ending the conversation before he could press forward with a witty comment. The crowd was dense behind her, pressing in, all rich, free, trapped human beings. Laenea shivered and wished them away. She wanted quiet and solitude.

Suddenly Kathell was near, stretching out her hand. Laenea grasped it. For Kathell, Kathell and her tiger, the guests parted like water. But Kathell was in front. Laenea grinned and followed in her friend's wake. She saw Radu and called to him. He nodded; in a moment he was beside her, and they moved through regions of fragrances: mint, carnation, pine, musk, orange blossom. The boundaries were sharp between the odors.

Inside the pavilion, the three of them were alone. Laenea immediately felt warmer, though she knew the temperature was probably the same outside in the open party. But the tent walls, though busily patterned and self-luminous, made her feel enclosed and protected from the cold vast currents of the sea.

She sat gratefully in a soft chair. The white tiger laid his chin on Laenea's knee and she stroked his huge head.

"You look exhausted, my dear," Kathell said. She put a glass in her hand. Laena sipped from it: warm milk punch. A hint that she should be in bed.

"I just got out of the hospital," she said. "I guess I overdid it a little. I'm not used to—" She gestured with her free hand, meaning: everything. My new body, being outside and free again . . . this man beside me. She closed her eyes against blurring vision.

"Stay awhile," Kathell said, as always understanding much more than was spoken. Laenea did not try to answer; she was too comfortable, too sleepy.

"Have you eaten?" Kathell's voice sounded far away. The words, directed elsewhere, existed alone and separate, meaningless. Laenea slowed her heart and relaxed the arterial constricting muscles. Blood flowing through the dilated capillaries made her blush, and she felt warmer.

"She was going to take me to . . . a restaurant," Radu said.

"Have you never been to one?" Kathell's amusement was

never hurtful. It emerged too obviously from good humor and the ability to accept rather than fear differences.

"There is no such thing on Twilight."

Laenea thought they said more, but the words drowned in the murmer of guests' voices and wind and sea. She felt only the softness of the cushions beneath her, the warm fragrant air, and the fur of the white tiger.

Time passed, how much or at what rate Laenea had no idea. She slept gratefully and unafraid, deeply, dreaming, and hardly roused when she was moved. She muttered something and was reassured, but never remembered the words, only the tone. Wind and cold touched her and were shut out; she felt a slight acceleration. Then she slept again.

Laenea half woke, warm, warm to her center. A recent dream swam into her consciousness and out again, leaving no trace but the memory of its passing. She closed her eyes and relaxed, to remember it if it would come, but she could recall only that it was a dream of piloting a ship in transit. The details she could not perceive. Not yet. She was left with a comfortless excitement that upset her drowsiness. The machine in her chest purred fast and seemed to give off heat, though that was impossible as that it might chill her blood.

The room around her was dim; she did not know where she was except that it was not the hospital. The smells were wrong; her first perceptions were neither astringent antiseptics nor cloying drugs but faint perfume. The sensation against her skin was not coarse synthetic but silky cotton. Between her eyelashes reflections glinted from the ceiling. She realized she was in Kathell's apartment in the Point Stabilizer.

She pushed herself up on her elbows. Her ribs creaked like old parquet floors, and deep muscle aches spread from the center of her body to her shoulders, her arms, her legs. She made a sharp sound, more of surprise than of pain. She had driven herself too hard: she needed rest, not activity. She let herself sink slowly back into the big red bed, closing her eyes and drifting back toward sleep. She heard the rustling and sliding of two different fabrics rubbed one against the other, but did not react to the sound.

"Are you all right?"

The voice would have startled her if she had not been so

nearly asleep again. She opened her eyes and found Radu standing near, his jacket unbuttoned, a faint sheen of sweat on his bare chest and forehead. The concern on his face matched the worry in his voice.

Laenea smiled, "You're still here." She had assumed without thinking that he had gone on his way, to see and do all the interesting things that attracted visitors on their first trip to Earth.

"Yes," he said. "Of course."

"You didn't need to stay . . ." But she did not want him to leave.

His hand on her forehead felt cool and soothing. "I think you have a fever. Is there someone I should call?"

Laenea thought for a moment, or rather felt, lying still and making herself receptive to her body's signals. Her heart was spinning much too fast; she calmed and slowed it, wondering again what adventure had occurred in her dream. Nothing else was amiss; her lungs were clear; her hearing sharp. She slid her hand between her breasts to touch the scar: smooth and body-temperature, no infection.

"I overtired myself," she said. "That's all. . . ." Sleep was overtaking her again, but curiosity disturbed her ease. "Why did you stay?"

"Because," he said slowly, sounding very far away, "I wanted to stay with you. I remember you . . ."

She wished she knew what he was talking about, but at last the warmth and drowsiness were stronger lures than her curiosity.

When Laenea woke again, she woke completely. The aches and pains had faded in the night—or in the day, for she had no idea how long she had slept, or even how late at night or early in the morning she had visited Kathell's party.

She was in her favorite room in Kathell's apartment, one gaudier than the others. Though Laenea did not indulge in much personal adornment, she liked the scarlet and gold of the room, its intrusive energy, its Dionysian flavor. Even the aquaria set in the walls were inhabited by fish gilt with scales and jeweled with luminescence. Laenea felt the honest glee of compelling shapes and colors. She sat up and threw off the blankets, stretching and yawning in pure animal pleasure. Then, seeing Radu asleep, sprawled in the red velvet pillow chair, she fell silent, surprised, not wishing to wake him. She slipped quietly out of bed, pulled on a robe from the closet, and padded into the bathroom.

Comfortable, bathed, and able to breathe properly for the first time since her operation, Laenea returned to the bedroom. She had removed the strapping in order to shower; as her cracked ribs hurt no more free than bandaged, she did not bother to replace the tape.

Radu was awake.

"Good morning."

"It's not quite midnight," he said, smiling.

"Of what day?"

"You slept what was left of last night and all today. The others left on Kathell Stafford's zeppelin, but she wished you well and said you were to use this place as long as you wanted."

Though Kathell was as fascinated with rare people as with rare animals, her curiosity was untainted by possessiveness. She had no need of pilots, or indeed of anyone, to enhance her status. She gave her patronage with affection and friendship, not as tacit purchase. Laenea reflected that she knew people who would have done almost anything for Kathell, yet she knew no one of whom Kathell had ever asked a favor.

"How in the world did you get me here? Did I walk?"

"We didn't want to wake you. One of the large serving carts was empty so we lifted you onto it and pushed you here."

Laenea laughed. "You should have folded a flower in my hands and pretended you were at a wake."

"Someone did make that suggestion."

"I wish I hadn't been asleep—I would have liked to see the expressions of the grounders when we passed."

"Your being awake would have spoiled the illusion," Radu said.

Laenea laughed again, and this time he joined her.

As usual, clothes of all styles and sizes hung in the large closets. Laenea ran her hand across a row of garments, stopping when she touched a pleasurable texture. The first shirt she found near her size was deep green velvet with bloused sleeves. She slipped it on and buttoned it up to her breastbone, no farther.

"I still owe you a restaurant meal," she said to Radu.

"You owe me nothing at all," he said, much too seriously.

She buckled her belt with a jerk and shoved her feet into her boots, annoyed. "You don't even know me, but you stayed with me and took care of me for the whole first day of your first trip to Earth. Don't you think I should—don't you think it would be friendly for me to give you a meal?" She glared at him. "Willingly?"

He hesitated, startled by her anger. "I would find great pleasure," he said slowly, "in accepting that gift." He met Laenea's gaze, and when it softened he smiled again, tentatively. Laenea's exasperation melted and flowed away.

"Come along, then," she said to him for the second time. He rose from the pillow chair, quickly and awkwardly. None of Kathell's furniture was designed for a person his height or Laenea's. She reached to help him; they joined hands.

The Point Stabilizer was itself a complete city in two parts, one, a blatant tourist world, the second a discrete and interesting permanent supporting society. Laenea often experimented with restaurants here, but this time she went to one she knew well. Experiments in the Point were not always successful. Quality spanned as wide a spectrum as culture.

Marc's had been fashionable a few years before, and now was not, but its proprietor seemed unperturbed by cycles of fashion. Pilots or princes, crew members or diplomats could come and go; Marc did not care. Laenea led Radu into the dim foyer of the restaurant and touched the signal button. In a few moments a screen before them brightened into a pattern like oil paint on water. "Hello, Marc," Laenea said. "I didn't have a chance to make a reservation, I'm afraid."

The responding voice was mechanical and harsh, initially unpleasant, difficult to understand without experience. Laenea no longer found it ugly or indecipherable. The screen brightened into yellow with the pleasure Marc could not express vocally. "I can't think of any punishment terrible enough for such a sin, so I'll have to pretend you called."

"Thank you, Marc."

"It's good to see you back after so long. And a pilot, now."

"It's good to be back." She drew Radu forward a step, farther into the range of the small camera. "This is Radu Dracul, of Twilight, on his first Earth landing."

"Hello, Radu Dracul. I hope you find us neither too depraved nor too dull."

"Neither one at all," Radu said.

The headwaiter appeared to take them to their table.

"Welcome," Marc said, instead of goodbye, and from drifting blues and greens the screen faded to darkness.

Their table was lit by the blue reflected glow of light diffusing into the sea, and the fish watched them like curious urchins.

"Who is Marc?"

"I don't know," Laenea said. "He never comes out, no one ever goes in. Some say he was disfigured, some that he has an incurable disease and can never be with anyone again. There are always some new rumors. But he never talks about himself and no one would invade his privacy by asking."

"People must have a higher regard for privacy on Earth than elsewhere," Radu said drily, as though he had had considerable experience with prying questions.

Laenea knew boorish people too, but had never thought about their possible effect on Marc. She realized that the least considerate of her acquaintances seldom come here, and that she had never met Marc until the third or fourth time she had come. "It's nothing about the people. He protects himself," she said, knowing it was true.

She handed him a menu and opened her own. "What would you like to eat?"

"I'm to choose from this list?"

"Yes."

"And then?"

"And then someone cooks it, then someone else brings it to you."

Radu glanced down at the menu, shaking his head slightly, but he made no comment.

"Do you wish to order, Pilot?" At Laenea's elbow, Andrew bowed slightly.

Laenea ordered for them both, for Radu was unfamiliar with the dishes offered.

Laenea tasted the wine. It was excellent; she put down her glass and allowed Andrew to fill it. Radu watched scarlet liquid rise in crystal, staring deep.

"I should have asked if you drink wine," Laenea said. "But do at least try it."

He looked up quickly, his eyes focusing; he had not,

perhaps, been staring at the wine, but at nothing, absently. He picked up the glass, held it, sniffed it, sipped from it.

"I see now why we use wine so infrequently at home."

Laenea drank again, and again could find no fault. "Never mind, if you don't like it—"

But he was smiling. "It's what we have on Twilight that I never cared to drink. It's sea water compared to this."

Laenea was so hungry that half a glass of wine made her feel lightheaded; she was grateful when Andrew brought bowls of thick, spicy soup. Radu, too, was very hungry, or sensitive to alcohol, for his defenses began to ease. He relaxed; no longer did he seem ready to leap up, take Andrew by the arm, and ask the quiet old man why he stayed here, performing trivial services for trivial reasons and trivial people. And though he still glanced frequently at Laenea— watched her, almost—he no longer looked away when their gazes met.

She did not find his attention annoying; only inexplicable. She had been attracted to men and men to her many times, and often the attraction coincided. Radu was extremely attractive. But what he felt toward her was obviously something much stronger; whatever he wanted went far beyond sex. Laenea ate in silence for some time, finding nothing, no answers, in the depths of her own wine. The tension rose until she noticed it, peripherally at first, then clearly, sharply, almost as a discrete point separating her from Radu. He sat feigning ease, one arm resting on the table, but his soup was untouched and his hand was clenched into a fist.

"You—" she said finally.

"I—" he began simultaneously.

They both stopped. Radu looked relieved. After a moment Laenea continued.

"You came to see Earth. But you haven't even left the port. Surely you had more interesting plans than to watch someone sleep."

He glanced away, glanced back, slowly opened his fist, touched the edge of the glass with a fingertip.

"It's a prying question but I think I have the right to ask it of you."

"I wanted to stay with you," he said slowly, and Laenea remembered those words, in his voice, from her halfdream awakening.

" 'I remember you,' you said."

He blushed, spots of high color on his cheekbones. "I hoped you wouldn't remember that."

"Tell me what you meant."

"It all sounds foolish and childish and romantic."

She raised one eyebrow, questioning.

"For the last day I've felt I've been living in some kind of unbelievable dream . . ."

"Dream rather than nightmare, I hope."

"You gave me a gift I wished for for years."

"A gift? What?"

"Your hand. Your smile. Your time . . ." His voice had grown very soft and hesitant again. He took a deep breath. "When the plagues came, on Twilight, all my clan died, eight adults and the four other children. I almost died, too . . ." His fingers brushed his scarred cheek. Laenea thought he was unaware of the habit. "But the serum came, and the vaccines. I recovered. The crew of the mercy mission—"

"We stayed several weeks," Laenea said. More details of her single visit to Twilight returned: the settlement in near collapse, the desperately ill trying to attend the dying.

"You were the first crew member I ever saw, the first offworlder. You saved my people, my life—"

"Radu, it wasn't only me."

"I know. I even knew then. It didn't matter. I was sick for so long, and when I came to and knew I would live it hardly mattered. I was frightened and full of grief and lost and alone. I needed . . . someone . . . to admire. And you were there. You were the only stability in our chaos, a hero . . ." his voice trailed off in uncertainty at Laenea's smile, though she was not laughing at him. "This isn't easy for me to say."

Reaching across the table, Laenea grasped his wrist. The beat of his pulse was as alien as flame. She could think of nothing to tell him that would not sound patronizing or parental, and she did not care to speak to him in either guise. He raised his head and looked at her, searching her face. "When I joined the crew I don't think I ever believed I would meet you. I joined because it was what I always wanted to do, after . . . I never considered that I might really meet you. But I saw you, and I realized I wanted . . . to be something in your life. A friend, at best, I hoped. A shipmate, if nothing else. But—you'd become a pilot, and everyone knows pilots and crew stay apart."

"The first ones take pride in their solitude," Laenea said, for Ramona-Teresa's rejection still stung. Then she relented, for she might never have met Radu Dracul if they had accepted her completely. "Maybe they needed it."

"I saw a few pilots, before I met you. You're the only one who ever spoke to me or even glanced at me. I think . . ." He looked at her hand on his, and touched his scarred cheek again, as if he could brush the marks away. "I think I've loved you since the day you came to Twilight." He stood abruptly, but withdrew his hand gently. "I should never—"

She rose too. "Why not?"

"I have no right to . . ."

"To what?"

"To ask anything of you. To expect—" Flinching, he cut off the word. "To burden you with my hopes."

"What about my hopes?"

He was silent with incomprehension. Laenea stroked his rough cheek, once when he winced like a nervous colt, and again: the lines of strain across his forehead eased almost imperceptibly. She brushed back the errant lock of dark blond hair. "I've had less time to think of you than you of me," she said, "but I think you're beautiful, and an admirable man."

Radu smiled with little humor. "I'm not thought beautiful on Twilight."

"Then Twilight has as many fools as any other human world."

"You . . . want me to stay?"

"Yes."

He sat down again like a man in a dream. Neither spoke. Andrew appeared, to remove the soup plates and serve the main course. He was diplomatically unruffled, but not quite oblivious to Laenea and Radu's near departure. "Is everything satisfactory?"

"Very much so, Andrew. Thank you."

He bowed and smiled and pushed away the serving cart.

"Have you contracted for transit again?"

"Not yet," Radu said.

"I have a month before my proving flights." She thought of places she could take him, sights she could show him. "I thought I'd just have to endure the time—" She fell silent, for Ramona-Teresa was standing in the entrance of the restaurant, scanning the room. She saw Laenea and came toward her. Laenea waited, frowning; Radu turned, froze, struck by Ramona's compelling presence: serenity, power, determination. Laenea wondered if the older pilot had relented, but she was no longer so eager to be presented with mysteries, rather than to discover them herself.

Ramona-Teresa stopped at their table, ignoring Radu, or, rather, glancing at him, dismissing him in the same instant, and speaking to Laenea. "They want you to go back."

Laenea had almost forgotten the doctors and administrators, who could hardly take her departure as calmly as did the other pilots. "Did you tell them where I was?" She knew immediately that she had asked an unworthy question. "I'm sorry."

"They always want to teach us that they're in control. Sometimes it's easiest to let them believe they are."

"Thanks," Laenea said, "but I've had enought tests and plastic tubes." She felt very free, for whatever she did she would not be grounded: she was worth too much. No one would even censure her for irresponsibility, for everyone knew pilots were quite perfectly mad.

"Don't use your credit key."

"All right . . ." She saw how easily she could be traced, and wished she had not got out of the habit of carrying cash. "Ramona, lend me some money."

Now Ramona did look at Radu, critically. "It would be better if you came with the rest of us." Radu flushed. She was, all too obviously, not speaking to him.

"No, it wouldn't. Laenea's tone was chill. The dim blue light glinted silver from the gray in Ramona's hair as she turned back to Laenea's and reached into an inner pocket. She handed her a folded sheaf of bills. "You young ones never plan." Laenea could not be sure what she meant, and she had no chance to ask. Ramona-Teresa turned away and left.

Laenea shoved the money into her pants pocket, annoyed not so much because she had had to ask for it as because Ramona-Teresa had been so sure she would need it.

"She may be right," Radu said slowly. "Pilots, and crew—"

She touched his hand again, rubbing its back, following the ridges of strong fine bones to his wrist. "She shouldn't have been so snobbish. We're none of her business."

"She was . . . I never met anyone like her before. I felt as if I were in the presence of someone so different from me—so far beyond—that we couldn't speak together." He grinned, quick flash of strong white teeth behind his shaggy mustache, deep smile lines in his cheeks. "Even if she'd cared to." With his free hand he stroked her green velvet sleeve. She could feel the beat of his pulse, rapid and upset. As if he had closed an electrical circuit, a pleasurable chill spread up Laenea's arm.

"Radu, did you ever meet a pilot or a crew member who wasn't different from anyone you had ever met before? I haven't. We all start out that way. Transit didn't change Ramona."

He acquiesced with silence only, no more certain of the validity of her assurance than she was.

"For now it doesn't make any difference anyway," Laenea said.

The unhappiness slipped from Radu's expression, the joy came back, but uncertainty remained.

They finished their dinner quickly, in expectation, anticipation, paying insufficient attention to the excellent food. Though annoyed that she had to worry about the subject at all, Laenea considered available ways of preserving her freedom. She wished Kathell Stafford were still on the island, for she of all people could have helped. She had already helped, as usual, without even meaning to.

But the situation was hardly serious; evading the administrators as long as possible was a matter of pride and personal pleasure. "Fools . . ." she muttered.

"They may have a special reason for wanting you to go back," Radu said. Anticipation of the next month flowed through both their minds. "Some problem—some danger."

"They'd've said so."

"Then what do they want?"

"Ramona said it—they want to prove they control us." She drank the last few drops of her brandy; Radu followed suit. They rose and walked together toward the foyer. "They want to keep me packed in styrofoam like an expensive machine until I can take my ship."

Andrew awaited them, but as Laenea reached for Ramona-Teresa's money Marc's screen glowed into brilliance. "Your dinner's my gift," he said. "In celebration."

She wondered if Ramona had told him of her problem. He could as easily know from his own sources, or the free meal might be an example of his frequent generosity. "I wonder how you ever make a profit, my friend," she said. "But thank you."

"I overcharge tourists," he said, the mechanical voice so flat that it was impossible to know if he spoke cynically or sardonically or if he were simply joking.

"I don't know where I'm going next," Laenea told him, "but you are looking for anything?"

"Nothing in particular," he said. "Pretty things—" Silver swirled across the screen.

"I know."

The corridors were dazzling after the dim restaurant; Laenea wished for gentle evenings and moonlight. Between cold metal walls, she and Radu walked close together, warm, arms around each other. "Marc collects," Laenea said. "We all bring him things."

"Pretty things."

"Yes . . . I think he tries to bring the nicest bits of all the worlds inside with him. I think he creates his own reality."

"One that has nothing to do with ours."

"Exactly."

"That's what they'd do at the hospital." Radu said. "Isolate you from what you'll have to deal with, and you disagree that that would be valuable."

"Not for me. For Marc, perhaps."

He nodded. "And . . . now?"

"Back to Kathell's for a while at least." She reached up and rubbed the back of his neck. His hair tickled her hand. "The rule I disagreed with most while I was in training was the one that forbade me any sex at all."

The smile lines appeared again, bracketing his mouth parallel to his drooping mustache, crinkling the skin around his eyes. "I understand entirely," he said, "why you aren't anxious to go back."

Entering her room in Kathell's suite, Laenea turned on the lights. Mirrors reflected the glow, bright niches among red plush and gold trim. She and Radu stood together on the silver surfaces, hands clasped, for a moment as hesitant as children. Then Laenea turned to Radu, and he to her; they ignored the actions of the mirrored figures. Laenea's hands on the sides of Radu's face touched his scarred cheeks; she kissed him lightly, again, harder. His mustache was soft and bristly against her lips, against her tongue. His hands tightened over her shoulder blades, and moved down. He held her gently. She slipped one hand between their bodies, beneath his jacket, stroking his bare skin, tracing the taut muscles of his back, his waist, his hip. His breathing quickened.

At the beginning nothing was different—but nothing was the same. The change was more important than motions, positions, endearments; Leanea had experienced those in all their combinations, content with involvement for a few moments' pleasure. That had always been satisfying and sufficient; she had never suspected the potential for evolution that depended on the partners. Leaning over Radu, with her hair curling down around their faces, looking into his smiling blue eyes, she felt close enough to him to absorb his thoughts and sense his soul. They caressed each other leisurely, concentrating on the sensations between them. Laenea's nipples hardened, but instead of throbbing they tingled. Radu moved against her and her excitement heightened suddenly, irrationally, grasping her, shaking her. She gasped but could not force the breath back out. Radu kissed her shoulder, the base of her throat, stroked her stomach, drew his hand up her side, cupped her breast.

"Radu—"

Her climax was sudden and violent, a clasping wave contracting all through her as her single thrust pushed Radu's hips down against the mattress. He was startled into a climax of his own as Laenea shuddered involuntarily, straining against him, clasping him to her, unable to catch his rhythm. But neither of them cared.

They lay together, panting and sweaty.

"Is that part of it?" His voice was unsteady.

"I guess so." Her voice, too, showed the effects of surprise. "No wonder they're so quiet about it."

"Does it—is your pleasure decreased?" He was ready to be angry for her.

"No, that's not it, it's—" She started to say that the pleasure was tenfold greater, but remembered the start of their loveplay, before she had been made aware of just how many of her rhythms were rearranged. The beginning had nothing to do with the fact that she was a pilot. "It was fine." A lame adjective. "Just unexpected. And you?"

He smiled. "As you say—unexpected. Surprising. A little . . . frightening."

"Frightening."

"All new experiences are a little frightening. Even the very enjoyable ones. Or maybe those most of all."

Laenea laughed softly.

They lay wrapped in each other's arms. Laenea's hair curled around to touch the corner of Radu's jaw, and her heel was hooked over his calf. She was content for the moment with silence, stillness, touch. The plague had not scarred his body.

In the aquaria, the fish flitted back and forth before dim lights, spreading blue shadows across the bed. Laenea breathed deeply, counting to make the breaths even. Breathing is a response, not a rhythm, a reaction to levels of carbon dioxide in blood and brain; Laenea's breathing had to be altered only during transit itself. For now she used it as an artificial rhythm of concentration. Her heart raced with excitement and adrenalin, so she began to slow it, to relax. But something disturbed her control: the rate and blood pressure slid down slightly, then slowly slid back up. She could hear nothing but a dull ringing in her inner ears. Perspiration formed on her forehead, in her armpits, along her spine. Her heart had never before failed to respond to conscious control.

Angry, startled, she pushed herself up, flinging her hair back from her face. Radu raised his head, tightening his hand around the point of her shoulder. "What—?"

He might as well have been speaking underwater. Laenea lifted her hand to silence him.

One deep inhalation, hold; exhale, hold. She repeated the sequence, calming herself, relaxing voluntary muscles. Her hand fell to the bed. She lay back. Repeat the sequence, again. Again. In the hospital and since, her control over involuntary muscles had been quick and sure. She began to be afraid, and had to imagine the fear evaporating, dissipating. Finally the arterial muscles began to respond. They lengthened, loosened, expanded. Last the pump answered her commands as she recaptured and reproduced the indefinable states of self-control.

When she knew her blood pressure was no longer likely to crush her kidneys or mash her brain, she opened her eyes. Above, Radu watched, deep lines of worry across his forehead. "Are you—" He was whispering.

She lifted her heavy hand and stroked his face, his

eyebrows, his hair. "I don't know what happened. I couldn't get control for a minute. But I have it back now." She drew his hand across her body, pulling him down beside her, and they relaxed again and dozed.

Later, Laenea took time to consider her situation. Returning to the hospital would be easiest; it was also the least attractive alternative. Remaining free, adjusting without interference to the changes, meeting the other pilots, showing Radu what was to be seen: outwitting the administrators would be more fun. Kathell had done them a great favor, for without her apartment Laenea would have rented a hotel suite. The records would have been available, a polite messenger would have appeared to ask her respectfully to come along. Should she overpower an innocent hireling and disappear laughing? More likely she would have shrugged and gone. Fights had never given her either excitement or pleasure. She knew what things she would not do, ever, though she did not know what she would do now. She pondered.

"Damn them," she said.

His hair as damp as hers, after their shower, Radu sat down facing her. The couches, of course, were both too low. Radu and Laenea looked at each other across two sets of knees draped in caftans that clashed violently. Radu lay back on the cushions, chuckling. "You look much too undignified for anger."

She leaned toward him and tickled a sensitive place she had discovered. "I'll show you undignified—" He twisted away and batted at her hand but missed, laughing helplessly. When Laenea relented, she was lying on top of him on the wide, soft couch. Radu unwound from a defensive curl, watching her warily, laugh lines deep around his eyes and mouth.

"Peace," she said, and held up her hands. He relaxed. Laenea picked up a fold of the material of her caftan with one of his. "Is anything more undignified than the two of us in colors no hallucination would have—and giggling as well?"

"Nothing at all." He touched her hair, her face. "But what made you so angry?"

"The administrators—their red tape. Their infernal tests." She laughed again, this time bitterly. "'Undignified'—some of those tests would win on that."

"Are they necessary? For your health?"

She told him about the hypnotics, the sedatives, the sleep, the time she had spent being obedient. "Their redundancies have redundancies. If I weren't healthy I'd be back out on the street wearing my old heart. I'd be . . . nothing."

"Never that."

But she knew of people who had failed as pilots, who were reimplanted with their own saved hearts, and none of them had ever flown again, as pilots, as crew, as passengers. *"Nothing."*

He was shaken by her vehemence. "But you're all right. You're who you want to be and what you want to be."

"I'm angry at inconvenience," she admitted. "I want to be the one who shows you Earth. They want me to spend the next month shuttling between cinderblock cubicles. And I'll have to if they find me. My freedom's limited." She felt very strongly that she needed to spend the next month in the real world, neither hampered by experts who knew, truly, nothing, nor misdirected by controlled environments. She did not know how to explain the feeling; she thought it must be one of the things pilots tried to talk about during their hesitant, unsyncopated conversations with their insufficient vocabularies. "Yours isn't, though, you know."

"What do you mean?"

"Sometimes I come back to Earth and never leave the port. It's like my home. It has everything I want or need. I can easily stay a month and never see an administrator nor have to admit receiving a message I don't want." Her fingertips moved back and forth across the ridge of new tissue over her breastbone. Somehow it was a comfort, though the scar was the symbol of what had cut her off from her old friends. She needed new friends now, but she felt it would be stupid and unfair to ask Radu to spend his first trip to Earth on an artificial island. "I'm going to stay here. But you don't have to. Earth has a lot of sights worth seeing."

He did not answer. Laenea raised her head to look at him. He was intent and disturbed. "Would you be offended," he said, "if I told you I am not very interested in historical sights?"

"Is this what you really want? To stay with me?"

"Yes. Very much."

Laenea led Radu through the vast apartment to the swimming pool. Flagstones surrounded a pool with sides and bottom of intricate mosaic that shimmered in the dim light. This was a grotto more than a place for athletic events or children's noisy beach ball games.

Radu sighed; Laenea brushed her hand across the top of his shoulder, questioning.

"Someone spent a great deal of time and care here," he said.

"That's true." Laenea had never thought of it as the work of someone's hands, individual and painstaking, though of course it was exactly that. But the economic structure of her world was based on service, not production, and she had always taken the results for granted.

They took off their caftans and waded down the steps into body-warm water. It rose smooth and soothing around the persistent soreness of Laenea's ribs.

"I'm going to soak for a while." She lay back and floated, her hair drifting out, a starnd occasionally drifting back to brush her shoulder, the top of her spine. Radu's voice rumbled through the water, incomprehensible, but she glanced over and saw him waving toward the dim far end of the pool. He flopped down in the water and thrashed energetically away, retreating to a constant background noise. All sounds faded, gaining the same faraway quality, like audio slow-motion. Something was strange, wrong . . . Laenea began to tense up again. She turned her attention to the warmth and comfort of the water, to urging the tension out of her body through her shoulders, down her outstretched arms, out the tips of spread fingers. But when she paid attention again, something still was wrong. Tracing unease, slowly and deliberately, going back so far in memory that she was no longer a pilot (it seemed a long time), she realized that though she had become well and easily accustomed to the silence of her new heart, to the lack of a pulse, she had been listening unconsciously for the echo of the beat, the double or triple reverberation from throat and wrists, from femoral artery, all related by the same heartbeat, each perceived at a slightly different time during moments of silence.

She thought she might miss that, just a little, for a little while.

Radu finished his circumnavigation of the pool; he swam under her and the faint turbulence stroked her back. Laenea let her feet sink to the pool's bottom and stood up as Radu burst out of the water, a very amateur dolphin, hair dripping in his eyes, laughing. They waded toward each other through the retarding chest-deep water and embraced. Radu kissed Laenea's throat just at the corner of her jaw; she threw her head back like a cat stretching to prolong the pleasure, moving her hands up and down his sides.

"We're lucky to be here so early," he said softly, "alone before anyone else comes."

"I don't think anyone else is staying at Kathell's right now," Laenea said. "We have the pool to ourselves all the time."

"This is . . . this belongs to her?"

"The whole apartment does."

He said nothing, embarrassed by his error.

"Never mind," Laenea said. "It's a natural mistake to make." But it was not, of course, on Earth.

Laenea had visited enough new worlds to understand how Radu could be uncomfortable in the midst of the private possessions and personal services available on Earth. What impressed him was expenditure of time, for time was the valuable commodity in his frame of reference. On Twilight everyone would have two or three necessary jobs, and none would consist of piecing together intricate mosaics. Everything was different on Earth.

They paddled in the shallow end of the pool, reclined on the steps, flicked shining spray at each other. Laenea wanted Radu again. She was completely free of pain for the first time since the operation. That fact began to overcome a certain reluctance she felt, an ambivalence toward her new reactions. The violent change in her sexual responses disturbed her more than she wanted to admit.

And she wondered if Radu felt the same way; he discovered she was afraid he might.

In the shallow water beside him, she moved closer and kissed him. As he put his arm around her she slipped her hand across his stomach and down to his genitals, somehow less afraid of a physical indication of reluctance than a verbal one. But he responded to her, hardening, drawing circles on her breast with his fingertips, caressing her lips with his tongue. Laenea stroked him from the back of his knee to his shoulder. His body had a thousand textures, muted and blended by the warm water and the steamy air. She pulled him closer, across the mosaic step, grasping him with her legs. They slid together easily. Radu entered her with little friction between them. This time Laenea anticipated a long, slow increase of excitement.

"What do you like?" Radu whispered.

"I—I like—I—" Her words changed abruptly to a gasp. Imagination exaggerated nothing: the climax again came all at once in a powerful solitary wave. Radu's fingers dug into her shoulders, and though Laenea knew her short nails were cutting his back, she could not ease the wire-taut muscles of her hands. Radu must have expected the intensity and force of Laenea's orgasm, but the body is slower to learn than the mind. He followed her to climax almost instantly, in solitary rhythm that continued, slowed, finally ceased. Trembling against him, Laenea exhaled in a long shudder. She could feel Radu's stomach muscles quiver. The water around them, that had seemed warmer than their bodies, now seemed cool.

Laenea liked to take more time with sex, and she suspected that Radu did as well. Yet she felt exhilarated. Her thoughts about Radu were bright in her mind, but she could put no words to them. Instead of speaking she laid her hand on the side of his face, fingertips at the temple, the palm of her hand against deep scars. He no longer flinched when she touched him there, but covered her hand with his.

He had about him a quality of constancy, of dependability and calm, that Laenea had never before encountered. His admiration for her was of a different sort entirely from what she was used to: grounders' lusting after status and vicarious excitement. Radu had seen her and stayed with her when she was helpless and ordinary and undignified as a human being can be; that had not changed his feelings. Laenea did not understand him yet.

They toweled each other dry. Radu's hip was scraped from the pool steps, and he had long scratches down his back.

"I wouldn't have thought I could do that," Laenea said. She glanced at her hands, nails shorter than fingertips, cut just above the quick. "I'm sorry."

Radu reached around to dry her back. "I did the same to you."

"Really?" She looked over her shoulder. The angle was wrong to see anything, but she could feel places stinging. "We're even, then." She grinned. "I never drew blood before."

"Nor I."

They dressed in clean clothes from Kathell's wardrobes and went walking through the multileveled city. It was, as Radu had said, very early. Above on the sea it would be nearing dawn. Below only street cleaners and the drivers of delivery carts moved here and there across a mall. Laenea was more accustomed to the twenty-four-hour crew city in the second stabilizer.

She was getting hungry enough to suggest a shuttle trip across to #2, where everything would be open, when ahead they saw waiters arranging the chairs of a sidewalk café, preparing for business.

"Seven o'clock," Radu said. "That's early to open around here, it seems."

"How do you know what time it is?"

He shrugged. "I don't know how, but I always know."

"Twilight's day isn't even standard."

"I had to convert for a while, but now I have both times."

A waiter bowed and ushered them to a table. They breakfasted and talked, telling each other about their home worlds and about places they had visited. Radu had been to three other planets before Earth. Laenea knew two of them, from several years before. They were colonial worlds, which had grown and changed since her visits.

Laenea and Radu compared impressions of crewing, she still fascinated by the fact that he dreamed.

She found herself reaching out to touch his hand, to emphasize a point or for the sheer simple pleasure of contact. And he did the same, but they were both righthanded and a floral centerpiece occupied the center of their table. Finally Laenea picked up the vase and moved it to one side, and she and Radu held left hands across the table.

"Where do you want to go next?"

"I don't know. I haven't thought about it. I still have to go where they tell me to, when there's a need."

"I just . . ." Laenea's voice trailed off. Radu glanced at her quizzically, and she shook her head. "It sounds ridiculous to talk about tomorrow or next week or next month . . . but it feels so right."

"I feel . . . the same."

They sat in silence, drinking coffee. Radu's hand tightened on hers. "What are we going to do?" For a moment he looked young and lost. "I haven't earned the right to make my own schedules."

"I have," Laenea said. "Except for the emergencies. That will help."

He was no more satisfied than she.

"We have a month," Laenea said. "A month not to worry."

Laenea yawned as they entered the front room of Kathell's apartment. "I don't know why I'm so sleepy." She yawned again, trying to stifle it, failing. "I slept the clock around, and now I want to sleep again—after what? Half a day?" She kicked off her boots.

"Eight and a half hours," Radu said. "Somewhat busy hours, though."

She smiled. "True." She yawned a third time, jaw-hinges cracking. "I've got to take a nap."

Radu followed as she padded through the hallways, down the stairs to her room. The bed was made, turned down on both sides. The clothes Laenea and Radu had arrived in were clean and pressed. They hung in the dressing room along with the cloak, which no longer smelled musty. Laenea brushed her fingers across the velvet. Radu looked around. "Who did this?"

"What? The room? The people Kathell hires. They look after whoever stays here."

"Do they hide?"

Laenea laughed. "No—they'll come if we call. Do you need something?"

"No," he said sharply. "No," more gently. "Nothing."

Still yawning, Laenea undressed. "What about you, are you wide awake?"

He was staring into a mirror; he started when she spoke, and looked not at her but at her reflection. "I can't usually sleep during the day," he said. "But I am rather tired."

His reflection turned its back; he, smiling, turning toward her.

They were both too sleepy to make love a third time. The amount of energy Laenea had expended astonished her; she thought perhaps she still needed time to recover from the hospital. She and Radu curled together in darkness and scarlet sheets.

"I do feel very depraved now," Radu said.

"Depraved? Why?"

"Sleeping at nine o'clock in the morning? That's unheard of on Twilight." He shook his head; his mustache brushed her shoulder. Laenea drew his arm closer around her, holding his hand in both of hers.

"I'll have to think of some other awful depraved Earth customs to tempt you with," she said sleepily, chuckling, but thought of none just then.

Later (with no way of knowing how much later) something startled her awake. She was a sound sleeper and could not think what noise or movement would awaken her when she still felt so tired. Lying very still she listened, reaching out for stimuli with all her senses. The lights in the aquaria were out, the room was dark except for the heating coils' bright orange spirals. Bubbles from the aerator, highlighted by the amber glow, rose like tiny half moons through the water.

The beat of a heart pounded through her.

In sleep, Radu still lay with his arm around her. His hand, fingers half curled in relaxation, brushed her left breast. She stroked the back of his hand but moved quietly away from him, away from the sound of his pulse, for it formed the links of a chain she had worked hard and wished long to break.

The second time she woke she was frightened out of sleep, confused, displaced. For a moment she thought she was escaping a nightmare. Her head ached violently from the ringing in her ears, but through the clash and clang she heard Radu gasp for breath, struggling as if to free himself from restraints. Laenea reached for him, ignoring her racing heart. Her fingers slipped on his sweat. Thrashing, he flung her back. Each breath was agony just to hear. Laenea grabbed his arm when he twisted again, held one wrist down, seized his flailing hand, partially immobilized him, straddled his hips, held him.

"Radu!"

He did not respond. Laenea called his name again. She could feel his pulse through both wrists, feel his heart as it pounded, too fast, too hard, irregular and violent.

"Radu!"

He cried out, a piercing and wordless scream.

She whispered his name, no longer even hoping for a response, in helplessness, hopelessness. He shuddered beneath her hands.

He opened his eyes.

"What . . . ?"

Laenea remained where she was, leaning over him. He tried to lift his hand and she realized she was still forcing his arms to the bed. She released him and sat back on her heels beside him. She, too, was short of breath, and hypertensive to a dangerous degree.

Someone knocked softly on the bedroom door.

"Come in!"

One of the aides entered hesitantly. "Pilot? I thought—Pardon me." She bowed and backed out.

"Wait—you did right. Call a doctor immediately."

Radu pushed himself up on his elbows. "No, don't; there's nothing wrong."

The young aide glanced from Laenea to Radu and back to the pilot.

"Are you sure?" Laenea asked.

"Yes." He sat up. Sweat ran in heavy drops down his temples to the edge of his jaw. Laenea shivered from the coolness of her own evaporating sweat.

"Never mind, then," Laenea said. "But thank you."

The aide departed.

"Gods, I thought you were having a heart attack." Her own heart was beginning to slow in rhythmically varying rotation. She could feel the blood slow and quicken at her temples, in her throat. She clenched her fists reflexively and felt her nails against her palms.

Radu shook his head. "It was a nightmare." His somber expression suddenly changed to a quick but shaky grin. "Not illness. As you said—we're never allowed this job if we're not healthy." He lay back, hands behind his head, eyes closed. "I was climbing, I don't remember, a cliff or a tree. It collapsed or broke and I fell—a long way. I knew I was dreaming and I thought I'd wake up before I hit, but I fell into a river." She heard him and remembered what he said, but knew she would have to make sense of the words later. She remained kneeling and slowly unclenched her hands. Blood rushed through her like a funneled tide, high, then low, and back again.

"It had a very strong current that swept me along and pulled me under. I couldn't see banks on either side—not even where I fell from. Logs and trash rushed along beside me and past me, but every time I tried to hold on to something I'd almost be crushed. I got tireder and tireder and the water pulled me under—I needed a breath but I couldn't take one . . . have you felt the way the body tries to breathe when you can't let it?"

She did not answer but her lungs burned, her muscles contracted convulsively, trying to clear a way for the air to push its way in.

"Laenea—" She felt him grasp her shoulders: she wanted to pull him closer, she wanted to push him away. Then the change broke the compulsion of his words and she drew a deep, searing breath.

"What—?"

"A . . . moment . . ." She managed, finally, to damp the sine-curve velocity of the pump within her. She was shivering. Radu pulled a blanket around her. Laenea's control returned slowly, more slowly than any other time she had lost it. She pulled the blanket closer, seeking stability more than warmth. She should not slip like that: her biocontrol, to now, had always been as close to perfect as anything associated with a biological system could be. But now she felt dizzy and high, hyperventilated, from the needless rush of blood through her brain. She wondered how many millions of nerve cells had been destroyed.

She and Radu looked at each other in silence.

"Laenea . . ." He still spoke her name as if he were not sure he had the right to use it. "What's happening to us?"

"Excitement—" she said, and stopped. "An ordinary nightmare—" She had never tried to deceive herself before, and found she could not start now.

"It wasn't an ordinary nightmare. You always know you're going to be all right, no matter how frightened you are. This time—until I heard you calling me and felt you pulling me to the surface, I knew I was going to die."

Tension grew: he was as afraid to reach toward her as she was to him. She threw off the blanket and grasped his hand. He was startled, but he returned the pressure. They sat cross-legged, facing each other, hands entwined.

"It's possible . . ." Laenea said, searching for a way to say this that was gentle for them both, "it's possible . . . that there is a reason, a real reason, pilots and crew don't mix."

By Radu's expression Laenea knew he had thought of that explanation too, and only hoped she could think of a different one.

"It could be temporary—we may only need acclimatization."

"Do you really think so?"

She rubbed the ball of her thumb across his knuckles. His pulse throbbed through her fingers. "No," she said, almost whispering. Her system and that of any normal human being would no longer mesh. The change in her was too disturbing, on psychological and subliminal levels, while normal biorhythms were so compelling that they interfered with and would eventually destroy her new biological integrity. She would not have believed those facts before now. "I don't. Dammit, I don't."

Exhausted, they could no longer sleep. They rose in miserable silence and dressed, navigating around each other like sailboats in a high wind. Laenea wanted to touch Radu, to hug him, slide her hand up his arm, kiss him and be tickled by his mustache. Denied any of those, not quite by fear but by reluctance, unwilling either to risk her own stability or to put Radu through another nightmare, she understood for the first time the importance of simple, incidental touch, directed at nothing more important than momentary contact, momentary reassurance.

"Are you hungry?" Isolation, with silence as well, was too much to bear.

"Yes . . . I guess so."

But over breakfast (it was, Radu said, evening), the silence fell again. Laenea could not make small talk; if small talk existed for this situation she could not imagine what it might consist of. Radu pushed his food around on his plate and did not look at her: his gaze jerked from the sea wall to the table, to some detail of carving on the furniture, and back again.

Laenea ate fruit sections with her fingers. All the previous worries, how to arrange schedules for time-together, how to defuse the disapproval of their acquaintances, seemed trivial and frivolous. The only solution now was a drastic one, which she did not feel she could suggest herself. Radu must have thought of it; that he had said nothing might mean that volunteering to become a pilot was as much an impossibility for him as returning to normal was for Laenea. Piloting was a lifetime decision, not a job one took for a few years' travel and adventure. The way Radu talked about his home world, Laenea believed he wanted to return to a permanent home, not a rest stop.

Radu stood up. His chair scraped against the floor and fell over. Laenea looked up, startled. Flushing, Radu turned, picked up the chair, and set it quietly on its legs again. "I can't think down here," he said. "It never changes." He glanced at the sea wall, perpetual blue fading to blackness. "I'm going on deck. I need to be outside." He turned toward her. "Would you—?"

"I think . . ." Wind, salt spray on her face: tempting. "I think we'd each better be for a while."

"Yes," he said, with gratitude. "I suppose . . ." His voice

grew heavy with disappointment. "You're right." His footsteps were soundless on the thick carpet.

"Radu—"

He turned again, without speaking, as though his barriers were forming around him again, still so fragile that a word would shatter them.

"Never mind . . . just . . . oh—take my cape if you want, it's cold on deck at this time of day."

He nodded once, still silent, and went away.

In the pool Laenea swam hard, even when her ribs began to hurt. She felt trapped and angry, with nowhere to run, knowing no one deserved her anger. Certainly not Radu; not the other pilots, who had warned her. Not even the administrators, who in their own misguided way had tried to make her transition as protected as possible. The anger could go toward herself, toward her strong-willed stubborn character. But that, too, was pointless. All her life she had made her own mistakes and her own successes, both usually by trying what others said she could not do.

She climbed out of the pool without having tired herself in the least. The warmth had soothed away whatever aches and pains were left, and her energy was returning, leaving her restless and snappish. She put on her clothes and left the apartment to walk off her tension until she could consider the problem calmly. But she could not see even an approach to a solution; at least, not to a solution that would be a happy one.

Hours later, when the grounder city had quieted to night again, Laenea let herself into Kathell's apartment. Inside, too, was dark and silent. She could hardly wonder where Radu was; she remembered little enough of what she herself had done since afternoon. She remembered being vaguely civil to people who stopped her, greeted her, invited her to parties, asked for her autograph. She remembered being less than civil to someone who asked how it felt to be an Aztec. But she did not remember which incident preceded the other or when either had occurred or what she had actually said. She was no closer to an answer than before. Hands jammed in her pockets, she went into the main room, just to sit and stare into the ocean and try to think. She was halfway to the sea wall before she saw Radu, standing silhouetted against the window, dark and mysterious in her cloak, the blue light glinting ghostly off his hair.

"Radu—"

He did not turn. Her eyes more accustomed to the dimness, Laenea saw his breath clouding the glass.

"I applied to pilot training," he said softly, his tone utterly neutral.

Laenea felt a quick flash of joy, then uncertainty, then fear for him. She had been estatic when the administrators accepted her for training. Radu did not even smile. Making a mistake in this choice would hurt him more, much more, than even parting forever could hurt both of them. "What about Twilight?"

"It doesn't matter," he said, his voice unsteady. "They refused—" He choked on the words and forced them out. "They refused me."

Laenea went to him, put her arms around him, turned him toward her. The fine lines around his blue eyes were deeper, etched by distress and failure. She touched his cheek. Embracing her, he rested his forehead on her shoulder. "They said . . . I'm bound to our own four dimensions. I'm too dependent . . . on night, day, time . . . my circadian rhythms are too strong. They said . . ." His muffled words became more and more unsure, balanced on a shaky edge. Laenea stroked his hair, the back of his neck, over and over. That was the only thing left to do. There was nothing at all left to say. "If I survived the operation . . . I'd die in transit."

Laenea's vision blurred, and the warm tears slipped down her face. She could not remember the last time she had cried. A convulsive sob shook Radu and his tears fell cool on her shoulder, soaking through her shirt. "I love you," Radu whispered. "Laenea, I love you."

"Dear Radu, I love you too." She could not, would not, say what she thought: *That won't be enough for us. Even that won't help us.*

She guided him to a wide low cushion that faced the ocean; she drew him down beside her, neither of them really paying attention to what they were doing, to the cushions too low for them, to anything but each other. Laenea held Radu close. He said something she could not hear.

"What?"

He pulled back and looked at her, his gaze passing rapidly back and forth over her face. "How can you love me? We could only stay together one way, but I failed—" He broke the last word off, unwilling and almost unable to say it.

Laenea slid her hands from his shoulders down his arms and grasped his hands. "You can't fail at this, Radu. The word doesn't mean anything. You can tolerate what they do to you, or you can't. But there's no dishonor."

He shook his head and looked away: he had never, Laenea thought, failed at anything important in his life, at anything real that he desperately wanted. He was so young . . . too young to have learned not to blame himself for what was out of his control. Laenea drew him toward her again and kissed the outer curve of his eyebrow, his high cheekbone. Salt stung her lips.

"We can't—" He pulled back, but she held him.

"I'll risk it if you will." She slipped her hand inside the collar of his shirt, rubbing the tension-knotted muscles at the back of his neck, her thumb on the pulse-point in his throat, feeling it beat through her. He spoke her name so softly it was hardly a sound.

Knowing what to expect, and what to fear, they made love a third, final, desperate time, exhausting themselves against each other beside the cold blue sea.

Radu was nearly asleep when Laenea kissed him and left him, forcibly feigning calm. In her scarlet and gold room she lay on the bed and pushed away every concern but fighting her spinning heart, slowing her breathing. She had not wanted to frighten Radu again, and he could not help her. Her struggle required peace and concentration. What little of either remained in her kept escaping before she could grasp and fix them. They flowed away on the channels of pain, shallow and quick in her head, deep and slow in the small of her back, above the kidneys, spreading all through her lungs. Near panic, she pressed the heels of her hands against her eyes until blood-red lights flashed; she stimulated adrenalin until excitement pushed her beyond pain, above it.

Instantly she forced an artificial, fragile calmness that glimmered through her like sparks.

Her heart slowed, sped up, slowed, sped (not quite so much this time), slowed, slowed, slowed.

Afraid to sleep, unable to stay awake, she let her hands fall from her eyes, and drifted away from the world.

In the morning she staggered out of bed, aching as if she had been in a brawl against a better fighter. In the bathroom she splashed ice water on her face; it did not help. Her urine was tinged but not thick with blood; she ignored it.

Radu was gone. He had told the aide he could not sleep,

but he had left no message for Laenea. Nor had he left anything behind, as if wiping out the traces of himself could wipe out the loss and pain of their parting. Laenea knew nothing could do that. She wanted to talk to him, touch him—just one more time—and try to show him, insist he understand, that he could not label himself with the title failure. He could not demand of himself what he could break himself—break his heart—attempting.

She called the crew lounge, but he did not answer the page. He had left no message. The operator cross-checked, and told Laenea that Radu Dracul was in the crew hold of A-28493, already prepared for transit.

An automated ship on a dull run, the first assignment Radu could get: nothing he could have said or done would have told Laenea more clearly that he did not want to see or touch or talk to her again.

She could not stay in Kathell's apartment any longer. She threw on the clothes she had come in; she left the vest open, defiantly, to well below her breastbone, not caring if she were recognized, returned to the hospital, anything.

At the top of the elevator shaft the wind whipped through her hair and snapped the cape behind her. Laenea pulled the black velvet close and waited. When the shuttle came she boarded it, to return to her own city and her own people, the pilots, to live apart with them and never tell their secrets.